Praise for
Bae Suah

"Bae Suah offers the chance to unknow—to see the everyday afresh and be defamiliarized with what we believe we know—which is no small offering."

—*Music & Literature*

"With concise, evocative prose, Bae merges the mundane with the strange in a way that leaves the reader fulfilled yet bewildered, pondering how exactly the author managed to pull this all off."

—*Korean Literature Now*

"A compact, personal account of anomie and withdrawal in a time of rapid social and economic change. . . . An easily digested short book that nevertheless feels much very substantial—a very full story. Impressive, and well worthwhile."

—*The Complete Review*

"The mystery, like the achievement of [*Nowhere to Be Found*], occurs not in space, but in time."

—*The National*

Also by
Bae Suah

A Greater Music
Nowhere to Be Found
Recitation

North Station

Bae Suah

*Translated from the Korean
by Deborah Smith*

OPEN LETTER
LITERARY TRANSLATIONS FROM THE UNIVERSITY OF ROCHESTER

Library of Congress Cataloging-in-Publication Data:

Names: Pae, Su-a, 1965- author. | Smith, Deborah, 1987- translator.
Title: North station / by Bae Suah ; translated from the Korean by Deborah Smith.
Description: First edition. | Rochester, NY : Open Letter, 2017.
Identifiers: LCCN 2017022257 (print) | LCCN 2017032524 (ebook) |
    ISBN 9781940953700 (e-book) | ISBN 1940953707 (e-book) |
    ISBN 9781940953656 (paperback) | ISBN 1940953650 (paperback)
Subjects: LCSH: Pae, Su-a, 1965—Translations into English. | BISAC: FICTION /
    Short Stories (single author). | FICTION / Literary. | FICTION /
    Contemporary Women. | GSAFD: Short stories.
Classification: LCC PL992.6.S83 (ebook) | LCC PL992.6.S83 A2 2017 (print) |
    DDC 895.73/5—dc23
LC record available at https://lccn.loc.gov/2017022257

*This book is published with the support of the
Literature Translation Institute of Korea (LTI Korea)*

*This project is supported in part by an award from
the National Endowment for the Arts*

Printed on acid-free paper in the United States of America.

Text set in Garamond, a group of old-style serif typefaces
named after the punch-cutter Claude Garamont.

Design by N. J. Furl

Open Letter is the University of Rochester's nonprofit, literary translation press:
Dewey Hall 1-219, Box 278968, Rochester, NY 14627

www.openletterbooks.org

Contents

North Station

First Snow,
First Sight

Yang had had countless harsh words thrown at him over the course of his life, and as these had tended to culminate in a curse on his very existence, whenever he discovered that one of his castigators was no happier once they were rid of him, in other words that there was no correlation between their misery and Yang himself, and that this lack of correlation might have been all that ever lay between them, his timid heart found it strange, and faintly baffling. For example, there was the letter that Mira, one of these castigators, sent him one day; sighing that her days were like a ruin—though her entire life had been just that—she said that she was planning to spend a few days in the city where Yang lived, and that they had to meet. Though my entire life has been just that; this noncommittal expression seemed to Yang like a prideful, ultimate desire, which Mira deliberately underlined in her letter to make him hear it as a shout, and it was as though he really did hear Mira's voice, commanding him to recognize the truth of this claim. But Mira's voice, that was something that he had forgotten long ago, and in fact he could picture her only faintly, and had to acknowledge that all he remembered of her was so vague that he doubted he could tell her apart from her mother. Having said that, it wasn't, of course, that he had absolutely no memory of the being known as Mira, simply that this "memory" was now only worth as much as any general, conventional expression related to human beings.

Though my entire life has been that. To Yang, this seemed to impose upon him the responsibility of having as exhaustive a knowledge of Mira's life as he did of his own, and on top of taking it as a warning not to act as though he didn't possess such knowledge, never mind whether or not he actually did, he also read into it a form of implicit criticism that was close to mockery; because there was no way for him to know even a fraction of what constituted this "entire life" of hers, any more than he could guess whether this life warranted the label, redolent as it was of melancholic previous-century lyricism, of a "ruin." Sufficient time had passed for their relationship to lose its validity—it had already been over eight years since they'd last seen each other, had any form of contact, or even had so much as a mutual friend who might happen to let them know, just by the by, how the other was doing—and so, rather than their friendship being one wherein Yang had once had a vast store of detailed information regarding her, but which he had now forgotten, each had from the start shown a complete lack of interest in the minutiae of the other's life, a life that was after all unrelated to their own and could be called absolute and unvarying—in that, at least, Yang could feel confident in his own memory—yet none of this was to suggest that they were indifferent to one another. It was just that the Mira Yang had known, Mira as she had been back then, had never once thrown that expression "entire life" at him. To Mira—or indeed, he thought, to anyone else—Yang was not someone who warranted deploying such a term. Back then, Mira had never even written "my life," or mentioned plain "life" in casual conversation, where its appearance would have gone unnoticed. Not only would such expressions, which comprehend time and human beings as a single, indivisible whole, have been inappropriate for Mira as an individual living a present of innumerable dimensions, they were also—and this Yang found especially unpardonable—utterly unoriginal. He read Mira's letter several times, it not being overly long; those ostentatious expressions—my entire life, and eternal ruin, sticking their heads arrogantly and impatiently out from in between the otherwise well-behaved sentences—meant that any kind of future connection they might have could only take the form of Yang's plunging into Mira's world and attending closely to its atmosphere of ruin, and so, shackled by an awkwardness and discomfort as though that high-handed and inconsiderate expression were a pair of handcuffs, there was nothing to do but write an equivocal reply, one that would avoid both definite consent and outright refusal.

Yang was lying supine by the lake. The water was surprisingly warm, given the cold wind, and in fact the heat was sufficient for the grass to give off a strange and sickening scent. The sun kept poking out from between the clouds, and as long as he stayed wrapped in his towel he wasn't bothered by any chill. The lake didn't have many swimmers that year, perhaps because the summer hadn't been as warm as usual. A handful of wild ducks were huddled unmoving not far from Yang, so as an experiment he tried tossing them the breadcrumbs left over from his lunch, but this didn't seem to interest them in the slightest, as though having to move for the sake of mere crumbs was too much hassle to even contemplate. Now and then there was a decent gust of wind, each one ruffling the ducks' long feathers so that their round bodies appeared even plumper, while the down on the backs of their bowed necks was swept briefly flat, gleaming like a pale gray blanket. Yang wanted to stay where he was for as long as possible. Hoping that his skin and general constitution would withstand the chill of the wind, he closed his eyes. The feeling of his whole body, from the crown of his head to the tips of his toes, being as light as the down on the ducks' necks, and thus being whisked away by the wind, that was it, as though in a dream—a dream, that is, of flying low and languid over the earth, sighing quietly at the sight that lies below, the seclusion of flat fields stretching on and on, low houses, people and their bicycles, looking friendly as toys—he struggled to keep that feeling. All the while, as though in a dream, he was taking care to regulate his breathing and not suddenly plummet down to earth, or lose the calm control of his orbit and go spinning away into the empty air like a baseball struck by a bat, governed only by centrifugal force. He was flying, and at the same time was sinking in a measure of fear and anonymous sadness—which was muted and mild enough to be enjoyable, and he felt the urge to shed actual tears. Tears warm as the gentle heat of an autumn evening, harmless as spiderwebs floating quietly in the November breeze. He tried to make the tears well up by calling to mind some concrete sadness, but it didn't work. He dredged up several lines of poetry: "Today, only today I am beautiful / Tomorrow all disappears / Death, death approaches." These lines had always seemed to him both beautiful and sad, but even they could not cause the tears to flow. Even while regretting this, the original sad-yet-tranquil feeling persisted. Of all the sadnesses he knew, the early morning kind when you've only just woken up, the kind against which there is no defense, for which you're never prepared, was the most poetic. Mornings when birds cried outside his window, the inside of his mouth was washed with salty tears, the distant drone of traffic sounded as though it had just started up, the street below echoed with the soft footsteps of people heading out early to work, a dog groaned in the kitchen, and none of it, not the leaves or sunlight or wind or the flowers on the balcony, was the least bit different from the day before; curled up in bed, he would often be gripped by a sadness so irremediable that only the day before it had threatened to make his heart judder to a stop; he would sleep for so long that he forgot it, and would forget even himself, as fully as paper dissolved in water, and would feel that kind of obscure sadness that seemed to have flowed far away on the river of oblivion, still further away, finally to be washed up here. The moment he opened his eyes, though the already-forgotten dream had given him an intimation of sadness, this was now, in his waking state, only a hypothetical sadness that could not be approached even through the contours of memory. Sadness and tranquility, which belonged to and yet were indifferent to him. In this state of willed torpor, Yang waited for evening.

Some time later, Yang opened his eyes to find a young man and woman lying down near his own spot, side by side. Their bodies were fully stretched out, and they were both extremely tall. Shockingly tall, in fact. Close to 190 centimeters, Yang estimated, or perhaps even more. Even sunbathing, the two of them hadn't removed their black, thick-framed glasses—for myopia, not the sun—and the parts of their bodies that weren't covered by their swimsuits looked firm yet sleek, such a vast pale expanse it was almost inhuman; the woman's legs were unshaven, so the splayed pattern of wet brown hairs clinging to her pale skin, plus the goose bumps on her thighs, was conspicuous. Yang had always liked tall people. Though of course, he didn't know how they thought of him from their perspective. And so, these tall people having taken his fancy, Yang wanted to look at them for as long as possible within the bounds of propriety. Aside from the issue of their height, their physical bodies harbored a factor that Yang had never before encountered in reality, a factor that could probably be called literary particularity. Because it felt as though those two bodies lying side by side were addressing him with incomprehensible words, like speech formed of some alien language. Like a song thrown together in dialect, like a wordless question, like a braying donkey. But at the same time, and despite the fact that, at least superficially, they made no gestures to indicate particular boundaries, their posture and facial expressions as they lay there with their eyes closed revealed a strong, primitive, animalistic awareness of their own borders, and an equally strong desire to safeguard these from seepage, to the extent that, for example, if they were to appear at a party holding hands, no one around them would dare approach as they crossed the threshold, their bodies formed one discrete region, solid and impermeable. They could not be called skinny, but it was true that their figures were spare, extremely ascetic. In the man's case, each time he took a breath the scaffolding of his ribs was clearly outlined, and those long, strong frames were ever so elegant, yet it was as though they were being borne on the currents of a strange and ineluctable fate. They looked like they might be brother and sister; more than in any similarity of facial features, the resemblance lay in their attitude and bearing, their movements and self-made mentality. The language of such acquired, a posteriori flesh made them seem like twins, closer even than brother and sister. Flesh of familiarity and homogeneity, shared exclusivity and extreme bashfulness. The transparent black-framed glasses, the woman's dully gleaming swimsuit, its thick black fabric patterned with water droplets, hair cut short as a duck's feathers, slightly protruding jaw, navel concealed neatly with both hands; large, flat hands that seemed to be clutching something wallet-sized, and long toes curled together in a way that looked both stubborn and shy. Reckoned in terms of sensitivity, the man was superior. He had both eyes closed behind his glasses and each time the light undulated his eyelids trembled perceptibly, their speed in precise proportion to the degree of that undulation. Though he was lying down undressed and with his eyes closed, he resembled "man thinking about anxiety" more than "man sleeping." Alongside the habitual, though very slight, forward thrust of his jaw, the look on his face was one of surprise. It seemed a private indication of his having come face to face with some abstract surprise that can be discovered only with one's eyes closed. As for the woman, she opened her eyes now and then to examine the situation with respect to the sunshine and her own body. She shifted her body a little at a time, stretching out both legs but taking care that her feet didn't touch the sand if it could possibly be avoided. In spite of the fact that the beach towels they had brought with them were extremely large, larger than Yang had ever before set eyes on, their feet stuck out over the ends. Just then two huge dogs suddenly leapt into the water at their owner's urging, panting heavily, and the startled ducks made for the hill on the opposite side of the lake. With no movement other than to open her eyes, the woman observed this brief disturbance. Though she must have felt Yang's watching her and her partner, her glance did not stray in his direction.

Just then it started to seem to Yang that he had met them both somewhere before. At first, the thought was like something in a dream, imagination and expectation tangled up and dim as the ground seen from a great height, but it gradually became invaded by echoing doubts, which might very well be facts. If Yang was not mistaken, they were that tall, odd couple who had been at the birthday party of the person living in the attic room that winter, who had stood there quietly side by side, practically glued to the wall, joined hands and did a little polka once the music started up, then gone home at the stroke of midnight, without at any point having spoken a single word to anyone else there. Since it was uncommon to encounter people as tall as they, Yang slowly became convinced that he was correct. At the party they had both been wearing sweaters; the woman with a sleeveless jacket on over hers, plus black stockings and a gray, pleated knee-length skirt. None of the other guests had seemed to know who they were, and were presumably none the wiser once the party had ended, but as Yang had

9

been standing close by when they'd exchanged greetings with the host he knew that the woman worked as an assistant librarian and the man was a college student. Just then it had begun to snow outside. It was the first snow of the year. The flat where the party was being held was on the top floor; the door to the veranda had been left open for the smokers, and the night was peering in through it, a night formed from keen rays of darkness, and within that only a chiaroscuro of what was dark and still more so; the lofty cityscape, comprised of the silhouettes of chimneys and rooftops, which were completely different entities at night than they were during the day, was casting a sharp eye over the room's interior. The rooftops, sloping at somber and beautiful angles, recalled iron warships floating mute in the sea of night, made with great toil but that were, having weathered a hundred years, desperately old. Yang loved the shadows of such rooftops on winter nights, and since whenever he encountered something he really liked there would stir in him a vague terror proportionate to the delight, intangible yet burdened with physical sensation, though in fact any experience of unbearable beauty will bring with it a measure of terror—in this case, the experience being the room full of people and the veranda that looked out over the rooftop nightscape—he had to be careful to make his body as inconspicuous as possible and not shock others with the pallor of his fear. That winter, the man had said he had to leave the party because he was working part-time clearing the snow from around the university office. Yes, that was it. Yang's memory began to revive from the dust of tangled unconsciousness, curling into animation gradual as a snail. Before the couple left, the woman got a book out of her bag. Yang could see it without moving from his place in the shadows, pressed up against the wall in the corner of the room. Not that he had stationed himself there in order to observe them; the two of them had simply happened to position themselves right between Yang and the open veranda door. Just then, Yang shuddered at the caustic sound of a hard, pointed talon scraping the metal handle of the apartment's front door. The sound grew louder as the music did, and disappeared when it died down. Though Yang surreptitiously opened the door several times to investigate whether some kind of wild beast was struggling to get inside, each time he opened the door to nothing but the stale smell of the old corridor, the saturated air raising goose bumps on Yang's face like being licked by a huge tongue.

The woman's book was from the library where she worked and had a classification code stuck to its spine. The blue stamp of the library's name was visible on the first page as she flicked through the yellowish pages. At the time, Yang couldn't see the book's title. It was clear that the couple were both extremely shy, unable to enjoy parties. They wore passive smiles that melted inconspicuously into those around them, and made an effort not to exclude anyone from their gaze, without actually staring at them. Yang furtively rubbed his finger, sticky from the sugary drink, against the wall. The scraping sound startled him, loud as a scream. Equally loud was the rumble then produced by his stomach, sloshing with drink; fearing stares, Yang tried not to attract attention as he rummaged through the host's son's toy box, hoping to find something that would muffle the sound yet seem like merely an amusing distraction, a pair of castanets maybe, but all he found was a yellow rubber duck that made a squeaking sound when squeezed, and a toy arrow. As time passed and the night deepened, Yang grew gradually more uneasy, seized by an ever-more inexplicable terror; whirled about by such emotions, oppressed by the scenery that lay before him, of the veranda and the snow-covered rooftops, their existence seemingly visible only to himself, and in order to slip still further into the antinomic pleasure of his heart smarting and melting as though pierced by the toy arrow, Yang did not stop deliberately pushing himself further into the center of the unease.

Even as he did so, he worried that his secret enjoyment would be unwittingly brought to an end by someone closing the veranda door, cutting him off from the sight of the rooftops, but luckily no one did. The woman gave the book to the host, who thanked her. The couple put on their hats and coats. They kissed the host on the cheek and said their goodbyes. They left, closing the door behind them as quietly as possible. Yang was shaking, but kept his gaze fixed on the veranda. After he'd calmed down a little he stepped out onto it, under the pretext of smoking a cigarette. The snow was piling up in the streets, and the shadows of the couple, seen from Yang's vantage point, were startlingly tall.

Later, the person who had invited Yang to the party asked him to return a library book for him, which he'd borrowed a short while before unexpectedly having to move house. He added that, though the initial due date had already passed, it wouldn't be a problem since he'd renewed the book twice for one-month extensions, but if there was some miscommunication and Yang did in fact end up having to pay a late fee, he would of course be reimbursed. The friend's need to move in a hurry made it difficult to find time for such errands, so Yang decided to do him this favor. There was no reason to refuse; the library was on his way to work, and returning the book wouldn't take much time. He went there a few days later. He'd been on night duty at the hotel, working at the front desk until the early hours and the gradual arrival of morning. When he got to the library he discovered that it wouldn't be open for another half hour. Coming back the next day would be easy, but he might forget, or the library's opening hours might be different, and if they didn't coincide with the time that he left work—since, for the hotel's temporary employees, these weren't fixed but depended on the circumstances—he might end up returning home only to have to head out again later, so he decided that it would be best just to wait, and get something to eat at a cafe nearby. There was no cafe serving breakfast in the immediate vicinity, but he was hungry, and in any case it was far too cold to wait out in front of the library. But the sparsely populated cafe he did find was barely any warmer than it was outside; the stingy owner must not have the heat on. After ordering toast and coffee, Yang got out the book and looked inside—the first time he'd opened it—finding there the blue stamp with the library's name, but neither this nor its title stirred any memories in him, as by then he had entirely forgotten the couple at the party. Yang read the first few pages while buttering his toast, drank his coffee, then opened the book again around the middle and read some passage or other, rummaged in his bag for his pen and notebook and continued reading, jotting down a few passages as he did. It wasn't that these had made any especial impression on him, simply that he liked to collect sentences this way, and tended to note down whatever caught his attention, as long as he had the tools on hand. Lacking a similar fondness for organized filing, however, meant that the quotes thus amassed were stored in a slapdash manner. Since the notebooks and loose paper where he wrote down random sentences were not kept specially for this purpose, and since, moreover, they were themselves not collected in one place but rather scattered here and there, he almost never looked at them twice, and in the majority of cases just discarded them for no reason whatsoever. Now and then he would stumble across them among his belongings, sentences he himself had written down, but which by this time he had entirely forgotten ever having read, never mind what they meant or which book they'd come from. Rather than lodging in his mind or being engraved upon it, these sentences were fated to be forgotten from the very moment he recorded them, and though the business of collecting them, being purely habitual, did not go beyond simple, repeated, profitless labor, discovering unlooked-for sentences recorded in his own handwriting, and in the most unpredictable places, seemed

13

such an intimate mystery that Yang could not bring himself to abandon the habit. Though there were almost no cases in which the sentences had a particular, significant meaning, he still wrote them down: on the back of the map he always carried around, the business cards of people he didn't know, the corners of the previous year's memorandum, in the blank spaces on receipts from ultimately forgettable restaurants he'd stumbled across in the course of a meandering stroll, here and there in the magazines he often flicked through, in newspaper margins, on flyers and pamphlets found on the bus, and on postcards he would never send. Sentences that even lacked a concrete subject, since he gained enjoyment from the mere act of recording them, and since, moreover, he attached the most importance to actions that were coincidental and impromptu, there were also cases where the sentences' simple, everyday nature—what was sometimes their mundane brevity—made them still more meaningful and enigmatic. Naturally, Yang no longer has the notebook in which he recorded several of the library book's sentences that time in the cafe. He is, however, able to recall something of the book itself; that it was a collection of letters exchanged between Voltaire and Emperor Frederick. Regrettably, Yang had understood almost nothing of what the book contained, for the simple fact that it was written in French. And so there is a strong possibility that what he transcribed, rather than complete, coherent sentences, would have just been flowery phrases and eulogizing fragments comparing Frederick to various heroes of legend. Yang had transcribed whichever sentence fragments happened to contain words he knew—for example, certain specific names—without any particular logic. "The young Solomon . . . or Socrates, were they here now, what is that to me, it is Frederick who I love." Though of course, Yang would have understood no more of this than Solomon, Socrates, love.

The library was busier than Yang had expected it to be so early in the morning. It was a fairly compact place, a French cultural exchange library operating out of the provincial government office, and didn't boast many visitors, but the handful of employees were so busily engaged in sorting documents, seemingly a task of some urgency, that none of them looked up when Yang walked in. While he stood there waiting he was able to enjoy the pleasingly crisp sound of paper rustling, and the rich smell of books common to small libraries where the reading room is not separated from the reception area. When Yang announced that he was there to return a book, one of the receptionists directed him to the next window along. The tall woman whom Yang had seen at the party, who stood there in silence the whole time, was nowhere to be seen. There was no notice board with information relevant to library users, perhaps with it being such a small-scale place, and no one was sitting behind the counter window the receptionist had indicated. As Yang's business wasn't all that urgent, he decided to wait until someone appeared. Just beyond the window were bookshelves, and a young man whose job was to return each book to its proper place in the classifications. There wasn't much else for Yang to do than watch the man at work. He looked very young, more like an apprentice than an official library employee. The youth was working clumsily; he clearly hadn't yet managed to master the locations of the various categories or the art of sorting the books efficiently, so each time he made some trivial mistake he would get himself into a terrible fluster, even though no one was there to harangue him. When he turned in Yang's direction and his face was revealed, Yang thought he couldn't be more than eighteen. It was a child's face through and through. Yang had been similarly impressed by a face once before, on the subway. A bunch of primary school kids had entered the car and begun chattering away about computer

15

games and anime films. No, not chattering, it would be more correct to describe them as bellowing at each other with all their might, with the blind aggression peculiar to children who have just begun to bloom. In the opposite corner from where Yang was standing, visible straight-on to him, a boy who made an unusually strong impression was tangled up with his friends; Yang's gaze was immediately captured by him. The boy seemed like a sprite from some mythical, light-flooded country, just now banished to the subterranean world of the train. The visual impression he made was of one formed not of solid materials like flesh, blood, and bone, but of pure luminosity and far-traveled echoes. Not because he was so very beautiful, but because his was the beauty of zero self-consciousness. This would partly be his youth, but he appeared utterly unaware of his own beauty, of putting on airs, of admiring himself in the mirror. He was a being who hadn't yet been reincarnated, an ignorant, foolish being who had, at least up to that moment, been ignorant of how he had to hold himself apart from the other objects of the world, alive at precisely that moment, so inadvertently beautiful that it made your heart ache. But this vacuum state, this total lack of consciousness regarding the world, would not last long. And precisely because it would be so brief, Yang was flooded with such heartbreaking emotion he felt his chest grow tight. He kept his eyes on the boy right up until the latter got off the train, disappearing into the crowd with his arms around his friends' shoulders, howling with laughter. And now, again, Yang shrank back and held his breath. Were the boy from the subway to have aged in an instant and be standing right there in front of Yang, this was precisely how he would appear. That is, if time were able to flow over the surface of human beings, self-contained and inviolate, with neither weight nor substance, neither affecting nor penetrating them. Or else, if time were an image inadvertently made, formed in the air by the radiation of such secret light, playfully scattering gold dust, receding into the distance while howling with laughter, this was the shape that would then be left in the air. No one would be able to touch it. Because it is only a shape, not some material thing existing in reality. Because it is only a certain function of time, made of light rays, luminosity, and echoes, formed of memories lost to oblivion, of hypothetical sadness and objectless regret.

As soon as the youth noticed Yang his face turned red to the lobes of his ears and he came toward him in such a rush, though there was barely a couple of strides separating them, that he almost broke into a run. And he apologized for there having been no one at the counter window, and his not having noticed Yang what with being in the stack room. His apology had an air of genuine contrition, a rare exception to the common rule whereby employees and visitors pay each other as little attention as possible, causing Yang himself to feel contrite for having caused this youth needless concern by standing there without a word. Once Yang had returned the collected letters of Voltaire and Emperor Frederick, the youth asked him imploringly if there wasn't anything else he needed. When Yang answered that he was looking for other documents related to this particular exchange of letters, the youth, blushing openly, replied that the library held many such documents, all in French of course, and there were also many magazines for which they had a regular subscription, several of which were related to literature or history, so it might be a help if he looked through some of those. In any case, he said, theirs was the most substantial collection of and on French literature in the whole city, with the exception of the university library, so if there was anything Yang was after in the way of specific publications, he himself should be able to help.

"But you must have already tried the university library?" the youth asked.

The flush had not yet completely left his cheeks. It had spread even into his eyes, so looking at them felt like looking at blue glass beads into which the sky and shining sun had been poured. At the youth's direction, Yang entered the periodicals room and gathered a large armful of magazines that he then carried away to read. Yang could make neither head nor tail of French, and since the documents the youth had brought him were all in this language, Yang had to occupy himself by flicking through until he found a picture, which he would then linger over as it though it contained some vital clue. The youth seemed unvaryingly gentle. Visitors generally addressed him first, and without exception received friendly guidance from him. It seemed he must have been this amicable by nature, but it might also be an attitude common to all vocational school students studying and working part-time at some corporation or other. During his time in the library, Yang learned that, as per his initial guess, the youth was there on an apprenticeship rather than as a regular employee, and did indeed study at a vocational school, from which he was soon to graduate. He also learned that the youth's name was Edmund. That day, Yang photocopied several sheets of documents that he absolutely didn't need, though he made sure that they were ones with photographs, and took out his first book from the library, a biography of Voltaire. When he filled out the form for a library card and presented this to Edmund, the latter said with a smile Yang? What a peculiar name.

Over the next four days Yang spent as much time as possible at the library. During those four days Edmund was assiduous in conveying this or that document to him, and Yang was equally unflagging in pretending to read them. If a given document didn't seem to arouse Yang's interest, Edmund would appear rather disappointed. He was a truly zealous apprentice. He threw himself in to whichever task was required of him, making an effort to comply with every possible breed of request related to books or documents;

to refuse or ignore these would have been alien to him. Yet the books themselves, beyond containing essays or documents that might be of use to Yang, didn't actually seem to interest him. His default response to the words "Voltaire" or "French literature" was an ordinary, professional smile, a far cry from any wild enthusiasm. Even when, in the course of discussion, the words Rimbaud or Aragon, surrealism, *Rilke in Paris*, etc., rose to his lips, he was every bit as cold and indifferent as when he pronounced the names "George Bush" or "Luciano Pavarotti." But at a request for "the October 1986 edition of magazine X," he seemed ready to clamber right up to the summit of the stack room, his cheeks flushed with genuine happiness. On the fourth day, Yang heard another of the library employees wish Edmund a quick "Happy birthday!" as they walked past him.

"Today is your birthday?" Yang asked, also quite casually. By this time, they were sufficiently intimate that their conversation could stray slightly beyond the formal exchanges of visitor and employee, though it was of course still bound by the domain of the library.

"Actually no, it's tomorrow; Mrs. Hella has a day off tomorrow, so she wished me happy birthday in advance."

"Ah, in that case I want to say happy birthday too. How old are you?"

"Nineteen. Thank you."

"And I'd like to give you some kind of present. Since you've been helping me so much."

Looking genuinely shocked, though with his smile as unwavering as ever, Edmund replied that there was no need for that, he was merely doing his job.

"All the same, would you mind giving me your address? I really would like to send you a present, as long as that's okay."

Edmund hesitated for a bit before acquiescing—"if you really want"—and writing his address in the notebook that Yang held out to him. Yang slipped the notebook back into his pocket. Edmund regarded Yang with a somewhat blank look, unsmiling. Then, when Yang met his eyes and said "bye then," he blurted out "bye" in response and awkwardly raised his hand, extremely flustered. Yang strutted out without looking back.

Each time he passed the gift shop, Yang's eyes strayed toward the china dolls. Never in his life had he possessed such an object, or even considered that he might one day purchase one. The majority of the city's gift stores were clustered along a huge road that stretched out to the west. When the evening sun was setting on those smooth milky brows, the dolls seemed like shy, flustered beings standing there at a loss, blushing, yet zealous and warm and surprisingly intimate. Yang was only too well aware of his own timidity, that he was always at least somewhat afraid. He'd always been that way, ever since his school days, but he'd never been able to understand why this timid disposition, perfectly natural to him, caused others to feel discomfort or awkwardness or even open hostility. To Yang, this defensive state of his was actually quite beautiful. Because it was another acute sensation only perceptible to himself. When he first spotted the china dolls in that shop, Yang had seen in them a single personality, irritating and intractable, like a fractious stepchild, but also pale and weak and frightened and beautiful. To Yang, this was by no means an unfamiliar combination. He found the china dolls' pose of pessimistic hesitation far more attractive than the gorgeous coquetry of Eastern European painted porcelain dolls. He used all the cash he had on him to buy a Meissen sleeping Venus figurine. Yang could spend some time in close study of the sleeping Venus, and still find that it aroused no greater a desire for access or possession than had those other surpassingly beautiful beings. The salesperson put the Venus in a box, gift-wrapped it, and finished it with a red ribbon that read "Edmund, a very happy birthday." The next day Yang bought nineteen yellow roses, and, walking slowly and clutching the note with the address, went to find Edmund's house.

It was getting near to evening, and the sunlight was so pallidly faint that there was almost no warmth to be had from it, and the ducks had all vanished somewhere, and when the wind grew even chillier the people began to fold up their blankets and leave their spots by the lake. The tall couple, along with Yang, were among the last to leave. They sat up side by side, adjusted their glasses, and brushed any remaining moisture from their swimsuits, pulled on T-shirts and trousers over their swimwear, stood up and into their shoes, then folded their towels and hung them over their shoulders. Though Yang wanted to address them with some brief word of parting, and ask whether she had stopped working at the library, almost as soon as the thought occurred to him he felt that it would be difficult and annoying to put it into practice and actually open his mouth, besides which, the couple would likely have responded with indifference, so in the end he just stayed quiet. Glancing at his watch, he saw that he would soon need to set off for home. Mira had decided to call on him around 8 p.m., so he needed to be back before then, though beyond that there was nothing, absolutely no reason to rush. Yang had let the time drag on in the hope that Mira might wear herself out and decide not to come after all, but these hopes had ultimately been thwarted. Though he had no reason to think so, at some point during this impatient passage of time Yang had begun to worry that Mira had him confused with someone else. It was possible. They hadn't seen each other in at least eight years, and whichever way you looked at it, Mira coming all this way to meet him, to meet Yang—she'd said it was just a passing visit but it was clear that he was the reason for her trip—simply wasn't credible. By the same logic, she might not even recognize him. Again, as it was so long since they'd last met, or even heard the other's voice, it was possible. Yang experimented with examining himself in the mirror, assessing to what extent his appearance had altered over the past eight years, but he couldn't even guess what he'd looked like so long ago. And surely Mira's memory would be equally poor, as in fact his was of her. Yang repeatedly reminded himself that Mira was a specific, material human being, a specific, material woman; sometimes this was strange and discomfiting, sometimes it seemed a joke so clumsy he wanted to laugh, and at one point he genuinely did laugh so hard he was almost doubled over. Eight years ago, Yang had been afraid of Mira. It was the same now. She was a magnificent-looking woman, strong-willed and fearsomely obstinate, and her assertiveness was uncommonly pronounced. But Yang's fear of her wasn't solely down to her powerful ego or will to dominate. It was because she had wanted him to fear her. There had been a period in his life when he had quailed at the thought that she might leave him. (The terror had been such that it seemed his chest would explode from the anticipation alone, and had gone on for such a long time at this same intensity that when Mira finally did cast him aside, in a dramatic scene entirely her own creation, it was actually less painful.) Back then Mira had hesitated, gently and patiently holding Yang's head to her chest. We fell in love at first sight, you know, in a way that had never happened before. And still you're afraid, what on earth are you afraid of? . . . Despite having arranged to come around at eight, it was past nine and there was still no sight of her. Yang sat on the bed and waited, watching the clock. Though strongly suspecting that she would arrive in due course, Yang fervently hoped that a last-minute change of heart might cause her to stay on the train and just pass the city by entirely. He didn't put the radio on, or the lights, didn't light any candles or make a pot of coffee. He simply waited, adopting unbeknownst to himself a posture of obedience toward some vague subject, preparing to receive the aggressor into the sphere of his shy soul. This was waiting only, without performing any action. At some point he fell asleep.

And then at some point he woke up; because he wasn't immediately aware that he'd been asleep, it took him some time to grasp why he was collapsed in bed with his clothes, even his shoes, still on, and what had then woken him up. In this state of his exhausted bewilderment he heard shoes shuffling across the floor, and dishes clattering in the sink, which went on for an uncomfortably long time. These rude, unpleasant sounds rubbed his nerves the wrong way, needlessly reviving evil memories like a coin dropped into a tin dish. And who was that crossing the unlit room? Mira had arrived. She had opened the unlocked door and come in, made herself something to drink—paying no attention to the sleeping Yang—and had just now emerged from the kitchen. This was a moment he had imagined time and time again, suffocating inside every time that he did, but now, seeing the shape it was actually taking, he was convinced that reality was no rare thing, was in fact nothing more than a poor imitation, dull and run-of-the-mill, of that imagination that anticipates everything. He was in no hurry to get up, and given that his body was deaf to his commands, leaving him unable to so much as turn his head, shackled to the air as is common in fever dreams, he could do nothing but continue to lie down as he was, watching Mira get some bread out of the cupboard, slice it, and spread it with margarine. Even in the dark Yang could see that Mira had grown yet more emaciated, as though a gust of wind might blow her away, and that her long hair was hanging down behind her back in a very ordinary way, tied in a ponytail. She was wearing a pale-colored wool dress, belted at the waist, and though her clothes didn't seem all that big, the material looked baggy on her hips. The fact that she had dwindled away like an aged, withering woman triggered surprise in Yang. Seemingly famished, she scarfed the bread down in the near dark, the only light from the moon shining in through the window. The sound of her swallowing was incredibly loud. And then she coughed for quite a long time. Ages ago, they'd been in line to buy train tickets when they first set eyes on each other; struck by an immediate attraction, they stood there hesitating behind the door to their respective destinations, pressing their ears up against it to hear whoever was on the other side; the bell rang to announce the train's departure. Doors opened and closed, and people appeared and disappeared quiet and courteous as funeral-goers, and the pianist struck up Chopin's Funeral March as if in response. (The music shakes Yang to the core. If not for that music, sadness would just be sadness; that was the kind of music it was.) The candle that had been placed in a corner of the room made the couple's shadows dance on the opposite wall, so tall it seemed they would touch the ceiling, and the wind that slid in through the door to the veranda flipped the pages of the book. On the wall where the shadows were undulating, Yang transcribed the sentences that so suddenly appeared, that were in a language he could not understand, that were all the more beautiful because of that. The snow was piling up on the rooftops; the stars shone mysteriously in the sky. A skinny black figure, broom in hand, was sitting next to the solitary outline of a chimney, and Yang gasped in surprise at the realization that he himself was the sole observer of this scene. The snow looked to be getting gradually thicker. "I'm the chimney sweep of sadness, I cry, cry, cry . . ." Yang grazed the pencil hesitantly against the wall. "I cry, cry, cry . . ." Taking care to get the spelling correct, he wrote it out again and again. "Cry, cry, cry . . ." Behind Yang, the shadow of the tall man was whispering, his words whisking out through the door: "But clearing snow is no easy thing. No, it's not easy at all." The voice receded, wavering with what seemed like regret, disappearing like a candle's last smolder. The woman took the man's hand and they passed over the threshold together.

Yang brought his lips to the wall, close as a shadow, found the sentences he had written and read in a small voice: "For twenty years I searched for such a place, where no one lives nearby, where the landscape is wide and rolling with meadows, hollows, swamps, solitude, forests, and the sky. Not even a village, just a tiny hamlet without a church. –Botho Strauß."

Mira got up from her seat and approached Yang.

And Yang knew that now, finally, it was time to let the tears fall.

Owl

There was an ambulance parked in front of the house. A pallid stillness lay over the whole scene, nothing moved, and the air was like a warm, transparent wall. A regular ticking sound pierced the silence of 33 degrees Celsius—as indicated by the wavering gradations of the rooftop thermometer. The lazy beat of a mechanical heart. Or else, was it the metronomic footsteps of someone running down a corridor in rubber-soled shoes, or the ticking of an unusually large wristwatch hanging from my ear? Perhaps the person living on the ground floor had turned on the washing machine, or maybe the sound was coming from a broken electrocardiograph. A man was being brought out on a stretcher to the ambulance. His shoes stuck out from under the blanket. Water was dripping from them. The house was a wrecked ship. I know that old man, with the huge green oxygen mask jutting from his head like a green dragon on a ship's prow, or I think I know him. I try to approach him but the nurses hold me back, their speech incomprehensible. When I turn the page of the picture book a toad and a red orchid are melting to a pulp in a flowerpot. The ruins of a castle appear as I keep walking, and a narrow stony road that rises at a steep gradient. There is the scent of hot grass and dry sunlight.

Just then, soaked in sweat, I look back over my shoulder and see a large damp reptile soundlessly following me. I can't recall its physical form. This is all a scene from a dream. I could only sense the warmth of its long black tail, which it held erect; warmth like that from stone steps burning in the heat of the midday sun. Someone took my hand. And suddenly the scene changed.

The old bookshop, which had no ventilation system other than its windows and door, was full of cigarette smoke. I sat at a table with an espresso cup on it; a corner of the square was visible through the open door, and I could see people sitting around tables by the side of the road in spite of the hot weather. I got the feeling that I was being watched intently by the countless books that lined the walls from the floor to the high ceiling, and by the stories within them. Strangely overwhelmed, I overcame my shyness and got up from my seat, looking up at the higher shelves as I wandered among them. It was the second time we'd visited this bookshop. The first time we'd arrived too late, after the bookshop had already closed for the day, and so could only stand outside for a while and peer in at the display stands. We talked as I examined the books laid out in the window display, pointing at the titles I recognized, but also at those I didn't. It was winter. The wind shook the awnings of the open-air cafes, and after midnight the snowflakes began to fly. But it was summer now, and we went inside the shop. They brought out small cups of an espresso that was thick as tar. A calm yet persistent scent eddied around us, made up of trees and stale dust, paper and the wooden floor, and cigarette smoke. You were talking with the owner about the difficulties facing small bookshops, about the pessimistic outlook; I finished walking among the shelves, and stepped outside the shop. The shop immediately next door was a florist's, with a single chair outside. I sat down and put on my sunglasses. Happily, I'd been given a book from the shop as a present. The first story in the book

27

was about five cities, and very short. The title, *Invisible Cities*. I began to read aloud from the beginning of the book. Time went by. Reptiles surrounded me, listening to the sound of my reading. They were curled up quietly, barely moving; only their raised black tails swayed slowly in the air, as a huge butterfly might, in that sunlight of late summer sliding into autumn. Heat radiated from their skin, which had been warmed in the sunlight and from the square's asphalt. This afternoon subsiding by degrees like a swamp. Asleep, I heard the sound of sleeping breath. Of one sleeping breath fumbling for another. They must be tangled with you, my breathing, my sleep, and my dreams. And I wanted to keep dreaming. Tears and sweat were flowing from me, wetting my face and watch and pillow. Sleep drifted about over lukewarm waves, like an anesthetic leaching in through veins, seized by sleep's phantoms . . . held within sleep, one eye makes a simultaneous record of what the other sees. Sleep, the soul's gelatinous component, the made-visible half-form of that which is unseen. Dreams and the embrace of dreams, which always stir up such sluggish, stunned sensations. This thing that stimulates my sleep, the respiration and waves of dreams, waves of breath and waves of water, that chord and note. And a silent song-cum-selfless-aria spun out on the keyboard. I passed back into the dream, back into the bookshop.

But you'd left, they told me. You were alarmed to find I'd disappeared and hurried outside to look for me, they said. And that it had already been over half an hour since you'd left. He left? While they were speaking I suddenly became alien to the dream, quite at a loss. All the books turned away with cold, sad faces, all the writers clamped their mouths shut and went back to being dead. The cold espresso dregs stained the bottom of the cracked coffee cup. He really left? I repeated blankly, clutching the book that had been my present. As though there was nothing more I could do. Which was true, in fact. I had been sitting in front of the florist's, reading aloud from the book. I didn't see you come out of the bookshop. And you didn't notice me either. I'd thought I was waiting for you. You believed I'd gone away. Like something that had always been spoken of, not knowing that it had not been true. In that moment when you failed to find me, I was reading *Invisible Cities*. I do not know where you live, and my house, though you know it, is too far away.

I liked to talk about dreams. For lovers, Freud was a gypsy of romance and sensual desire, part fortune-teller, part lute-carrying poet, and the manufacturer of a wonder drug. At some time or other, I told you about the beautiful yellow bird I held in my hand. The sense of a being delicate as a spider's web, suggested by the heat from its fierce warm breast, its slender weak toes and the soft down on its skin. About the wingbeats that had seemed shockingly strong in spite of such delicacy, the feel of its muscles tense and tremble beneath the skin, the ruddy memory of its chest suddenly springing up at that smallish yet explosive wriggling. At that, you pronounced my dream both enjoyable and extremely well behaved. I didn't know the reasons for your conclusion. I wasn't a student of Freud like you. But I could guess that the reason you found it enjoyable wasn't because of what Freud himself had taught. You dismissed such provisional explanations, given purely for the sake of carnal intimations, as "Freudian versification." Imaginary poetry that looks forward to a time overflowing with amusements.

Believing (incorrectly) that I had grown sad and left, you found yourself all alone. You must have been hungry—it having grown quite late by then—and might have gone to a restaurant, even without a companion. There were plenty of places lining the square, as in the small streets that radiated out from it. The kind of place, in other words, that people felt was highly suitable for evening dates, especially fashionable Friday evening ones. After peering inside several of the restaurants, I quickly realized that I had miscalculated—you would never have chosen to eat alone amid such a cheerful clamor. The square was a place for what is commonly called "going out." The parties and pairs clustered at each table all had smiling faces and cheeks slightly flushed. There were no tables with single occupants. My search so far had been in vain, and it was clear that someone with your firm sense of self-respect wouldn't be drifting around like a loner. I gave up on the restaurants, but couldn't think where to try next. I saw the lights of a taxi rank—you must have taken one. And left. I've experienced the emotion of love twice in the time that I've known you. The first time is long past, the second is still ongoing. Both times it happened with writers, and both times I fell in love with them without ever having met them in person. Though you yourself were somewhat acquainted with the first of the writers. To be precise, you told me that your acquaintance had only lasted for a brief while, a very long time ago, but now and then you would make a vague plan to go and see him again. Using this as a pretext, we put together a fairly concrete plan for the two of us to visit that first writer. He lived far away, and though we managed to obtain his address and get an appointment with him, we weren't sure whether the trip would require a passport or visa. Only once we'd gone to the harbor to catch the ferry were we told that a passport was necessary. I had mine in my handbag, but you'd left yours at home. We watched the ferry depart without us.

After that, I would sometimes dream of going to meet the first writer. You told me that, a very long time ago, you'd traveled to that city, the city where the first writer was now living. You said that the tolling of a distant bell was audible in the ruins at the heart of the city, a place so little-frequented that even the shadows of passersby were rarely seen. It had been a curious experience. You were sitting halfway up a tall flight of crumbling stairs, and the

wind blowing in through the gaps in the ruined stone walls carried
with it the sound of the bell. But as for the creaking of a nearby
window-frame, or the scrape of carriage wheels over paving stones,
there was nothing. Ah, this was still a little while before such typical tourist things had appeared in that city. Might the whispering
of lovers on the other side of the wall, blending creole and patois
in their speech, have sounded to you like the ringing of a bell? But
that is merely conjecture, with only the faint possibility of truth.

You once asked me to write about my dream. Not just an offhand mention of a certain scene, but to describe the whole thing
in as much detail as possible, and send it to you. I said nothing
at the time, but privately decided not to. It would be comparatively easy to write about only one particular scene, or one aspect
of the dream that had made a strong impression. But recording
it in its entirety from beginning to end—if dreams can be said
to have beginnings and ends—was another matter entirely. Not
only had the dream lacked a sequential plot, but its story was not
a rational one, it didn't fit with consistent logic. I was unable to
judge precisely where it had started or come to a close. No, I was
unable to remember. A dream, once dreamt, is soon forgotten. The
lifespan of the dream, still vividly remembered when I woke up in
the middle of the night, was not all that long. On touching the
surface of consciousness, the mosaic of the dream rapidly oxidized
and crumbled away, and my mind filled in the blank spaces with
colored tiles of its own invention. The dreams I can still recall at
least in part are, without exception, the ones that I recounted to
you. Through the telling, those dreams found a foothold in my
consciousness. But in doing so, the dream would have inevitably
altered, becoming tainted with deliberate contrivance. The dream
degenerated into that which was not a dream. It was impossible
to tell whether it was a dream or something imagined while sleeping. And more than anything else, my own belief is that there are

many cases in which dreams are fundamentally void. For the most part, what appears in dreams are no more than relics, imagined or recalled by the eyes of day, presented at random without relation to either time or will. And so, dreams can be neither a divine revelation nor a prophecy. The dream says nothing about me, no more than it does about you. It bears as little relation to reality as the fortune inside a fortune cookie. Even if you believe what the dream seems to show, that doesn't alter the fact of its nullity. And so, even if I were to spy on myself, record the entirety of my dream and send it to you, ready and willing to disclose myself, such a record would clearly lack the ability to disclose or betray anything of this self. You strongly opposed my belief in the nullity of dreams. Since when have dreams been nothing? That's evidently not true. Hints and paradoxes, caves and reptiles, never mind what you call it, they clearly have some kind of psychological meaning. To interpret a dream, you need more than the dream itself, more than a mere process of mechanical unraveling; rather, you need the counseling process, in which the concerned party and the interpreter collaborate. People who declare that dreams are nothing simply do not want to believe them, or are frightened of doing so.

In my opinion, it's more appropriate to say that whatever psychological meaning a dream has is more to do with the one who interprets it than the one who dreamt it. And so, interpreting a dream rather than disclosing one would be the more effective way to disclose oneself. Only some time later did I come to understand that, by treating dreams as an amusing pastime, you were largely aiming to provoke. You might also have fostered that light, benign atmosphere as a way of setting me at ease, so that I wouldn't be afraid to disclose my dream. Wanting, as you did, for me to put it down in the form of an essay, as a full and coherent literary composition rather than some series of fragments.

The dream was nothing, but at the same time it was also me. Because the dream was my fabrication, my lie. I was aware of that fact and did not conceal it from you. Even while recounting the dream just as it had unfolded, I believed I had prepared an escape route by continually suggesting that it was all a lie, broken free from the control of self-consciousness.

There is a dream, one that ceaselessly recurs for me, a dream related to water and snakes.

But to hew to my theory, that dream's hidden psychology would necessarily lack any concrete connection to either water or snakes. Water or snakes would just be chance symbols, improvised keys that fit no lock. And so, any attempt to attach ourselves to the figures of the dream, to the faces within it, would be like trying to open a door with the wrong key.

A newspaper ran an interview with my second writer. You sent it to me in the mail. The envelope contained page 17 of the newspaper—plus page 18, inevitably, printed on the rear side—the entirety of which was devoted to the interview, and which you had torn out as a full page and folded into a square. You hadn't enclosed a note, as far as I could see, or even jotted something down on the newspaper itself.

Mr. H, what do you generally get your inspiration from when you write?

Back in the day, my subjects were almost always beautiful women I admired, you know. But now, the meaning of a "subject" has itself paled. It can be a mailbox or trash can. The subjects from which I draw inspiration now are precisely those that ensnare me in confusion . . . that ambush me in an utterly unpredictable fashion. That I can neither prepare for nor calculate in advance. Like dreams . . .

Like dreams, that part was underlined. Your method of underlining is so very familiar to me. You always applied more strength than necessary, ruthlessly and impetuously, like drawing an arrow. I never knew you to use a pencil. Sometimes you would draw a big circle around one word, sometimes your underlining would be so excessive that I couldn't make out the sentence itself. And then it would come to an awkward end, breaking off in some crude, incomplete shape as though you had snatched your pen away, having abruptly thought of something else. Next to the underlined passage there would generally be an exclamation mark, triangular in shape, gouged deeply into the paper. The kind of underlining that clearly had decades of egoism behind it.

At some point I was standing in a long immigration queue. Even though I turned to look in all directions, the only thing to see was the throng of people drifting around distractedly, so many they filled the large entrance hall. You couldn't even tell where the immigration counter was. A uniformed man (presumably a policeman) had planted himself firmly halfway down the line, standing with arms crossed and legs apart, to prevent everyone rushing forward en masse. In their jodhpur-style trousers, the policemen reminded me more of colonial prison officers or detention camp guards than they did of ordinary policemen. The concrete construction of the wharf entrance hall amplified noise. The extraordinary din of the crowd made me feel as though my head had been shoved inside a clanging steel bell. The people in front of me suddenly began to run. They were running blindly forward, all carrying bags, some holding the hands of little children wearing little backpacks. Without knowing the reason for all this, I too flowed into the crowd. As soon as we turned the corner, the immigration counter became visible. The instant they had that reassurance, ah, now we're here, those who had been running stopped in their tracks. Once again, policemen were blocking the way in front. We were unable to move any closer to the counter. It was the turn of the group who had slipped through the other gate to approach the counter. Only then did I figure out the control system. Each line had fed in through a different gate, and now they were all rayed out in a semicircle, the people in them staring piercingly at the immigration counter. The policemen were fixing the throng with some truly intimidating looks, while there were those who accepted the system as familiar, and presumably had their reasons. Inside my bag was the notebook containing the first writer's address, and when I recalled that fact my courage revived. As long as he is still living in this city, if he remembers the past appointment, I would be able to meet him. Perhaps, if I mentioned your name, I might receive some small welcome. He would ask how you were doing, and I would tell him.

I thought that the city, though it was a city, would have looked suburban for the sake of those foreign aliens who came from rural areas. Befitting an exotic Special District. This was down to the brief, fairy-tale impression I'd gotten from you. I was vaguely expecting that if I came out from the harbor and took the bus, after a few stops I would be in the heart of the city, the square and ruins would appear and, without even knowing the name of the street, I would be able to recognize it at a single glance, with the feeling of ah, here it is. And my first writer was living in some apartment nearby. In that room with a potted red orchid and where the balcony window, hung with a rattan blind, looked down onto the ruins where a bell could often be heard.

But what you'd told me was very different from what I found. The fact that quite a few years had passed since your visit needed to be taken into consideration. After finally escaping from the harbor area I managed to make it to the bus stop, constantly jostled in the great tide of bodies, and caught a bus with the driver's seat on the right-hand side. The bus was small and there were many

35

passengers, so I had to stand and cling to the handrail. Each street we passed through was packed with such an enormous mass of people that my eyes widened in shock. I thought of the mass of immigrants I'd seen at the harbor. If the throng that had passed through immigration was at this very moment heading for the narrow sloping alleyways of the old quarter, or the downtown shopping district, or to take souvenir photos in the tiny square with the fountain, this—the entire city looking as though it had been occupied by a swarm of scurrying ants—would have been the natural result. The bus cut through the city center, which was dense with malls and department stores. I had no idea where I needed to get off. More people crowded on at each bus stop, and I was gradually pushed farther to the back. I craned my head with effort to look outside the window, but couldn't see a single street that might be part of the old district. On top of that, I didn't know for certain the name of the ruins where my first writer lived.

A long time ago, and a longer time ago still, two people I knew each came on a separate trip to this city. They sat on the steps of the ruins. What they saw was the last remaining colonial wreckage, a breeze soft as young rice, and in the heart of it a beautiful, young, yellowish-green woman who turned calmly toward them in the light, and the open window of some nameless apartment. A potted red orchid had been placed at that window. At each gust of wind the laundry hanging from the balcony, a white handkerchief, fluttered. All the balconies were ships leaving port. They were fixed there but forever departing, and with no way to return. All were the things of 1999, an awfully long time ago.

For a long time now I'd been thinking of him as someone incredibly old. According to the common expression, someone "with one foot already in the grave." But this was an illusion. Not that the first writer was old, but old people like him already have one foot in another world, hear voices from that other world and put them into their writing. Only later, when I was as old as him, did I realize how mistaken I had been in this. The first writer was still among the living. I'd been greatly attached to him for several years, but could not have described his face in any detail. All I had was a photograph, one that had been taken some twenty years ago and printed in a book. Beyond that, there were only the photographs that accompanied his newspaper interviews, and they all seemed impersonal, sterile. Those images of him with his white hair, wearing black sunglasses and carrying a cane. All that anyone could tell from such a picture was that he was very old, that he wore unattractive, shabbily cut suits, was slightly stooped, and relied on a cane. But it was neither the cane nor the sunglasses that allowed me to recognize him at first glance. What stood out for me was his tempo. Because it was the tempo I'd come to love through reading his work. True writers emanate their writing from their body. And so his tempo is the same as the respiration of what he writes. It is neither faster nor slower than that of other people. At the same time, neither is it not faster nor slower. That was an error shining with self-conceit, quite out of touch with reality. A mistaken assumption made by millions of people, tiny yet persistent. At some point, in a magazine interview, he had answered the question "if you weren't a writer, what would you be?" with "I would have gone mad and killed myself fifty years ago." A wavelength that breaks up and becomes broken up, a lunatic wavelength. A tempo that reveals sickness and transcendence at the same time. His sentences, pulse, and tempo, made up of words that have slightly different meanings than they do in the dictionary. And only then did I realize that the small space filled with people was the entrance to the ruins, where I needed to get off. I pushed my way between the other passengers, and rang the bell.

In his youth, he liked to gamble.

He wagered everything that could be wagered. After having an appendectomy, he gambled his own appendix, preserved in formaldehyde, and a few days later his family had him dragged off to the psychiatric hospital.

Even after he became quite well known, there was a time when he was always pressed for money.

Content found on Wikipedia. He came here on a trip with his girlfriend, then set down roots, never returning to his hometown. More than twenty thousand dollars remained of the debt he'd accrued there, a sizeable amount at that time. Although he'd had no lawsuit taken out against him, even after having built a solid reputation as a writer he was unable to shake the stigma of having fled gambling debts. When he received the Andreas Gryphius Prize at the end of the 1970s, his creditors announced that they would officially write off his debts, happy to be magnanimous if it meant sponsoring a famous writer. The prize money and his success as a writer made it possible for him to settle his debts, but he didn't, and never went back to his hometown, even after his last remaining creditor, who had at one time been his friend, died some time ago at the age of ninety, without a legal heir.

"The morning after I'd lost all the money I'd taken to the casino, I was strolling the dew-damp streets of the ruins; I thought I heard the blue-tinged sound of a bell coming from between the martyrs' graves. Though there was no way of explaining whether I really had heard it, or whether it was only an auditory hallucination produced by the climate peculiar to that place. We both stopped walking at almost the same time. Sighing lightly, she described it as the cry of a greenfinch searching for its mate. Whatever it was, we'd both heard it at the same time, there in that place. Turning to me, she asked 'what if we lived here . . . ?,' speaking as though to herself. At that time I had failed at everything I'd attempted, my heart was constantly torn to pieces, and I had no money, so I felt as though each day brought me closer to the brink of disaster. Worse, I would think to myself that even she whom I loved so much might leave my side at any moment. Because she was beautiful, the daughter of a rich family, and young to boot, only just past twenty, while on the other hand I was a flat-broke writer in his forties who had experienced one setback after another. But the moment I heard her say those words, I felt an abrupt, unlooked-for assurance that I was not alone. If I lived here, why, I could have it all, that kind of thought. All meaning both her and writing. At that, a feeling of relief swept over me, filling me up. Fulfillment such as I'd never known . . . it's been a long time since then, and now, as you can see, my circumstances are very different from what they were. I broke up with her, and married a Mandarin-speaking woman who came here after 1999. My wife writes poetry, you know. My life back then, and the way this place looked then, will sound strange to you as I describe it now. Over the past few years, there's been a huge increase in the number of mainland tourists who descend upon this place. Though it's true that I have no plans to leave, I don't want to say that it became my hometown at some point. At least to me, 'hometown' has long been nothing more than a word in a dead language."

At some point or other, I stopped loving the first writer. And the second writer became "my writer." We made plans to go and visit the second writer just as we had with the first. This time you had a good knowledge of the locality where the writer was living. You called it the supreme land on earth; meaning, of course, that the natural environment was beautiful. In the meantime, I was drunk on anticipation. It swelled my body and tongue, made the rain fall endlessly in my dreams. Even while asleep, I had to wipe away the grass-scented rainwater flowing down over my forehead and cheeks.

One day you asked me what question I would ask the second writer if I did manage to meet him. I said there were two, and that one was about the relationship between writing and ecstasy. Of course not the drug ecstasy, I was referring to the word that derives from the state of religious rapture that can be achieved through meditation. And added that my question had absolutely nothing to do with everything that word generally connotes. You confronted me then, claiming that the state of religious longing that arises from piety—in other words, from the desire to be submissive that human beings have always known, and which can on the surface be something obscene—is also and thus a comic struggle to make a clear division between ekstasis and ecstasy, though in any case both have the same meaning, with the one being the Greek, Latin root of the other. "And one more vague thing that's impossible to distinguish. I doubt whether your 'first writer' and 'second writer' are really two different people. I'm starting to think that the reason you so abruptly switched to thirsting for your second writer was that you were trying to overlay him onto the first writer, and thus conceal from yourself the fact of their separate existences. In other words, you selected both the first and second writers on the grounds of their being people you had never met, people with whom, from your individual point of view, your 'association' can only be indirect, given that they are both so famous, and who must always be plural, and fatefully far away, thus satisfying the desire for non-specificity; though you keep saying that it has always been your dream to meet them, deep down you fear that meeting them in person would bring to an end the sense of distance and one-sidedness that establish the relationship's necessary tension. Of course, the reason you need these individually ordinary human beings to be vague and mysterious is that this will amplify and perfect their perceived greatness, a greatness that you deeply long for. Do you remember what your first writer said in one of his interviews? 'The point in time at which writers like myself acquired a kind of greatness was that at which human beings stopped believing in a god, and came to want a substitute for divinity.' Most ordinary people would call that nothing more than vague envy. Envy has always had the character of a daydream. And persistent envy is a flight from something inside oneself." You continued. "To you, then, is it a flight from ecstasy, or an ecstatic flight?" I told you then that you were no better than a porn addict, that you were unable to talk about dreams without making them into something dirty and vulgar. I could see that you were pleased, though too shy to want to show it.

I spat out what was inside my mouth. The taste was unbearably poisonous and bitter. I didn't know what it was, but its absolute inedibility was clear. The thing that I'd spat out was quite a large lump of excrement. I was shocked. The lump fell onto the widespread expanse of an enormous petal. The balcony was crowded with brilliant-hued flowers, but I kept feeling as though I would vomit . . . I thought. A while ago I put a poster up on the wall right next to my bed. It was a photograph in which the light-and-dark contrast of shade and sunlight was clearly defined. The shade was a black that looked deeper than darkness, thick and viscous, and the part where the sunlight shone was brighter than streaming sugar, and whitened as the real sun's yellow light fell softly upon it. If I briefly woke up in the middle of the night, my eyes would always drift to that poster. Of course, in that kind of hazy dreamstate in which you haven't completely woken up, I am never aware of it as a poster. It seems to be something other than the image I know from the daytime. And each time something different. It would generally be connected to something I'd seen in a dream, or an extension of the dream unaltered. If I started awake from a state of dreaming the bright part of the photo glowed a brighter white, jumping out at me as a different being each time. That night it appeared in the form of a luminescent well. The well from which light was streaming stretched slowly up into the air, becoming a huge pair of pale lips that seemed to suck me in. Though afraid, I stretched my hand out toward it. I don't know why. But when I did, my fingers bumped up against a cold, hard wall. No, it was your wristwatch. A wristwatch with a large, round face. As soon as I took hold of it your wrist elongated like a butterfly's feeler and before I knew it was pursuing me to the balcony, which was crowded with pots and planter boxes. I hurriedly gathered some petals to cover the disgusting excrement I'd vomited. But it struck me that I'd never be able to cover it completely, that you'd see it and I'd plummet into an abyss of shame and despair . . . There was only one way to avert disaster, nothing else for it but for me to swallow it back inside me. Making my mouth into the shape of a bird's beak, I bent down toward it . . . Just then, the first writer carried tea into the room adjoining the balcony.

If the world were to become a place in which books are forbidden, and the only way for humans to have a relationship with literature was to learn entire books by heart—this is a hypothesis connected to Ray Bradbury's novel—my first writer unhesitatingly gave two names when asked which writer's works he would memorize, or which would be worth the effort even without such a hypothetical ban, and even though it would seem absurdly laborious: Shakespeare and James Joyce. But, he said, the writer I personally admire is Goethe. Though regrettably, he continued, laughing softly, his death makes it impossible to visit him and take tea together. He made a brief mention of Goethe's house, now a museum, and added, still laughing, when I visited that house I stood in his study and could picture the writer sitting there at his desk, composing his works. When he lived there, Goethe generally employed a secretary to transcribe what he dictated, rather than putting pen to paper himself. I was surprised by this, and responded that in that case it's hard to believe his sentences are entirely his own, as his secretary would have been able to improvise some minor edits in the course of his transcription, and since Goethe himself could not have remembered every sentence precisely as he'd dictated it, down to the punctuation, even on examining what his secretary produced, it's possible that he wouldn't have been able to spot any cuts or alterations. But the real cause for my surprise was that such a method, whereby another personality can squeeze its way into a creative work, was strange to me. The first writer immediately refuted this, saying that such a thing could not be. What makes you so sure? It's not as though you yourself are Goethe. It's unimaginable that a writer could compose a piece "through another's pen."

"The 'cornerman,' who was one of those secretary-cum-assistants, took it upon himself to arrange Goethe's manuscripts, you know. But he wasn't just an assistant, as people commonly think, who looked after Goethe's needs or ran small errands for him. Though his reputation has been thoroughly besmirched, a misconception that persists even today . . . the 'cornerman' was himself a poet, and had been one before he ever met Goethe. Though of course, some people devalue his poetic worth by labeling him 'Goethe's parrot.' He was the son of a poor peddler, and lived in poverty his whole life. His fellow poets would never accept him into their own artistic rank. But it's simply impossible to think that he would have put his hand freely to Goethe's manuscripts. He was Goethe's helper, but he was also his friend. I cannot think of him as someone who practiced petty deceptions while sitting at Goethe's side. And since such a thought can, on the other hand, occur to you," here the first writer broke off for a short while, as though pondering whether it was really admissible to speak his mind so frankly. "I think you must have never actually read Goethe's original writing. Or books about him, such as *Conversations with Goethe*. If you want to make claims about a certain writer, you have to have read his books. If only you'd known the extent to which his writing pursues strictness and exactitude."

After this discouragement, the first writer fixed me with a look of obvious disappointment. He'd probably supposed that I was an academic, faithful to the classics. I'd thought I knew a lot about him, but had completely forgotten his ardent worship of Goethe. What I knew of his career history and personal inclinations had actually led me to suspect the opposite.

"Are you suggesting that professional assistants could only work if they were always shut up in a corner? And that's why they were called 'cornermen'?" I'd hoped to avoid any further criticism by going off on a tangent, but he hurriedly dismissed it with a wave of his hand. "No no, that's just a coincidence." As though meaning to apologize for having been overly touchy, he arranged his features into an expression of tolerance, of choosing not to make an issue of my outburst. "His name really was 'cornerman.' Eckermann. It was a genuine surname, inherited from his father's father's father."

"Oh," I said, clamping my mouth shut after that short sound.

We drank lemon-leaf tea in his study. The pale green leaves floated in the teacups. His study also served as his bedroom, workroom, office, dining room, and living room. The apartment comprised this single decent-sized space with a balcony, plus a small cooking area and bathroom. Apparently he and his wife each lived in a different apartment in the same building, so that each could have their own creative space. In the center of the room were three longish desks, each of a slightly different size, shape, and even height to the others, the three arranged in the shape of the letter ⊏, and littered with books and mail, documents and photographs, a standing clock, a typewriter and an ashtray, a penholder, a glasses case, a notebook, a lamp, pills, a tape recorder, a vase, a candle, a wine glass, a fountain pen, one bottle of ointment and one of ink, a muffler for windy days, a flyswatter attached to a key ring, a fax machine and telephone and, next to these last, a pair of socks, tossed there casually. The bed was pushed into the corner where the ceiling sloped down, the one section of wall that hadn't been colonized by bookcases. The impression the first writer gave was not much different to what I'd gleaned from the photograph in the book. Granted that, according to him, it was twenty-two years since that photograph had been taken. In the photograph he was already gray-haired, a man with a short, sturdy neck and long, thick eyebrows, his lips curled in dissatisfaction. When he first removed his sunglasses, his gray-blue eyes appeared small, set in a face so deeply wrinkled it seemed strewn with dry straw. They were eyes that saw deeply, yet at a slant. Even the faint evening light seemed to dazzle him, causing him to blink repeatedly. Holding his teacup, this time he was the one to question me. But what it is that you do? Are you a journalist, or a writer? I grew terribly flustered; I was neither, and had been unable to prepare any response that might be suitably impressive.

Contrary to your expectations, you never went back to the first writer's house. The orchid's petals and the empty birdcage were swaying in the wind. The balcony with the laundry hung out to dry, the brass candlestick clattering on the table, the chirping of unfamiliar language pressing in through the open window, the noise of tourists thronging the alleyways, and of motorbikes, formed the scene. And what it hinted at was a curious waiting. The kind of formless waiting that takes place within a long and hazy nap, when your schedule for the rest of the day is free. The first writer was remembering your name. But he was unable to recall when it was that he'd seen you last. It might have been several years ago, or several decades. He was remembering you as a broad-minded journalist who wrote pieces for newspapers and radio. Though as far as I knew, you hadn't written an article for a very long time. What is it that you do? Are you a journalist, or a writer?

I looked the first writer straight in the eye and said, I've been a fan of your writing for a long time, more than a fan, in fact, and so I've been hoping for a long time to meet you, and even, if possible, to translate your work—as this is the only possible way of bringing me closer to you, that I could dare to ask for. Though my love for him was perfectly true, the idea of translating his work was something I'd plucked from thin air on the spot. "Oh, so you're a translator!" the first writer exclaimed, his face becoming open and welcoming. "I'd sensed you were something of the sort, you know. And I was correct." I was in fact nothing of the sort, had never done anything you could call proper translation, but once the words had popped out of my mouth it somehow felt as though I genuinely did have a long-held wish to translate his book. I made a promise that when I went back to my hometown I would translate his work into my mother tongue and find a publisher worthy of bringing it out. I really was planning to do this.

The two of us exchanged many letters. If emails were included in the tally, the person with whom I've maintained the most extensive correspondence would be none other than you. It was already enough to fill a fair-sized book just a year after we first met. Of course, there were plenty of brief notes and postcards with just a single line like "thanks" or "okay." You were an especial fan of letter writing. Each time you went traveling you sent several postcards back to friends, and your job meant that you spent more than half of each year away from home. My mailbox became crowded with your letters and postcards, not to mention the records and photographs, the essays and poetry collections. Once, you even tore out a newspaper advert you'd come across while eating breakfast in a hotel restaurant, and sent it to me, still permeated with the faint fragrance of tea. It was an ad for a tourist destination that the two of us had once visited together. You'd drawn an arrow in pen pointing to the bench in the photograph, with the words "We sat right here!" You also sent me any interviews you came across with either the first or second writer. Even when I went to Berlin for a while, you asked for my address there so you could keep mailing things. Some mail arrived for me there even after I'd moved out. One was an essay you wrote for a magazine, which you'd sent from America. The Berlin landlord forwarded it on, but it took almost eight months to get to me, having remained in Shanghai for several months in the bag of the person who was supposed to send it on. We called it the essay that had circumnavigated the globe. You sent quite a few letters even after we'd broken up. At the end of the final letter, you recommended a film, urging me to see it. You also wrote that I should go and visit the second writer, as you'd told him who I was. At this point, the second writer was already ill. A magazine carried his last interview, which he gave just before he died; in the photograph that appeared with it, his melancholy and ill health were evident in his face, in his huge sunken eyes. He wore suspenders to hold up his trousers, and his hands gripped the straps where they ran over his shoulders. As if they were a slender lifeline still tethering him to existence, the last such bond remaining.

Mr. H, how do you feel about these articles that talk about your cancer? Does it cause you to lose peace of mind, or start panicking?

I'm not exactly pleased about it, of course. It's true that such articles make you shudder when you first see them. But all the same, I don't start panicking or anything like that. The only one who panics is my wife. And so, I try to comfort her, you know. Saying "Darling, this is all a part of nature."

The first writer and I watched the film together.

There was a scene in which the man said, my whole life, I've been afraid of being alone and being unable to write, those two things.

We were sitting in the theater. Once the male protagonist finished delivering those lines the first writer grasped my hand. He turned to me and said, "Those pitiful lines could have been spoken by me. I've spent my whole life failing to break free from them." "But I envy you. You've accomplished everything there is, both as a writer and as a human being, and you've managed to keep yourself free from some things—economic necessity, for example. It seems there's nothing left for you to fear. Your world is insanely enviable." "For god's sake please don't say 'accomplished everything.' It sounds like 'finished with everything.'" "All lives come to an end, including those with no such accomplishments. I could write a great deal about that other kind of life." "You're so pessimistic about your future!" "And you aren't?" "I'm aware that there's no further future for me. But that doesn't make me a pessimist." "There's only one kind of future I wish for. One where I can free my soul from the mud suffocating it to death! But the more time passes, the clearer it becomes that both a soul and freedom are equally impossible."

"If only you knew what an uncertain, indeterminate thing the 'soul' is, that it leaves us helplessly ignorant of how to look after it, even at our final hour!" He brought his face closer to mine and lowered his voice, speaking almost in a whisper. "Come and see me like this once a year." The faces on the screen undulated in the uneasy darkness, a composite of light and dust. The dream's wavelength spread. Bright white ekstasis flashing like lightning. That metallic dream pierced through me as it passed, and I felt a kind of pain that no longer hurt. "Come and see me once a year. For your sake, and for mine. Each year, around this time, come to this city and see if my name is still written by the door to this house. If it is, that will mean I'm still here. Then open the door and come right in, put down your bags, and spend a couple of weeks here. I have an old typewriter you can use for translation work. The kitchen is pretty cramped, but you can make yourself a basic breakfast, or something simple like soup. In the alley directly below there are lots of restaurants for tourists, and you can buy fruit, bread, dumplings, and delicious coffee in the shops, whenever you like. You can keep the windows open all year round here. Go for a walk around the ruins in the evenings. You can keep your orchid in this room if you like, or a bird. Even if you give them names in your language and speak to them every morning, I won't mind in the slightest. I'll sit with them for hours, waiting for that moment when you address them in your mother tongue. You'll give water to the orchid, food to the bird, and your language to me. To me, it will sound like a love song without lyrics. And you're welcome to leave your bags here between visits. Do you know those kinds of popular songs? If you come back to visit after leaving your bag, even if a year has passed . . . We won't have that much time together, but there'll be so much else for you to share in. And at night the two of us will sit side by side drinking lemon tea and I'll read my writing to you. So you will be my first reader. Just a small gift that I can give to you. Come and visit me once a year, like that. Take a vacation in this city. And while you're here, dream of the other cities you've not been able to go to. Write something about them. Travel together through dreams. Then, one year, when my name is no longer outside the door, think, then, that I am no longer able to welcome you, that I cannot even remember you any more. Cannot read to you, cannot listen to you. After that, there will be no more need to come and visit, not even the following year, as I will have ended up unable to write. I will be truly alone, and so, I will no longer need you."

I get out of the taxi and enter the house with its small garden. The house is at the far end of the church tenement block; it stretches back quite far, but has a narrow facade. The front door has recently been painted. Next to the house is a spruce, and on that tree a young owl sits with its eyes half closed. For several weeks already, at around this time of day, that owl has flown from the nearby wood of Chinese thujas to this spruce right by your house. It is dusk.

I remember the day we were together on the boat. In the ash-gray air, dense with murky fog, the harbor scene spread out as a wet painting. There weren't many tourists on the boat; though it wasn't especially cold, it was constantly sleeting. We were the only ones on deck. You were wearing a baseball cap you'd bought at a Busan street stall, and I had the hood of my coat up over my head. The coat's waterproof material and the flag of the company that ran the sightseeing trips both produced a rough flapping sound. The flag bore writing in the shape of a shield. The whistle announcing a cargo ship's departure hung heavy and drawn-out in the fog. Gulls cried as they wheeled in the gray air, and lights flickered on the hill near the harbor, the windows of rich people's houses. It was the middle of the day, but it was as overcast and dusky as evening as far as the eye could see. The boat was making directly for an orange lighthouse visible up ahead, producing the monotonous repetition of water splashing then sucking each time it passed a hulking cargo ship. It occurred to me that I needed the bathroom. When I made to go down below deck, you told me you would never forgive me if I left you up here alone. Not meaning a quick trip to the bathroom, of course. You laid particular emphasis on "if you leave me alone." *My dear*, if you left me alone in this desolate place I would never forget it. And I would never forgive you, you said, with a faint air of theatricality, standing tall on the deck behind me as I, heading to the stairs, tossed out over my shoulder that I was just going to the bathroom and would be back in a moment. I thought how strange it was that I wasn't angered by your words. Hadn't you always been the one to leave the other alone? The blue iron stairway was slippery with water. The smell of boiling coffee seeped out from the boat's empty bar. On the other side of the window, its glass blurred with condensation, the bar worker was leaning against the wall in the small galley, smoking a cigarette. The boat pitched and rolled, and a damp mouthful of coarse-grained fog rushed into my throat and lungs. I coughed. It was the kind of weather that called to mind extreme sadness and impulsiveness.

You go up to the first floor and open the study window. And, perching on the windowsill, stare fixedly at the branch where the owl is sitting. The owl is still as a statue, stuck fast to a branch of the tree. The light breeze fails to ruffle a single feather, not even a single one. Where had the young owl learned to hold so still, as still as the sleep of kitchenware, lying unused in the dead of night? As the owl was almost the same color as the tree, and largely concealed by a fretwork of twigs, it would have been difficult to pick out had you not been aware of its daily visits, the fact that it came to that tree at the same time each day and perched there for a while, facing your room. Keeping your eyes fixed on the owl, you get an old film camera out of one of the drawers. You point the camera at the owl, zooming in as close as possible, and take the photograph. You didn't even enjoy photography as a hobby, never mind being skilled at it. It simply wasn't your kind of thing. You didn't even own a digital camera, like almost everyone else these days. But in that one vague yet revelatory moment, that moment, abrupt and specific as though in a dream, of wanting to breathe in *being* itself, to draw it deep inside yourself, *being* with the sluggish, ponderous mass of a whale, already regretting the inevitable disappearance of such a moment, its vanishing into the words of some abstract concept like every other fleeting inspiration, you photographed the owl that was there before you, then heard someone calling up from the floor

51

below to say that dinner was ready. You open the bathroom window and lazily brush your teeth as you sit on the toilet, completely naked. The white froth of toothpaste bubbles and expands inside your mouth, dropping to the floor. A line from Walser's poetry: "Night, the dream beetle crawls into my open mouth."

In dreams, looking into a mirror is a hair-raising experience. The empty black holes looking back at you, so threateningly strange and ravenous. A river flows in bed, and on its bank stands a single tree. Its branches stretch out horizontally, and your wristwatch hangs from one of them, ticking. It will still go on telling the time when we have disappeared from the earth. We, now lying down, black-and-white bodies delving deeply into each other. Until we eventually transform into fossilized tree scarabs, with only our shells remaining.

The dream's fade-out.

52

For a long time all I received in the mail were bills and advertising flyers. If I didn't pay the bills on time they were sent to me again, printed in successively larger and more splendid type, seeming paradoxically like presents. One day I opened the mailbox and discovered an owl inside, watching me. Its round body was patterned with dappled shade, and you could see its eyes between tree branches, cast darkly down. It was the photograph of the owl, printed out and glued to the front of a postcard. The owl in the photograph had been enlarged into a clumsily pixelated version of itself, unnaturally inflated like an overstuffed specimen. There was a faint scratch on one corner of the photograph's sleek surface, and the air between the branches was a dull purple, the color of dusk. On the back of the postcard was my address, a date stamp, and an airmail sticker. The sticker had been stamped with the post office's seal, four neatly waving lines. Imprinted over the word "airmail," it could double as the owl's left wing, a modern hieroglyph denoting both distance and continuity.

The bed is beneath the sloping ceiling, in the shadows in the corner of the room. I drop my bag at the entrance and go straight to it, lying down without removing my shoes or coat. I curl up facing the wall, pulling my knees right up to my chest, and close my eyes in this position I know best, of slow intimate waiting. It is some time or other, some monsoon afternoon when the hot din of the sunlight and the radio is incessant. The bird seller passes through the alley, balancing a cage on the back of his bicycle. In this moment, some people will be buying a ferry ticket for a rendezvous with the dead. Others will be beginning to write an essay relating to dreams. But I want nothing to do with any of this, only sleep.

North
Station

My silk moth, my moonwalker, my inkpot, my meadow
tree, my sleepyhead, my evening light, my scatterbrain,
my reverse counter.[1]

*H*e, seized with tension, will kiss the woman before the
train arrives. But how? She keeps her eyes downturned,
flustered and awkward as melted wax dripping messily
from a candle, and holds herself perfectly still; the clock on the
platform has just passed midnight. Their bodies are angled in the
direction from which the train will come; both are so incredibly
on edge that if a blind and disoriented pigeon were to nose-dive
in front of them, they would mistake it for a passing train—the
train they will have missed, the train they will have failed to catch.
His mind is taken over by the memory of a city one summer in
the 1970s, when the scent of seltzer was strong in the air and the
hot, humid streets swam when he looked down on them from the
balcony. The memory of the rattan bed and its thin blanket, the

---

1. Friederike Mayröcker, "What I Call You When I Think of You and You Aren't
Here."

tiled bathtub, and the enormous rusted tap shaped like a cross. The woman's address was all he knew of her; and the woman lived in that city. When she had first handed him the scrap of paper onto which she had written her address, at the time when their fate— which would eventually leave them each remembered by the other as no more than an address—had just been set in motion, he felt the memory of that city, which he'd thought he had long forgotten, rise up inside him as a damp rainbow, accompanied by a single cry. Like an aged peacock winging wearily up above the treetops, some early morning in India. When he spent a week lodging on an unfamiliar balcony, battling clouds of mosquitos and sleep thin yet sticky as a swamp, the footsteps of the woman as a young child might have passed through the alley directly below him. Had she appeared again after all this time, here in this place, waiting for the last train? It was barely a day since his first sight of her, and confusion still gripped him; still, he was tormented by the illusion of having been pursuing her all this time without knowing it, and of the various cities he'd since traveled through—ever since the one he hadn't at the time known was hers—having been for ages in this long pursuit, as he fumbled after the footprints of the woman he had unknowingly left behind.

55

Now the backdrop that frames the woman's head and shoulders is a night festooned with spiderwebs, a corner of this world knitted from disordered electric wires, awaiting the train's departure. The train ticket in the woman's pocket gives wordless testament to this world. Externally, it is the world of the platform's information board, where the train times flash up, of the enormous round clock whose minute hand inches forward with a click, of billboards for beer and french fries, and of the lit balconies lining the rail tracks. That world, patient as the hunched elderly. A world of pipes, ducts, and conduits. A world of pipes that grope their way forward in the darkness, electric wires and water pipes and measuring instruments and fiber-optic cables and transmitters, existing for the sake of drainage, ventilation, and the night strolls of ladybugs, a place for a pigeons to roost or a guiding device for the blind. But upon closer inspection it revealed its connection to the world of the bathhouse's mini radio, which had played Telemann in the mornings, of the glasses and wallets and pen nibs he'd lost, the various addresses that had been given him, the cities and countless streets to which those addresses had silently pointed, the secret alleys and neighbors whose faces he hadn't known. Now, this hour, fragments of all the trivial worlds, all the scenes of his life he'd swept past with such indifference, captured his consciousness, invading his memory in one great rush. As everything that makes up life and lifestyle, they were the origin of all the countless memories, thoughts, and impressions he'd ever jotted down, casually, even unconsciously, the secret museum of every inspiration his life had ever known. They were the eyes of the innumerable totality of objects simultaneously fixing him with their stares. And, at the same time, it was an incredibly simple action, formed from a single melody, nothing other than the sleep of the world. From a single melody where both the eyes and the mind are closed. Closing one's eyes, an action of surrendering oneself to the world, and the peacock shade beneath shuttered eyelids. The act of sleeping, the conscious awareness of it, came so close to something pure and absolute as to provoke an internal cry: "For god's sake stay like this!" Just as he, looking up at the platform clock this very moment, longed to command time to stop in its tracks.

The woman has her cold, firm hand resting on the platform bench, and his own palm presses gently down on it. Rigid in these positions, they both face the direction from which the train will come. How he'd longed for a single night's worth of sleep on the woman's balcony. Once again, he recalls the rattan bed. The depth and warmth of that night of mosquitos, that night of fog, that sour smell hanging low over the ground . . . He was lying down. Drinking in the soft snuffle of the woman's breathing, with his face, his own sleep, buried in the nape of her neck. Each gust of wind produced a furious crackling from the tarp stretched over the balcony. He thinks he can hear rain. He is lying down on the fold-up bed beneath the tarp with his clasped hands resting on his stomach, his senses half-open to the foreign language drifting up like the low hum of insects, the clamor of the market and the smoke from the mosquito coil, the strong warmth of unfamiliar spices rising from the kitchen. If he could somehow find himself back there again, perhaps he would fall asleep after shouting "stay like this!" out loud. Sleeping, he will fly through the distant streets as he clings to the woman's bosom, and her eyelids and the night will tickle his sleeping toes.

The clock is wound for a long time, rattling in his ears. A huge wheel clatters over the cobbled, tree-lined street and, in the wake of that autumn, leaves flush red and die. "What is that attitude of the November leaves, so passionately in thrall to the wind? They do not cry out loud, do not whimper to themselves. What should it be called, that which is neither whispering, murmuring, dancing, singing, laughing, nor giggling, neither trembling nor kissing their wind, feeling the contact as a sweet relief?" The leaves depart their melancholy home, was how it had sometimes occurred to him while overcome with sorrow or absorbed in thought. He understands the gestures, the speech of the leaves. He understands the language of their sadness! But the proper name for it eludes him, and so he begins again. "The leaves of the trees do not cry out loud. It is not that they whimper. They do not whisper, do not murmur . . ." The road stretches out ahead, and the wheel clatters on. Fixed direction and uniform vibration, and one decisive word, which refuses to reveal itself even after a whole life spent wandering in search of it. It's not certain exactly from what point, but he has long accepted it as a part of his life. "I will go to my grave without knowing what it is birch leaves do. I know what it is, but I can't put it into words," and he recalls again the words of that exile and depressive Kurt Tucholsky, who killed himself! "I can't put it into words. The word won't come to me." At that, it seems as though he really can hear the sound of the birch leaves, quivering in the wind in some distant wood—though woods and the like are entirely removed from the place where the two of them actually are, a platform in the middle of the huge train station—and he cannot help but strain to listen. As a youth, he had always been somewhat envious of those who killed themselves. Especially during those frequent periods when he felt his mind grow strong and sharp, the writings of suicides had been his only support. Surely those who did not kill themselves could not speak about freedom, or humanity's absolute condition. Because, however you interpreted it, they had compromised, chosen conformity. He had at one time pondered whether, like Tucholsky, who had died from an overdose of sleeping pills while exiled in Sweden, he had not long since arrived at the point of being unable to say or write anything, had been rejected by everyone and banished from their sight, and thus been brought to a pathological state from which it was impossible to return.

Yet another memory seized him, of a clock in the classical style, bulky yet elegant. He had seen it in the display case of a secondhand store, next to some chipped teacups, a rusted manual typewriter that looked more like a sewing machine, public school textbooks from decades ago, a 1960s photo album that was never going to sell, and a rather poorly-bound edition of Tucholsky's essays—that's right, Tucholsky again! He leaned in close to the store window and, as he peered inside, a handful of pigeons landed on some breadcrumbs scattered on the pavement opposite, where a police boat was docked by the bank of the canal. As this was some-what out of the ordinary, several passersby were milling around expectantly, thinking that the police must be fishing something out of the water; after a while, when nothing had happened, they dispersed, disappointed. He straightened up, and walked on past the secondhand store. He directed his steps along the canal-side path, a place of swans and mud. A long time ago, having moved here after retirement and sought out the best route for a regular stroll, he marked on a map in colored pencil the course he had settled on. The route went through the old alleyways of the canal area, which boasted a cluster of used book and other secondhand shops. In the distant past, when mass production had yet to catch on, craftsmen and artisans had had shops stretching the entire length of the alley. He stopped on the corner between a glassblower's workshop and a leather bookbinder's. Bicycles and the wind swept on ahead of him, and the bright clarity of children's voices soared up from the cemetery, into the winter sky's chill blue. His eyes followed that ascent. There, his memories swelled and expanded, outpacing his present. Running on ahead of Tucholsky and the swans, of the woman's sleeping lips, all the way to the north station, and to the woman's house.

He, too, is living in the city, and at the same time in another, five hours away on the express train. Now and then he would go to an even more distant city, where he stayed at the house of an acquaintance. That house, where he had stayed in his university days, he now remembers without name or countenance, only as a room, that attic room with its unusually low ceiling, a bathroom below the landing, the sofa he had used as a bed, the incomparably quiet hours he'd spent there. There, in the house of his acquaintance, he had almost always been alone, and thus even more keenly aware of his immediate environment, its light and temperature and airflow. The light that never shone with the same color or degree of brightness twice in any given day, the wind that had seemed always to have blown in from the golden hills of early autumn, and the long interior hours, each totally unique, of days when he didn't have lectures, their constant subtle shifts like the colors of a sunset, their atmosphere of gentle repletion like the feeling of having just eaten a meal of warm potatoes, hours he had spent writing letters. Outside the window, the narrow roof and sloping walls stood with their backs to him, square and rectangular windows facing out into the wind. The memory of those stained old walls. Walls that had originally been painted a deep yellow, but had faded over time and grown patches of mold-green moss. Walls which still, now and then, when rays of winter sun sliced down between the clouds, were momentarily revived, glittering brightly as though scoured by a lithographer's chemicals, each individual brick given its own color and shading, fragrant orange or chest-tingling rose, glossy olive or fresh pea-green, rain-damp charcoal or the murky sheen of tar. And the poems that he had read there, limbs folded into the long, narrow alcove of the bathroom window. Their stanzas followed the wind out of the open window, to whirl around the confusion of chimneys and television antennae that made up the aerial forest, then disappear off toward the gray-shrouded city center. When was it that he had last kissed a woman so ardently, his lips as passionate as when they pronounced poetry? In that city or this, at the house of his acquaintance or on the platform in the north station, while waiting for the train. On the window seat where he read poetry, in the shadow of the walls, or on the path by the canal. Outside the door or inside it. Or a woman who had just crossed the threshold. Embracing a blazing heart, and longing for it to stay like that. Like water boiling in a teakettle, a whistle resounded in his chest. According to the timetable the train would arrive within the next few minutes. It would be the last train of the evening.

Who would have first used the expression "to capture someone's heart"? A hunter, perhaps, who would know deeply how it feels to capture a beating heart, a living thing, how the one doing the capturing finds himself captivated, in thrall to the sense of his own omnipotence? Like capturing a fawn or kit still warm from its mother's heat. Someone who, like the hunter, introduces himself into his victim's eyes at such an early stage. Who deploys his imagination to render in his mind's eye that state of utter despair to which the lack of any exit, the terrible clarity of this fact, gives a paradoxical sweetness. Who reproduces this state through what we call a verbal expression. In such a way, the expression would have been born not through those who are captured, but through those who do the capturing. Since the victim has no time for song. And because, in depicting the emotional state of suffering, the one who stands outside it as opposed to being gripped by its claws has the freedom of objectivity, is better able to use his imagination to turn such grim fatality into song. Such is the work of sprites; using a song to hold sway over the heart. Carnivorous sprites, who have dwelled inside human beings since time immemorial, are the ones who sing the heart. They are suffering's only surviving witnesses, its only interested parties. The sprites who create suffering, and who thus eventually learned to feel empathy, were able to experience suffering for themselves through their own songs, and, moreover, wished to do so. To capture the heart, to rattle the heart, to steal the heart away—for him, such expressions strongly evoked long-held carnivorous habits, human being as predator. Right in front of his eyes, a young woman is waiting for the train, a young woman who, as a predator lusting after his flesh and blood, is fated to empathize with him as her potential victim and end up made pregnant with his song. Young women of a certain type were both recurring characters in his life and predators who preyed on him, and even now he remembers them well. The frighteningly young mother and the coquettish nurse; the music teacher who, despite her cold, unfeeling exterior, would frequently fall into a depression; an accountant with a stutter, who danced slowly as though

underwater; women who had been both unlucky boss and innumerable harem, big-hearted jailer and a bashfully-blushing actress
in a suggestive play; lesbian, nymphomaniac, and nun, all at the
same time. The one thing that had remained common throughout
was that these "young women" acted like enzymes, reawakening
a song for him through their own unconscious singing of it. And
so, unbeknownst to themselves, those women were both his sprite
and his song. His song was indebted to his women, his Eurydices.
Ultimately, his so-called "self" was equally dependent. His heart
produced a quavering tune in line with their vibrations and, in
accordance with this wavelength, thousands of verbal expressions
performed his existence. His so-called self knows nothing of the
process by which these expressions are made, knows them only in
their outward-facing guise. Those expressions that ultimately come
from women, of which a single decisive word could inform him of
the truth, a truth he knows and understands but is unable to put
a name to, and thus will die in a state of ignorance. "Young lovers
do not cry out loud, do not whimper to themselves. What should
it be called, that which is neither whispering, murmuring, dancing,
singing, laughing, nor giggling? They do not tremble, do not kiss
the wind and feel the contact as a sweet relief . . . I will go to my
grave without knowing what it is."

He has no idea that at some later date, when this present-now
resurfaces in his memory, he will scarcely pause at the moment just
before the last train departed, that moment when his lips had just
grazed those of the woman, like warm air hastily scudding past—
pretending not to be lips but breath gone astray—before proceed-
ing onward. In truth, that moment lasted no longer than it took
the platform clock's second hand to move a single click, but to him
it lay outside the flow of time, was instead the fossil of an enormous deep-sea whale—yes, a fossilized whale!—remaining in his
mind as a discrete moment, forever delayed. When the train pulled

into the station, the woman's hand and his reflexively moved apart. And their hands again verified the feel of the other's palm, in order to shake; a still more formal pose followed this polite gesture, an attempt to conceal the extreme fear and fretfulness which wracked them both—comprising the fear "we might never meet again," the mute questions "will you really write to me?" and its partner "will you really wait for my letter?," and a continuous flood of wordless doubts each following on the heels of the other. The woman's lip quivered as though she might burst into tears. "Are you afraid?" he asked. Without even asking "afraid of what?," the woman hurriedly shook her head. And turned toward the train as she did so, one foot raised to step up into the train. Struggling to conceal a look of frustration, her face contorted into a strange shape. The conductor, wearing a red hat, was standing outside the door to the train and peering at the platform clock. The wind mingled the faint scent of oil with that of coffee from the dining car and of train carpets dirtied by muddy footprints, stimulating their sense of smell. At almost the same time as the conductor's second whistle broke the platform's frozen silence, signaling departure, he bent over the woman's lips in a stiff, hurried movement. And wished her a safe journey.

At some later date, when this present-now resurfaces in his memory, arriving each time at the memory's end, he would instead take the woman's hand and climb up into the train with her. Passing through the carriages, down the narrow corridor adjoining the passenger compartments, they end up in the dining car, its air sullied with steam. Their bodies vibrate at the same frequency as that of the juddering train. Their wordless whispers, blind stares, and paralyzed lips perform this regular back-and-forth movement, rattling along with the scenery framed by the window, the timetable hanging in the corridor, the cutlery and crockery. All these vibrations taken together produce the wavelength of distress. From right to left, and from left to right. Their eyelids and hearts oscillate at this identical rhythm. A slow acceleration soon arriving at a steady speed, creaking and rocking whenever it rounds a bend, and at those parts where the track is jointed together, as though arrived at the very edge of the world, the body of the train jolts along while the wheels below growl and shriek. In no time at all, slender glasses are filled with clear yellow alcohol and handed out to the irritable passengers. They fall asleep leaning on each other, with their glasses still at their lips. Every now and then when the train comes to a stop, a long sharp blast from the conductor's whistle will shatter their restless slumber. This hand and that, these lips and those, that do not pull apart even in a sleep achieved with open eyes, this dream and that, overlapping. This is how the journey goes, for countless weeks and months. Passing platform after platform, each deserted as a barren steppe, they travel toward the city where the woman lives. Toward one of the countless cities that lie between this, which he had arrived at quite by chance, and that, and another city beyond these two, a pall hanging over these cities' existence, which labor under the weight of anonymity until they finally succeed in obtaining a name. Before he left that city, people had said "Though we are living in the same century, we never know what on earth goes on in that distant province—in the border regions of the world, in village after nameless village where the national boundaries are constantly changing, in one of the countless cities on this earth that today fights for Stalin and tomorrow against him." But he would seek out the woman's house. He would go to the farthest corner of the farthest corner and knock on the door he found there. A whole life spent seeking the house of a young woman in such a distant place. And so only knocking on the door. And even if it were Stalin's name he found there, there could still be no substitute. The woman is living next to the desk in his room . . . but as her address only, the address that he'd pinned there to the top of a pile of notepaper, her home address. And since at the same time the woman will also exist somewhere in this alley with the strange-sounding name, all of this—the labyrinthine alleys, corners where dogs loiter, bicycles, the fruit stall where he will ask for directions—will be, to him, a plum of ripe yearning. Midsummer of 1970-something, sweet, deeply purpled plums whose flesh is critically overripe, seemingly about to burst out of themselves in the heat of the sun. Given that lips to which a song had once risen speak unbidden until they die, no gesture would be able to prevent his dream from strolling billions of kilometers and reaching the woman's corner, the woman's plum. His lips were forever flying toward hers, even after the train had pulled out from the platform, had been sucked away into the darkness in one deep gust. Like a butterfly flitting its way across the sea, a dead swan finding the water of the canal, like a remembered autumn sliding on into November, and as though all the trains in the world ran toward the woman's address. Always at some later date, when this present-now resurfaces in his memory.

He woke up in the middle of the night. Slowly, the bodied forms of furniture revealed faint shapes in the darkness. He hadn't been dreaming, hadn't heard something, wasn't thirsty, didn't need to go to the bathroom. He'd simply woken up. That awakening had a different character to opening your eyes in the morning. He hadn't slept entirely soundly, and was still deep in the ravine of sleep's vacuum. He turned his head on the pillow, thinking that he would fall asleep again almost right away. But it wasn't possible. He knew what it was, the root of this fretfulness that had gone on for several months now. He had hope. And this hope was a frightening thing. For example, there can be no peace for the condemned criminal who clings to the hope that his execution might be stayed. And no freedom either. The day before the execution,

65

would the convict be able to sleep? His mind was swept up in a vortex of raging thoughts. How old would he have been when the newspaper printed the shocking photograph of the Turkish dictator Adnan Menderes hanging from the gallows? In the museum of postwar history—where he had first met Ann, whose mother had been working there at the time—Ann had just so happened to be standing right of the photograph of the executed dictator. She had been very young (he had felt certain that, like other young women her age, she would never even have heard of Adnan Menderes); her plump figure was not unattractive, she had her longish hair tied in braids, and crude rubber boots like those worn by sailors. As she turned her head and looked at him, the corners of her lips turned sharply upward. The way she was standing next to the photograph made it seem as though those red lips were a spearhead aimed at Menderes. At the same time, as though the look on her face were nothing special, merely chance, she said "I don't know who that man is, but I'm sure the one who should be hanged is you. Am I right?" Practically as soon as they met, they were packing their things and setting off on a trip to Malaysia. Once they reached their destination, not a single moment went by without Ann finding a way to start arguments, in which he was fated to be ever the loser. He could not resist Ann. They'd assumed they were done with each other after that trip, but that wasn't how things turned out. In fact, he'd gone to see her only the day before. A signature had been necessary in the matter of inheriting a relative's house, and though this could have been solved quite easily by mail, he'd chosen to drop by Ann's office. She didn't like him, and she didn't bother to conceal that. Ann stood with her back to the wall. Sometimes, while making a gesture of explaining a project to a customer, she would shuffle sideways along the wall, for no particular reason; it was a ponderous movement, like forcing swollen feet to walk in too-small shoes, and made her appear barely able to move under the weight of her own mass. Though she knew that he had entered the office, Ann did not look at him. Her lips and chest were thrust out in front of her, like someone on the point of a voluminous sigh. Though the cut of her black skirt was demure and classy, she was so squeezed into it that the slightest movement sent a ripple through her bell-shaped lower half. She'd put on weight since a few years ago when he'd last seen her; now, her skin glistened noticeably, and even her hair looked to have grown thicker, more lustrous. As ever, she looked more like a strapping opera singer fresh from a production of Verdi, or a tall Viking maiden standing spiritedly at the prow of a ship (wearing the distinctive horned helmet and carrying a round shield and curved ax, as though about to charge at something and smash it to pieces) than the financial officer of a credit institution. He and his world were clearly included in the list of things this youthful woman was itching to smash. "Oh, it's you," she spat out eventually, when his proximity meant speech could no longer be avoided, her words filled with a sense of obligation, the sense that she might as well get it over with as quickly as possible, seeing that it had to be done. And clasped her hands neatly in front of her belly button.

He wanted to fall asleep again, but he couldn't. Very far away—though clearly somewhere within the building—a wall clock was chiming three in the morning. He thought about sleep. Sleep, a word symbolic of forgetting, lightens the load of the night that has fallen through forgetting and forgetting again, and sends it flying away. He was accompanied by a sleep that was an experience of the soul, both an imitation of and a rehearsal for death. Sleep, the asceticism practiced by a Buddhist monk, everything falling under the designation "alone" . . . his whirling thoughts gave rise to vertigo, and a longing whose intensity shocked him. At some point, the firm, dry form of a woman's hand had lain beneath his own. A small, warm hand. A bird flying into his palm. With a

hard beak, a warm belly softly feathered, and glassy eyes recalling the hard, smooth surface of amber. Overlaid in this way, their
hands crossed vast plains, stony deserts, and high mountain ranges.
They exhausted all the realm of time, passing over to dimensions
beyond. Their hands flew over Moses's reed bed and the strait that
divides this world from the next. This side of the earth was the
woman's exposed breast, and on the far side were the scenes that
that breast was dreaming. He opened his eyes to scan the terrain.
But the world hovered over by their linked hands was nothing but
a land of darkness. Where is this? Where on earth! The breast's
sweetness leaked like honey from out of the dream's private jar. His
imagination was wandering, had lost its way; the woman's house
appeared abruptly at the very end of a road. The stony road sloped
gently upward. He was sweating inside his winter suit, and the
buildings lining both sides of the road recalled public schools or
national museums. There was an airfield nearby, formerly used as
a barracks, and the noise of planes taking off or landing could be
heard at regular intervals. In the darkness that enveloped his surroundings entirely, making it impossible to tell whether it was day
or night, the woman's house looked down on him with a solemn
countenance. The house looked like a deep-sea whale beached on a
sandbank, moments before death, and also like the Papal window.
In front of it, he stood and shook violently for a while. In this
deep, viscous stillness, known by none.

The concerto still wasn't over, but his headache was too unbearable
for him to stay seated any longer. Gritting his teeth so as not to
let out a moan, he tried, as he slipped out of his row, to gain some
measure of comfort from the conviction that he hadn't been enjoying the performance anyway. The air in the packed concert hall,
its smells of clashing perfumes, deodorized underarms, starched
fabrics, hair products, varnished instruments, and rosin—merely

recalling it was enough to make his throat feel tight. Each breath was a struggle. After forcing an apologetic smile in the direction of the usher, he hurried across the lobby and down the spiral staircase, the whole place decked out to the nines. He remembered that he had once loved these very stairs, these smells that were now choking him. Wasn't it none other than the scent of Friday evenings, which had never before seemed less than lovely? It was the scent of ink from a freshly-printed score, of air freshener that lingers on the collar and in the hair, of leather shoes permeated by the seven o'clock fog, of a restless heart, of wine and cigarettes, and, more than anything else, of well-dressed women. He got out his handkerchief and mopped the sweat from his forehead, then, after collecting his coat from the cloakroom, pushed open the main door and went straight out into the street. Once he had inhaled a deep draught of the fresh, cold air, his vision started to unblur itself, along with the contents of his head. It had been overcast all evening; when he'd arrived, the thick clouds had been so low they'd seemed about to smother him. Now, it was snowing. Fine-grained as sand, the snow struck angrily at his eyelids and brows. He blinked rapidly and a little of this snow melted, the water tracking downward over his cheeks. He paid no mind to his lack of a hat, just went and sat down on the nearest bench, practically collapsing onto the slats. Leaning back, he stretched his arms up over his head. He continued to struggle for breath, though he no longer felt on the brink of suffocation. He didn't want to go back inside the building. In fact, he wanted to leave the area entirely. One day, people would stumble upon him somewhere quite different. In a Chiang Mai orphanage, for example, teaching English to children orphaned by AIDS or tsunamis. A long time ago, an old friend who was working to set up such a school there had told him of the need for trained teachers. And an even longer time ago, he taught English and linguistics in a secondary school, albeit for a very brief period. What was stopping him from taking up that line of work again? Given that there were places in need of his skills. And given how easy it would be to get on a train and just leave. From the north station, where all the world's trains were bound for a single address.

He stayed at home the next day. When he heard the mailman's bicycle jolting over the bumpy paving stones, the leaves were all rustling on their branches. The air was filled with the damp moisture of the earth and the scent of young shoots. He opened the window halfway. The mailman thrust a letter into the mailbox, swung his leg back over his bicycle, and peddled off. The clattering of the mailbox's metal lid was still reverberating even after he had disappeared, and a dog barked twice as though in answer. Then the echoes died down, and silence reigned once more. His hand, clutching a pencil, hung motionless over the paper. There was still the creaking of the chair. But aside from that, the world was liberated from sound. In that moment, he slipped the moorings of himself. He listened hard, concentrating, as though he was a hunter trying to pick up the sound of a bird laying an egg in a distant coppice, several kilometers away. There was no sound to be heard. Though he was clearly alone, he was seized by an intense shyness, leaving him unable to move. This shyness proceeded from boastfulness, from private expectations, and from his inability to put any of this into words. Without needing to consciously formulate the thought, he knew the address from which it had come flying, that letter which the mailman had left in the mailbox with a clang, and which was the only letter to have arrived that day, when any letter at all was a rare occurrence. It was early spring, the days continuing to be oddly mild. Around noon, when the light morning fog had dissipated and the sun briefly showed its honey-colored face, there were even times when a breeze blew soft as a quilt.

It was a very long letter, twelve pages, handwritten. It had been sent in a business envelope rather than the smaller one used for letters. Each page had been meticulously numbered, and the body of the letter itself had several sections in which the ink and handwriting looked slightly different, as though it had been written over a number of days. The handwriting, which at first flowed with a schoolgirl's affectionate ease, seemed to reach a sticking point every few sentences, tensing up and trembling uneasily. I shriek! the handwriting confessed. It took him around an hour to read the letter from beginning to end. There were some parts that he read several times. The sun set completely in the course of his reading, so he had to get up halfway through and switch on the light. The hour which formed the border between evening and night did not last the letter's single exhalation. The shadow of him holding his head in his hands smothered the book-lined wall. Once night had fallen in earnest, the temperature dropped markedly.

At the end of the letter the woman wrote that she wanted to see him again, just one more time. "For god's sake, please give me permission to visit you. Please decide everything for me, I mean. I need to be decided." He paced up and down in the chilly room, his hand to his forehead. Swept up in some terrifying passion, his senses were so disarranged that he'd forgotten to close the window. Before he'd even read the letter through he knew how he would answer the woman's entreaty, and the result was not at all to his liking. If only it were possible to alter his decision. But how? If only it were possible to turn back time, he would return to the north station platform where he'd been standing several months ago, follow the woman up into the train and travel far away with her, to somewhere very different from the place he now found himself. To an oh-so-eternal yesterday. Was it the woman's fault? No. It wasn't because of her at all. He shook his head as though confirming his own firm resolve. "It's entirely natural for one person to form a relationship with another. Even if that relationship is the fruit of error and uncertainty. No—or is it that the closer a human relationship is to error, the more perfect, the more natural it becomes? It's no one's fault when a relationship doesn't proceed straightforwardly from one person to another. Even when the individual is captivated by himself rather than the so-called object of his affections, such an object is still needed, if only as a convention." He couldn't claim to be a stranger to those relationships that are formed without the need to fall in love, of that elegant intimacy and tranquil companionship, that comfort and affection, unease and insufficiency, passivity and resignation, of the constant fretful need for psychological escape. His life, like many others', was a garden blooming with these exact relationships. He was well aware of what the woman was currently experiencing. Though she would not yet have realized this, it was a congenital disease of those who are by nature already liberated. It was the stench inevitably caused by moving in the direction of freedom. Just then, he recalled that he had become a father through absolutely no will of his own, that it had taken almost twenty years for him to learn of the existence of his daughter, and that her name was Ann. Ann's mother had telephoned out of the blue and demanded that he take his now-adult daughter with him on this trip to Malaysia. Becoming a father through no will of your own could be every bit as appalling as inadvertently becoming a mother, even granting that no one had forced any responsibility on him. To put it boldly, it was a basic human right to be protected from such a thing. In his own case, he was too free from mother and daughter for "avoidance" or "rejection" to be an option; such terms cannot apply when no claim is being made. And it was too late to run away, there was no need to anymore. He was being swept to the shore of mothers and daughters, borne there on fate's slowly-contracting tides. The sadness and discomfiture of that time, the scrabbling for purchase, the odd little despairs of the breakfast hour. The vain and feeble attempts, always thwarted somehow, to love the mother and daughter. He was nothing more than a stranger to them, just as he had always been . . . Several years passed by in this way, with no object he could leave or even want to.

In just the same way, he could imagine how sad and discomfiting the woman's hours must have been ever since she met him. "It's not my fault!" the woman wrote. "It's not my fault!" A protest that announced itself through the deep indents the pen had made in the paper, the sweat stains from nervous hands. But eventually, unable to reason it out in a logical fashion, her trembling hand had written "It's not my fault! But it's also not something other than my fault . . ." Her earnest desire to deny this statement, though such a thing was impossible, was revealed between the lines, an unmistakable accent of desperation. And the woman wrote "though it seemed I would burst with longing at every moment" "this meaningless thing" "turned each of my footsteps toward the grave." What he knew of the woman's life, of what she carried with her from her personal history, was mostly a void. Just as there was no one who really knew his own life, his own private burdens. They'd exchanged no personal information other than their respective addresses. They had held hands only, walking side by side above the clouds. Their stares were vacant, their conversation silence. He had closed his eyes and walked into a daydream. The pendulum that swings between nothingness and infinity, absence and absence of limits. The woman, born in the city that spread out beneath the balcony he had long since left, took only two steps to cross over to this place, yet in the meantime decades of time had flowed by. "In order to catch up with you I run swift as a hunted deer. I run a little faster every day." To the man with whom the woman now lived, he would have been one of the things that threw her into confusion even though there were no bonds of any form. In certain moments, his ability to leave becomes a trap itself, clamping down around his ankle, and he forgets his tolerance and hefts an ax to his shoulder. The friendly fire that breaks out between those who find themselves together in the same place! The hours of death ensconced in a close life! (Just as the Malaysia trip with Ann had been for him! Just like the long, failed struggle to love Ann!) The train had already departed; the woman who has fallen in love has nowhere to go. The countless cities listed on the platform timetable, each one becomes a bird and soars up out of the north station. They will fly all the way to the region of the polar easterlies, and alight on the aurora. Skipping ahead to the conclusion, we can say that the woman could in fact have left at some point or other, could have made some kind of decision for herself and put it into action. (Just as he himself had done! Oh, the unending shamelessness of free human beings!) But her simultaneous inability to do these things was because for her, belief was a prerequisite for action, and she instinctively yearned to have faith in her own freedom. Otherwise, the birds would flutter back down again between the trash cans on the platform. Once again building their nests on the dregs, just as they had always done.

To remain only as neighbors of the past. Thinking that she had to loosen some bond if she was to achieve decisive liberation, the woman wandered in search of that exit that is both nowhere and everywhere, constantly thwarted until eventually, arriving at the very brink of suffocation, she reached out her firm, dry hand to him. She wrote him a long letter. Oh, you poor soul.

City and cities. This city and that, a city whose name gets spoken, and names that go a whole lifetime without being pronounced. Those names which, therefore, are to certain people no more than sounds, infinitely meaningless. The evening lights of the city, which spread out presently when the plane attempts to land; the houses and stations looming faintly; the parks and fountains that stagger like sick pigeons in the pallid white darkness; the shapes of buildings—why do they all look so tired and sad? The scenery is spread out like a quilt, as though with an invisible flick of the wrist. Now is the hour for sleep. But in dreams there are only longing lips. Fog, mosquito swarms, and the lips of the monsoon, and lips that bloom amid a crowd of flies, whimpering over watermelon juice. The sensual sleep of some brief moment, with the woman on the balcony, that he was always trying to depict, though only in his imagination. The bed's rattan frame, the light summer quilt, the breeze that used to press itself persistently against the flesh, and the swaying of the flower-patterned fan . . . When he first set out for that place, the events of 1967, the eleven who had been tried as spies after being extradited from a foreign country, and subsequently sentenced to capital punishment, were still fresh in people's memories. And so none of his colleagues would answer that city's call for university scholars. He alone had gotten on the plane and flown out there for the seminar, had agreed to being photographed, and signed his name in the guestbook, and been guided around palaces and various folk performances, and attended dinners here and there, and made conversation with people from the university, who all had their hair cut short. Eventually left alone, he slipped out of the central hotel where they were putting him up and took a bus around the market and old quarter, with no clear objective. It was an extremely strange week all told, like being an asteroid temporarily broken free from its orbit. A city encountered quite by chance, abrupt and easy as turning a corner; whose name, he had thought obscurely, would likely never rise to his lips again. A city with the pronunciation of a crooked tongue and uncommon throat. He recalled all he had seen at that time, the narrow, kinked alleys, the people, handcarts and buses, the elderly and children. A teacher of classical languages, getting on in years, who had invited him and some university students to his house—and how proper and correct they had been, more like soldiers than students—and made a bedroom for them on the balcony. Ah, what was his name . . . As the plane slowly began its descent and the city's wrinkled face fanned out, the river revealed itself, meandering like the long tracks of tears. Why do cities all show such similar faces when seen just before the plane lands? Faces with eyes half-closed, the look you wear on beginning to resign yourself to something, of having experienced too much too young, of having been woken too quickly or of falling asleep too soon, the point at which reality gets confused with dreams. The sky, shot through with the pink haze of the setting sun, hilly districts seen from far away, the blank face of the runway, and the artificial chill leaching into your knees. In some cities there were jungles, too. Whose clouds had sharp, distinct contours, like handkerchiefs spread out onto the sky. Against that still-pallid background, the clouds' deep red was unsettling. A buoyant moon above them, huge and nearly crimson. A single thread of gray smoke rose up from the jungle. That smoke gave off not the warm scents of a village at evening, of rice cooking in the pots, but one of helpless, sorrowful oblivion, as though the last nomads to leave the jungle were burning what possessions they could not carry. Passing through this subtropical city, worn with an exhaustion that belied its age, his plane groped in search of the runway. He'd been able to travel much more frequently since retiring, from one sunset city to the next. Each place had its own unique scent. But airports, airports were different. Each time he stepped out of an airport roses were invariably withering nearby.

"Whenever that time comes back to mind," the woman wrote in her letter, "I think the ghost has come to call again, the one that held me captive that day I rode the train back home, and is sitting soundlessly by my side, pressing its flesh against mine.

A ghost with no smell or body heat, that knows neither touch nor respiration. At first I thought it was a product of our parting. But now the ghost seems more and more like you yourself, and I grow ever more frightened. Frightened by the thought that ever since we parted that day at the north station, the you whom I had known, those brief hours we spent together, have all been nothing but ghosts, never again to be known in reality. This is how everything really exists; why is our world so unreal, a mere ghost of existence?"[1] Perhaps, in the course of writing the letter, the woman had slowly come to realize what his answer would be. In the letter's final stages, the tremors of shuddered breath seemed ever more apparent in her handwriting, shaken at the last by a growing unease. "But for god's sake, don't give in! I won't!" He read the letter again many times after that first day, and each time he came to the end his chest would be throbbing with a cruel unease every bit as a severe as the woman's. He had only to recall that final passage and his heart would be crushed by the misfortune of loss. Above the exhausted letter hung the vague, blurred lights of the north station's platform. Above the two of them as they waited for the last train, at an hour when even the pigeons were asleep, the woman being bludgeoned by the struggle inside her. "For god's sake," the woman wrote again, over and over like a tic. "Don't think about anything else, just let me come see you!" "But for god's sake, don't give in!" he whispered as though he sat at the woman's side. Stretching out his hand as she had done to the ghost who interrupted her writing. Who was it that had shown him such a gesture? "Ever since we parted that day at the north station": he reads the passage that begins thus several times, out loud, as though repeating a refrain. After reading it several times back to back, it really does come to feel like a song. Like his own song, which the woman

---

1. Albert Ehrenstein: "Everything exists; only this world does not."

had been pregnant with. Like his song which goes as follows: "It was only our ghosts who parted at the north station that day; the real us left together on the train, and are together even now . . ." The plane was now in mid-descent, sliding toward the evening city whose final look was one he had seen countless times in the course of his life. The city and its jungle were visible beneath the clouds, shrouded in the smoke of evening, their countenance curious and brimming with melancholy.

"Ever since we parted at the north station that day."

It had reached the point where he practically knew the letter by heart, could recite large chunks of it with his eyes closed. But he still carried it with him at all times, never putting it away out of sight. On the last day of his trip, he had left the hotel and been walking for quite some time when he began to read that passage. He quickly flicked his eyes up from the letter to take in the scene in front of him. A group of tourists on their way back from a mountain temple surged across the road in front of him, moving like a strong current to where their bus was parked. Despite being surrounded by such a mass of people, a simultaneous racket of myriad languages, his view was entirely filled with the vivid red of the bougainvillea, a riot of color against the deep-blue skyscape. He read the woman's letter several times, and thoughts of her ran through his mind. Those thoughts were extremely specific. He'd been a brilliant student at school, though that was a long time ago now. He'd never skipped a single piece of homework, and got top marks in every exam. He'd been a voracious reader, and even considered it a matter of course that he would die with his nose in a book. When he grew up and started to have relationships with women, more than in the women themselves, he reveled in that specific emotion that could only be evoked by such clandestine relationships. It was common to those whose experience of the world has for the most part been through reading. He put great stock in the fact that pleasure or sensuality were not merely something to be enjoyed, but could be noble objects evoking a specific song. Once he was old enough to reason, he naturally began to think of himself as an explorer. Ordinary explorers wander in search of beautiful undiscovered islands, of flowers found only in special regions, of highly-prized parrots with gorgeous plumage or as-yet-uncivilized primitive tribes. Because such objects would then be named after their so-called discoverers. His own task, which he himself had decided upon, was to search for the most unique song, "the one and only song." Since that song would be none other than the song of the discoverer. "Then again," unable to tear his eyes from the bougainvillea, he was struck by a thought. "Then again, the greatest beauty and significance might not actually belong to the fruits of such labor, or to the long process of wandering itself, but to something we already know quite well. Something so incredibly natural that we are aware of it as a matter of course, like the moon or stars, or the songs we sing every day. What if we're unable to see it simply because we can't hold it in our hands or put our own name to it? Because it's not something that we can possess? And so we just pass it by, pushing on into the heart of the jungle. As though we have no need of whatever we cannot own, no need to cultivate an appreciation for the variety of life. What if countless unique things—the moon and stars, flowers and parrots, even that one unique song—had already skimmed right past us, so that we never even noticed they were there? If that were the case, I would know so many unlucky people, myself included." At that, he felt that he had become lost in certain thoughts as a means of experiencing the pathos of happiness and sadness, joy and despair—those being fundamental human passions regarded as worthy of admiration—no, for the sake of the woman herself, a weak and imperfect being. Pure, affectionate compassion for both himself and the woman . . . It was such a simple, plain thing, yet it brought such an immediate sense of fulfillment that the cry was on the tip of his tongue: "For god's sake stay like this!"

He carried on walking, going against the current of people. Now both sides of the road were a jungle. A small truck that had come to pick him up was parked at a fork in the road. Tourists visiting the school usually came in small or large groups; that day, he was the only one. Crouching in the severely rattling truck bed, choking on the dust that it threw up from the unpaved road, he was jolted along for more than an hour and a half, in the middle of which was a brief rain shower. He pulled a tarp over himself to keep the rain off, but the rough material kept sliding around him, and the raindrops beating vigorously against it sounded like a round of gunfire. The thick veil of vapor produced by the rain isolated him from real time. Within the haze, some dim thing raised its head. Some faint, opaque, yet decisive thing, which could have either been extremely significant, or have passed by him entirely without him even noticing. Something that passed him by without his putting a name to it. But the moment when, red rising into the mosquito bite he was scratching, he tried to apply himself to thinking about what that thing might be, the clouds abruptly vanished from the sky, some last plump rainbow-colored drops ricocheted in arcs off the leaves, and the rain came to a stop. Once again able to make out the muddy dirt road, he was overwhelmed by the green swathes of jungle surrounding it. Before long, they arrived at the entrance to a small village, a residential area deep in the mountains near Chiang Mai. The sound of laughter could be heard as the truck pulled up in a clearing, coming from children playing in the yard adjoining the school and dormitory buildings. A cool breeze blew in the wake of the rain, and a rainbow bridged two blades of grass, strung together by the small world of a spider's web. The silk-weaving spider, slender as a needle, had fallen from that bridge into the muddy yellow river that had collected in the truck's tire tracks. Floating along with a look of despair, it must have been thinking that it would be carried to the world's end; in that moment, he felt himself become the spider, his thoughts the spider's thoughts. Desperately thrashing his limbs, he made a vain attempt to stave off death. In that moment, the spider's despair, the spider's world was clear and distinct in his mind. Despair and desperation. Yet on the other hand, such an inexorable fate can bring with it a certain measure of peace, not unlike the willing surrender of those of us who are blessed to reach old age. After clambering down from the truck, tottering with dizziness, he began to walk slowly over to the school building. It was the School for Life, where he was to volunteer as an English teacher.

The
Non-Being
of the Owl

*D*ecember 2ⁿᵈ, 2008, Bielefeld: there's been nothing much to report today. All I wanted to tell you is that the two large firs that stood near the house have been cut down. I suppose you realize what that means? It means that now when I go out onto the balcony, no longer the pleasantly shady spot it once was, the absence of those close, companionable trees, which had shielded me from the wind and any prying eyes, leaves me completely exposed, defenseless, open to the road. And that isn't even the worst of it—the house opposite, which had always been concealed by the firs, now assaults the eye with its unsightliness. I never realized before how ugly it is. One of those typical '50s monstrosities, glaringly white all over, its exterior gaunt and desolate. Now, when I sit at my desk and let my attention drift from my work over to the balcony, you can imagine what a hideous sight I'm confronted with! It seems whoever owns that house had the trees cut down so that his living room could get more light. Naturally, that kind of decision is up to the homeowners, and since I'm only renting I couldn't protest. And after all, I'm the only one who's being put out. How can a drab rectangular wall not set one's nerves on edge? Forcing a human being to stare at that sort of heinous architecture every day is practically a form of punishment! It really is a shame that those firs are gone. Remember, it was only last summer when the owls would come to roost there every evening. They would quietly watch me for hours on end, absolutely still, and I took a photograph of them with that old-fashioned film camera I have. I was pleased with how the picture turned out, especially as you yourself really liked it. But the owls won't come back here now that the trees are gone. Well, aside from that there's nothing else of note. I wrote a review of a new work by my old friend Ludwig Harig; the days are still as bitingly cold as ever; tomorrow I'm off to spend another couple of days in Berlin and then Munich; nothing aside from that. I'll probably be quite busy while I'm traveling, but all the same I'll email you again if there's anything I particularly want to tell you. So, goodbye for now. Yours sincerely.

After the funeral was over, Werner asked me if I wanted to take a walk into town. A good long walk, he added, all the way to the center. I looked up once more at the sky. Although the snowstorm hadn't set in, the sky remained a pale ashen color, clustered with low smoke-like clouds. However, everyone else had already begun to make their way to a restaurant, where a simple meal had been arranged. This scene was slightly in contrast to how it had been before the various formalities were over. Earlier, everyone had formed an orderly queue, thrown his flowers down onto the casket and sprinkled a handful of earth from a jar, then made way for the next person, who would then repeat the procedure in exactly the same way. Now that the ceremony was over, people turned away from the covered grave and headed straight to the restaurant. The cemetery attendants in their epauletted uniforms watched us with an exceedingly patient air. Their expressions amply demon-strated their understanding of and consideration for our situation, stemming from a combination of businesslike familiarity and a necessary sense of detachment. The hole was very deep; even if you reached in you probably couldn't touch the casket. The casket was a light brown color, the grain of the wood running in wide, distinct striations along the sides. Of course, this is the same for all caskets, but it gave such a strong impression of solidity, of substance. And that hole. That unforgettable hole. I have never seen another so deep in all my life. So deep, perhaps, that I could be buried in it standing up on the casket. Perhaps I had already been buried. Early morning on Thursday, March 12th, the interior of the damp red hole strewn with flowers, clumped together like the day-old snow piled up here and there in the corners of the cemetery, but soon to be filled in with earth. As I stood by the grave, hesitating, the others urged me to come to the restaurant now that we'd said our goodbyes, tempting me with promises of weisswurst from Bayern. I'm not fond of weisswurst. I never have been.

Early this year, when you sent me Kafka's *Dream,* I was pretty excited. Not only because it was a book that in form very closely resembled one that I myself had been thinking about writing—not just recently but for a long time now, as long as I can remember— but also because I had a hunch that it would end up having a big influence on what I wrote in the future. Of course, the book you sent me wasn't an individual work of Kafka's entitled "Dream," but rather a compilation of the passages from his various jottings and memos, letters and essays, etc., which were related to dreams. On opening the book, I found the following sentence had been used to begin the preface: One morning, when Gregor Samsa awoke from an unsettling dream, he discovered he had turned into a cockroach. The first sentence of *The Metamorphosis.* It affects the reader in the manner of a strong hint. A hint that the story this novel recounts is actually a nightmare the protagonist is having, or else a nightmare that Kafka himself had recalled after awaking from a troubled sleep.

After that, the very first thought that came to mind was, of course, connected to hints. Hints bubbling hot as lava inside the cold red hole, the thought that wordly relationships are in actual fact almost all formed through fragmented, anonymous hints. Hints that self-generate from someone's offhand remarks, or from metaphors that coalesce entirely at random; hints from which all sense of genuine premonition has been removed. It seems that, perhaps, the point at which the two differ is that the former seem ignorant of their own import. And so today, too, we can write, quite casually, in a letter: I am hurting. And so I hope you're not too surprised that I haven't contacted you for a while . . . "But it isn't a dream," the preface continued. "It isn't a dream. Kafka makes this point clear to his readers. Thus, from the very first he denies the possibility of a straightforward interpretation for an outlandish phenomenon that it is difficult to make readers accept as being realistic. And so, we are forced to accept the fact of a man having turned into a cockroach as precisely that, a fact, or at least as something that has truly taken place in reality."

People hurt, and after experiencing the sudden death of a friend are riven with an anxiety and loneliness difficult to express in words, and thus fall deeper and deeper into depression, a depression that is incurable because you fear to examine its cause too closely; and you work, after all, you have spent your whole life working, except that now you are working like someone possessed, of course you are, and one day the realization comes that the work you have thrown yourself into is utterly meaningless, will never amount to anything more than a mountain of paper covered in your own poor scrawl, and that everyone passes away at some time or other, and that one day there will be no one left to recognize this handwriting as your own; then, though privately in the grip of a breakdown, a fiercely personal and somewhat obscure breakdown that you cannot explain to anyone else, nevertheless in spite of this you find yourself drawn back to the desk, ready to devote yourself to work once more; but then one day you open the paper and another friend has died, died suddenly and incomprehensibly; as if, drinking tea together, you turn to find that the friend who was there is there no more, they have parted from you forever without leaving even a single word behind, their mind was sliced through with a blade but no cry of pain issued from their mouth; you torment yourself with unanswerable questions, and you travel as though you have spent your whole life wandering, taking planes and trains, sometimes crossing oceans and continents and, turning to look out of the airplane window, your vacant stare is arrested by the view; a sequence you often repeat, causing melancholy to silt up inside you; and on one of those rare days when the sun is shining, you carry flowerpots out to the balcony and arrange them there; at times you crack a joke, and sometimes even smile; you write an email to someone in a foreign country, and go down to the post office to send a postcard; there is even the odd occasion when you are invited to some bright, cheerful place, and sometimes you even go; and you also write, of course, and think of friends, both the dead and the living, meaning the dead and those who have not died yet but will; you fill your time with various appointments and engagements, attending exhibitions and recitals, going to the theater and, more than anything else, reading books; and on returning home, before settling down to work you stare once more out of the window, and think of the snowstorm, of faraway things, and of things that cannot think of themselves—and then you think of that thought; and you work all day; and before going to bed you stand holding the receiver in your suddenly trembling hand, but the long-distance call won't connect; and eventually, one day, you hurt, again.

"I'm sorry this is rushed, but I just wanted to let you know why I haven't been in touch for a little while"—that was how your email of October 9ᵗʰ, 2007 began. "At first it was simply a quick, work-related trip—to Leverkusen, in fact, in the Rhine area. It's just a run-of-the-mill industrial town, but there was some kind of literary event going on, and there were these two writers who were to be awarded prizes, you see. The atmosphere was very good, and the food at the event was fantastic, so I was thoroughly enjoying myself. And just then I heard the news that a close friend of mine, the poet Walter Kempowski, had died. And so I had to go up to Lottenburg in north Germany straight away, via Bremen, in order to attend his funeral. Walter had had cancer for over a year, it had been no great secret, and now at last he had gone to his eternal rest, amid the grievous mourning of his friends. The funeral ceremony was conducted by one male priest and one female (since Walter was Protestant, just as I used to be). And by god's grace we even had a day of fine weather. Well, it didn't rain, anyway. After the burial, we left our places and went to drink coffee and eat butter cake. And it was only the night before that I'd left Frankfurt. The express train rattled through the night, speeding monotonously over the tracks, and I spent the whole time engrossed in a book. I'm staying at my sister's here in Frankfurt; you met her that one time, if you remember. The Frankfurt Book Fair is just getting started, and no doubt I'll keep myself well occupied wandering about between all the parties and other events, just like every other year. All the same, I hope you won't infer from this that I won't have time to think about anything else. I sincerely hope that you are well, and that your writing is going smoothly! Just now in the *Süddeutsche* I read a review of those diaries of Walser's that were published this year. It was really very positive. I will bring the book for you when I visit Korea this November. With my greetings."

Kafka's dream world evoked exactly the same thoughts and feelings for me, almost as though we were twins; and at the same time it was so unusual, unique and neurotic, unbearably empty and beautiful. Our views on the subject of dreams had originally been so completely divergent that we had even gone so far as to quarrel over it. In contrast to my deeply-held belief that dreams are the stuff of literature and the imagination, for you they could be comprehensively and conclusively analyzed as a kind of seepage or inadvertent betrayal of one's innermost self. And so, when I revealed to you that I wanted to write a book that would be entirely the product of my own dreams, you enumerated your misgivings one by one, first expressing your skepticism regarding the formation of such a literary work, and secondly, your belief in the rashness of a writer exposing their own personal psychology, then, after thus wounding me, you sent a much gentler email in order to qualify those previous criticisms.

Last night I walked past Munich's university and art academy—beautiful, stately buildings that had at one time been capable of seizing hold of my very soul, and yet I passed them by entirely unmoved, like some barbarian. I was looking up at the black rainclouds, straining my eyes as if searching for something in the dark-drenched sky, but I'd come out without a hat and before I knew it water was trickling down through my hair. It was then that I discovered that those viscous raindrops, clearly outlined as they streaked down through the black void, were not in fact black themselves. I was on my way to meet Werner, and as I went down into the subway station to shelter for a moment or so, a woman who was coming up the stairs clutching some flowers in a paper bag asked me if it was raining outside. The Münchner Freiheit station was under construction. Sitting perfectly still on the platform bench and listening to the low buzzing of a power saw, which hummed like a swarm of bees, I watched as several trains in turn pulled into the platform then departed. The trains came at regular intervals, and the passengers boarded them with the same unvarying repertoire of movements; reflected in the carriage windows, and leached of color, their faces slid by like ghosts, and like ghosts they were distorted; the forces holding particles in their arrangements broke down as light and speed were pushed beyond the everyday, the web of veins surrounding the heart became clotted with sadness, and all disappeared into the deep tunnel.

One cold, dark night, Werner and I wandered here and there along Leopoldstrasse. We didn't have any particular destination in mind. The first place we happened to drop in at was a sports bar, where they were showing a soccer game on a large wall-mounted television. After we sat down, by horrible chance some soccer fans began to pile into the seats behind our table, meaning we ended up sandwiched between them and the screen, which was directly above us. While we talked and talked, the fans kept their eyes riveted to the screen. The waitress was kind and friendly, and we ordered two glasses of wine. "It was as though a big lump of lead was suspended from my heart, weighing me down," Werner said. "Until now, whenever I wrote something, I always imagined him reading it at some point in the future. He read the composition I had to write for my Abitur, and even quoted from it in one of his own books. Afterward, we remained friends for twenty-nine years. That was the kind of friend he was—the kind you don't meet twice in a lifetime. And now a black hole has opened up inside of me. I suppose it will feel like this forever. We—both of us, now—have one other kind of sadness to contend with, unique among all the many sadnesses that exist in this world—that incomparable loss: 'Jörg's non-being.'" Leaving the sports bar, we wandered here and there around unfamiliar corners until we went in through the open door of another tavern and ordered another two glasses of wine. Werner kept up his monologue. "I've already watched my father die, and my older sister, too. She suffered for two years beforehand: breast cancer. And as for my grandparents, one morning in May 1945, right after the war ended, they were attacked out of the blue

by the inmates who had been liberated from a nearby concentration camp (they had come to rob them, you see), murdered in their
bed. My grandfather's farm was a tumbledown place in an out-of-
the-way village; my eight-year-old father saw the bullets pierce his
parents' chests. The bed became a kind of black mire, fouled with
their blood and chunks of their flesh. My young father had to witness all that. And so believe me when I say you mustn't be sad that
you couldn't see him at the end. On the contrary, it will turn out to
be a blessing for you. I decided a long time ago, that every human
should try and bring something into being from out of this loss,
which wounds our hearts and afflicts our lives, and which we must
nevertheless embrace. Something even more beautiful precisely
because of its stemming from such loss, something that can touch
us even more deeply because of it." The waitress approached to tell
us that she was sorry, but it was already closing time. Though it
had stopped sleeting, outside was as cold and dreary as ever, and
now the wind had picked up. The entire street fluttered like a black
flag. Once more, we began to drift along Leopoldstrasse, which
appeared larger and wider now that it was completely deserted.

Perhaps for you, dreams are themselves the fearful language that
Werner and I poured out to each other that night, but for me
they are the darkness that shrouded Leopoldstrasse, and the rain
that came down in that darkness. Considering that, unlike Werner, I only write in Korean, I could never expect that you would
read any of my works. Wasn't that a matter of course? Werner
and I, who can in a certain sense be considered as the children of
your literature, connected you to our own writings in that kind
of contradictory fashion. We constantly wrote in relation to you,
yet I was certain that you would never read what I wrote, which
was somewhat ironic. And I had no doubt that in the future, too,
we would continue to write in this way. I didn't tell you, but I
had already revealed my dream, our hidden dream, to the general

public. Had already been thinking of revealing it. I knew it would be like this. This is how it is, already.

When I stepped inside, the restaurant near the cemetery was already warm with the bustle of the funeral-goers. People were taking off their black scarves and black coats to hang them up. On the dining table were wicker baskets filled with pretzels, and as soon as we sat down warm china plates of weisswurst were passed round. Someone put on that stirring Ernst Busch song, "The Ballad of the Old Pirate." Several men even sang along with the refrain in their booming bass voices. The conversation was on anything and everything. For example, Mr. and Mrs. Rusch, from Frankfurt, who were sitting next to me, announced that in a few days they would be taking a vacation in America. Obama's America, that is, Mrs. Rusch added brightly. And there was a whispering in my ear. In France this Ernst Busch song would perhaps be called a "chanson," it said, as it sets Brecht's poetry to music, but here in Germany it's less certain as to which particular genre it should be included in. And take a look over there, why, it's only Alexander Kruggerand, the famous writer and film director, *and* eminent intellectual, and lawyer to boot. Even you must have heard the name once or twice, no? A man recited the memorial address and a woman read out a letter. Mrs. Rusch showed me her personal method for neatly removing the casing of the weisswurst. Karin went straight up to the restaurant owner to tell them how pleased she was with the food and table settings. Turning to me, she asked if I had been to see the Kandinsky exhibition while it had been on in Munich, and which had closed the weekend before. Apparently one of her friends had waited outside in the cold for two hours in order to get to see that exhibition. When I told her that I had barely been out of the house, never mind Kandinsky, she tossed her hair, her expression plainly saying that I had been foolish to miss such a precious opportunity. They looked like truly experienced mourners.

They were crying, of course, but in a seemly fashion, so as not to stain their collars. Just say goodbye now, Rusch had said to me as I stood by the grave, before promptly leaving the cemetery.

Since it had happened so quickly, so suddenly, it might be that even the person concerned had been unable to clearly recognize it for what it was until the very last moment. It had happened at lightning speed. In spite, of course, of such speed being unnecessary. I had the feeling that I had glimpsed such uncanny speed once before. If that were the case, could it have been a vague, nameless hint, formed only from silhouetted gestures from behind a dark curtain? Hints speak to me, kiss me. Arms locked with one another. It's like I am forever embracing and re-embracing these hints thick as fog. That is the way it seems. Pure hints, unrelated to each other, with not even a sliver of foreshadowing to enrich them.

They flutter, flowing against time, and I follow after them. That day, we said goodbye at Karin's house in Munich. The day was overcast, somber and melancholic, and you had arranged to go to the train station. I can't remember where you might have been taking a train to. Maybe Frankfurt or Leipzig as usual, Weimar or Zurich, or else Vienna, some other city, or if not then perhaps Bielefeld. As you dragged your bag down from Karin's third-floor apartment, the sound of it thudding against the old wooden stairs grew gradually fainter. You always rushed down those stairs, which were wide but slanted to one side, in that house, Karin's house, which was orderly and proud, the well-tended flowerpots arranged neatly on the gleaming wooden floor giving it a fresh look despite its age. Always rushing, so that it made you seem impatient, as if you felt a great, unreasonable rage at the fact of other people being able to watch you as you leave. Perched on the windowsill of the third-floor room, I watch as you slip out of the front door and disappear down the street. Always with that black New Zealand baseball cap jammed down on your head, the hem of your bright trench coat flapping wildly, holding a suitcase in one hand—even though the zip was broken you took it traveling with you all over the world—walking briskly, rapidly, with an air of soldierly resolution. That year, summer in Munich was particularly cold. The streets funneled the wind, and the scene beneath the overcast sky was one of bowed heads, lips drained of color, and hair wildly disheveled. You had not yet turned the corner, and in that moment I suddenly remembered something, something that made me want to rush down the stairs and out into the street to catch up with you. What was it I remembered then . . . had there been something I wanted to say to you? But if so, what? You were coming back to visit Munich next month, meaning we were sure to meet again very soon—what could be so urgent that I had to tell you right then? That though as I watched you and could see you were almost running, you didn't have to since you were still in good time for the train; that in fact, for us everything was already too late; or that nothing will ever now be late again. But one does not hurtle down old wooden stairs, treacherously slanted and slippery with wax, just to share such a trivial thought. And besides, you are already about to turn the corner, where you will see the entrance to the subway directly in front of you. You will jump on the train and it will take you straight to the central station, whisking you away from in front of my eyes. The ghosts' faces are visible on the other side of the carriage window, translucent like congealed cheese, their forms slightly distorted from flowing rapidly into the dark cave, their density momentarily diluting, visible around the middle of light and form, these final faces that for some reason make us stop and stare. It's only natural that it should be so, but all things are already too late. Already they will end up being much too late. The world where nothing will ever be late lies just over there on the far side of the river; a day of uncommonly bright sunlight, revealed to us briefly amid the fog rolling off the river, only for the enticing

93

vision to be veiled again behind water and shadows, even before the stirrings of longing have yet to pass off. And thus, it seems, are we caught, rapt, by this unidentified yearning. I was aware of this quite clearly at the time; strange that then, unlike now, it caused me no confusion.

The airport. It's an unbearably sad place to discuss, a place forever tinged with sorrow. When the tense wait is over and the fuselage finally thuds down onto the runway—something is over, and yet, something has begun; the intersection of two mutually indistinguishable feelings that gesture from across the dark void. This goes without saying for a Korean airport, or for Hong Kong's; and for the huge, old dinosaur that is Frankfurt airport; and for the much more carefree Munich airport; and for Berlin's cold, confusing Tegel airport; and for Boden's Friedrichshafen, comically dwarfed by the lake next to it; and for the now-defunct Berlin Templehof, too. Walking down the long corridors of the impressive Templehof complex, on my way to meet you, the very first words that always sprang to my mind were "concentration camp." If the airplane is the steamship, then the airport is the harbor. These jokes immediately before the ship's departure. The airport cafeteria immediately before a plane's departure. The constant clinking of china teacups, the shop assistant's monotonous drone, the click of camera shutters, and the squeak of suitcase wheels, mingled with the somewhat restless bustle of the travelers. I always get the feeling that time flows differently, and has a different character, according to place. Because of this, this place will always be different from that place. Even this place's "us" and that place's "us" will inevitably differ. I cannot help but write differently in that place than I would in this one. While one time flows out of us through the right ear, another time enters in through our left. Now and then it pierces even the heart. The movement of that piercing is slow. Now and then it will always be passing through us. As a writer, I am drawn to that mysterious time difference, unique to every person. I am always wanting to talk or write about it. It is somewhat nebulous at present, but I have a premonition that it will soon coalesce into some kind of form, and this will suffice for now.

And your email one winter's day in 2006. "You asked why my letter sounded so sad. Well, it was because one of my friends— a mere 53 years old—had suddenly died, and so, you see, I was immersed in all the complexities of grief. But there's no need for you to worry on my account. You know how people always say that weeds cling to life? Well, my constitution is every bit as tough and tenacious as that of a weed, and that's how I've made it this far." My own time is always spreading slowly toward that place, like an encroaching swamp. "That place" being the name I have given to a certain vacuum in time. That place, where nothing will ever be late. One day I received an airmail postcard with the photograph of the owl attached. It's been pinned up over my desk ever since, along with the sentences of immaterial time which I wrote myself: "It visited me like this once a year; if one year my name is no longer outside the door to this house, then I will no longer be in sync with you, and I doubt whether I would even be able to remember you." The owls were the autobiography of a certain moment we shared, and since one cannot turn back time when it has already been written in an autobiography, what I did in that place amounted to crucifying the owls on the now-vanished trees. I crucified myself along with the owls. But it seems that you will never at any future time be able to read about the owls that we loved—though of course, this was the case in the past, too. And memory tends again toward elegant hints. Perhaps, as some physicists believe, our future is already out there waiting for us, pre-determined. However, if we can never know what this future holds, what difference does it make for us whether or not it is determined? In my autobiography of October 26th, 2006: after saying goodbye to you in Weimar, I spent a few days in Bonn before coming back to Berlin. Every time I saw my friends in Bonn I ended up thinking about that simple, warm-hearted life that humans lead, about the loving feelings that constitute these lives as we think of and rely upon each other. Whatever kind of life I dream of is not clear, but somehow it still has the power to move me. Even though she had her hands full with the child, his wife made up a lunchbox with a baguette for me to eat on the train, and he drove me to the central station. As there was nowhere to park around the station, he had to quickly pull into a spot reserved for residents. He helped me carry my bag down, and even came with me onto the platform, but then he had to go back and find a proper place to park. "But I'll come back when I do," he reassured me. "I'm incredibly grateful for all this," I told him, "but my train will be here any minute, and I've taken plenty of trains in Germany before now, so I know what I'm doing. So please don't feel like you need to rush back." But he wouldn't hear it. "The thing is," he said, "I won't be able to feel like I've seen you off properly until I can see that you've found a seat on the train." The train came around five minutes after he left, and just as I had found a seat I saw him reappear on the platform. We waved goodbye from opposite sides of the glass window. It seemed a very small, insignificant episode, but strangely enough I was greatly comforted by it. I mean, comfort rather than something empty, you know. The day after I arrived back in Berlin, I was sitting in an Indian restaurant on Oranienburgur Strasse. Through the restaurant window, I saw that Berlin's autumn was just passing its zenith. It was flowing away, time, I mean, and what did the future hold for me? Now, if I were to attempt a quick description of that atmosphere, it would probably get lost behind the formal sentences. But after I came out of the restaurant and was walking down the street, I stepped on a huge dead bird that had fallen from the sky; that's all I really want to tell you. Right now, as I'm writing this, I'm back home again sitting at the desk beneath the window in my room. In the fading autumn light on Friedrich-Engels-Strasse, when high up in the sky the final lingering luster is painting shining contours onto the city's rooftops, and twilight is spreading its skirts in the street below, the time of day when those two shadows we call light and dark merge and blend, every leaf on every tree is exchanging gestures of farewell. It cannot be called by any other name. Small birds ride the currents of the wind, and only in this very moment, in which it seems as though this autumn has brought itself into being, do they appear to be exchanging whispers with each other, light and quick as a single breath, murmured conversations tossed into the wind. It is impossible to overhear their secret voices. And so I will never be able to know the secret of the wind, that wind that makes emotions blaze up while remaining calm as the cadence of breath being shared by these children of autumn. Greetings, from Berlin.

But there are those, citizens of this life that seems a colony of death, who try to overcome that personal suffering while maintaining a severe sense of distance. For example, in the case of the writer Walser who, when I dashed off an email in an Arabic Internet cafe after arriving in Munich, answered with the following sentences. "Dear Ms. Bae Suah, it cannot but feel cruel, since man is so powerless in this case. Silent assent and acceptance is our lot. And yet, we try vainly to resist. No matter how useless. The kind of loss you are now experiencing is like a screaming, bloody wound. But you absolutely must stop tormenting yourself with the thought of becoming an orphan. Since, at some time or other, our parents will inevitably leave us, please bear these words in mind: since there is only one of two possibilities; either, whoever we are, we are all of us—and always—orphans, or else we are fated to be unable to become absolute orphans . . . I'm sorry, it is impossible for me to talk as though I am an expert on this matter. All I can say is this:

you absolutely mustn't be too distressed on account of suffering. Because if you dwell on suffering then my heart my will suffer too; and by no means do I wish for any more suffering in this life. Yours, Martin Walser."

Until then it had been thoroughly abstract for me, nothing more than one particular written character with the sound "death." Though it was dark, it was the dark shadow of strangers passing by. If I am to make an even more truthful confession, it was a wholly artistic, literary thing. Though all sorts of other people often spoke and even wrote about it in that way, I didn't know what it was, had not even the vaguest premonition as to what it might be like. It might be the kind of "truly, no longer existing" of one whom we had known as living. And it might mean suffering and loss of the kind that "can in no way be undone," placed between life and death. I didn't like cultures that ignore death or consider it taboo. In Korea I had once paid 3,000 won, a tiny amount, for a suit of rough, hemp mourning clothes, which I later wore to a funeral in Berlin. At the time I had a vague desire to know what it was, that thing we call death. Someone at the funeral asked about the clothes, wondering what their particular characteristics—exceptionally rough fabric, sloppy needlework, exposed stitches and conspicuously loose finishing—could have to do with mourning. I didn't know the answer back then, but perhaps now I can say: we wear this sort of clothing because a person's death is our fault. We have a guilty conscience because, in other words, those who are living are the cause of death. Because someone gets old while we are still in the prime of our life. Because they become ill while we remain in good health. Because they end up dying while we are still alive. Because life is in debt to death. Because one person dies, and in that way the deaths of those remaining are postponed. If this world were to be summed up in a single sentence, it would be this: nature maintains its equilibrium, and man grieves.

For a long time now I have thought about what my death might be like, and have even tried writing these thoughts down. This is the conclusion I came to: "One day, just like any other day, I fall asleep, and when I wake in the middle of a strong wind, I am dying. I am on a high, lonely mountain peak, with only the brass-colored wilderness extending endlessly in all directions, without a single plant or tree to break the monotony. I watch myself dying. Then, I hear a sound coming toward me." But the "I" in this passage is someone already dead and therefore already released from suffering, not someone having to face up to death itself. There is no flesh or blood in these words. In terms of real, flesh-and-blood death, the death of an actual person, I knew nothing.

When the clock showed exactly 2 P.M., Werner and I left the restaurant. By that time, most people had already gone home. Luckily we didn't have any of that drizzly kind of weather that day. Just like on the day of Kempowski's funeral, which you told me about in your email, it came to me. "Well, at least it didn't rain," you wrote. Werner and I walked together without the need for words, relying on our mutual silence. We left Haidhausen Cemetery, walked along Einsteinstrasse, and crossed the Isar River over the bridge by Maximilianstrasse. Cafe Roma on Maximilianstrasse was where Werner and I first met, do you remember? It was at that cafe, which featured in Walser's novel *Angstblüte*, that you introduced me to Werner Fritsch, the talented, extraordinary writer and independent film director. On the same day, the three of us went to the Academy of Fine Arts in Munich; on your recommendation, Werner was being made a member of the academy. Werner's and my feet took us to Cafe Roma as if by appointment. There, we would sit at the same table as we had in the summer of 2007, perhaps with you joining us as you so often had back then, and drink espresso. However, as we turned onto Maximilianstrasse we were surprised to see that there was now a Gucci store where Cafe Roma had previously stood. A cafe selling coffee on Maximilianstrasse, the most expensive part of the city, must have been uneconomical.

A few days before coming to Munich, while taking a solitary walk in Korea, I suddenly became aware that it would soon be spring. Although in objective time we were still in the grip of winter, and the weather was indisputably chilly, it was as if the trees felt with their whole bodies that their time was coming round again. The moment of being suffused with nature's love, which we call spring, and breathing, and life. Expressed through a delicate trembling, the moment of their zenith is awash with secret, private intimations. In this moment, while drawing near each other and not pulling away, the trees understand love. Their highest branches rustling in the slow current of the air, they are as calm as if they were dreaming. There they stand, gesturing that they know why they are there in that moment. I may find myself in circumstances that cannot realistically be called easy, but nevertheless I will not lose courage or be daunted. I believe that I am independent and strong, as I would wish to be, and so even while I am inwardly proud, I have at least some happiness. Because abundant spring will come, that season which embraces within its heart an internal impulse that cannot be refused, and a gentle wind will blow, a sensation as though the air has been made flesh, and in keeping with this I will keep on living, unchangingly, just as I do now. Because, just as I am now, I will keep on walking facing into the wind, unbowed and unshaken. At that, my heart became so much more at ease. And I decided to write a letter to you who would be buried in work.

Before all that, I had been thinking about writing an essay on Elfriede Jelinek's *Lust*. No, actually I'd already written it. Not only that, but I'd even translated it into German and sent it to you.

You proofread it for me; this was the last week of February. When you became interested in Jelinek, who is not dissimilar to myself as a writer, even though her work contains an element of the fantastic you very much enjoyed it, unlike with Kafka's *Dream*. While writing the essay, I read an interview with her in a magazine from 2004. There were several key points in her frank radicalism that moved me: that whether a woman is a Nobel Prize winner or whether she works behind a shop counter, the way in which she is judged is identical, i.e. according the market value of her body; and of course, as she gets older, this value suffers a precipitous decline. "Peter Handke and I were both born in Austria, but we are not at all alike. Handke seeks inspiration in our daily lives, whereas by contrast I already know that everything will just turn to ash." "Life and writing, these two things absolutely do not go hand in hand."

When I asked him how on earth it had all come about—these wicked lies, his worst joke, these obscenely malicious rumors I'd gotten wind of—Werner, stammering, unburdened himself of the knowledge he had recently acquired. I knew that over ten years ago he had had bypass surgery. But one day he went to the hospital—he hadn't been feeling well for a couple of days—and the doctors discovered that one of the three bypass tubes was blocked. They then said that they would have to take action in order to open it up; if they did nothing he would suffer a stroke, which would lead shortly afterward to cardiac arrest. That was what lay behind the rumors I'd heard. So, you're telling me he's *dying*? I couldn't understand, and blankly repeated the question. Someone who, more than anyone else, had always overflowed with a burning lust for literature and life, an incredibly singular individual? Could this alone be the sum of what we are?

The sloping fields around Werner's hometown Wondreb appeared from behind the woods. The yellow fields, where the hay had all been cut and only the tough lower stems remained, extended to the edge of the horizon, the afternoon sun beat down on our backs, and the shadows stretched their bodies out beneath our feet. The three of us, all women, clothed in black, red, and white, have to slowly make our way across the fields with the sun at our backs, framed against a background of the endless furrows, which rise and fall like waves, the tall cedars, and the sky. We walked slowly, maintaining the spaces between us, our gazes fixed on the middle distance. Ahead, Werner is aiming his camera at us. I was being photographed for Werner's film, but I didn't know what part I might be playing. All of this will be nothing more than a rough sketch. It's a foundation, until I discover the image I want, Werner had explained briefly. In that case, what sort of proto-image do you have in mind? The image of someone's life, he answered me, images of the soul, which will not be fitted together until directly before death. Images of dreams, and drawn-out weeping, and rain, falling against the background of the black woods. Thoughts of the Wondreb riverbank, a very long time ago. This person, sitting by the river and looking into the water, absolutely cannot forget that they can never again at another point in the future be exactly that person who now, in this very instant, had been looking down at the water, lost in thought; and so at the same time he will forget both self and river, because that self will soon itself become that water. Stream combines with stream to reach the sea, and the strong, rough current swirls in our consciousness, rolling out to all the shores of this world. Such are the images in *Faust Sonnengesang,* which begins anew from exactly that moment the words "stay like this, time, this is truly beautiful" are spoken, the moment we call this noble "present-now."

After the funeral was over, Werner asked me if I wanted to take a walk into downtown Munich. A good long walk, he added.

I cannot understand death, I confided to Werner. Now, for the first time in my life, I cannot understand death. A certain person

suddenly disappeared. As if artistically erased from life's canvas
without any warning whatsoever. One dazzlingly bright summer
morning, I was sitting with them at the breakfast table, under the
linden trees by the Bodensee; I added milk to my coffee, and he
fetched the paper; then, on turning my head at a certain moment,
he is nowhere to be seen. The coffee and newspaper are as they
were, but he is gone. Invisibility, and that word, non-being. Birds
whose names I didn't know, hidden from sight within the branches
of the linden trees—oh, but I *had* caught sight of those birds,
one other time—uttered low calls at regular intervals, like on any
other ordinary day, and the silence was complete, without a single
crunching footstep; a physical experience of the ghastly hallucination we call "non-being," which doesn't exist in reality. He had
withdrawn from the church of his own accord, and did not believe
in the soul or afterlife, so it is ironic to search for traces of him in
mysterious experiences or the domain of religion. Bearing that in
mind, where is he now? Tell me, Werner, where is he? Yesterday,
they told me that his body hadn't been embalmed—and now he
has already been dead a week and his casket has been locked forever, and no one can see him anymore, and do you know what this
means? Biological extinction of the flesh, no? And if that were the
case, I, along with Mozart's *Lacrimosa*—people had informed me in
advance that the music to be used at the funeral had already been
decided on, no doubt someone would set up a way to play the
music where the funeral was to take place, someone else would get
hold of the record, and food would be served after the ceremony.
They just chattered on like this about other things, even though I
kept on asking where he was—I cannot think that he will be there
forever, in his casket, buried deep within the earth. His flesh, which
had confirmed his existence to us and stirred up our affections,
would rot away to nothing. And now I am swept away into confusion, like an orphan who has lost its way. Could he be in heaven, as

the old songs have it? On my way to Munich, I scrutinized heaven through the airplane window—that is to say, the materially visible atmospheric heavens, a constant blue above the clouds. I want to say that I caught a glimpse of him, but that was only the imagining of my confused mind, and in fact I saw nothing at all, nothing but the sky. Do the dead remain with us? Are they by our side? Do they think of us, in the same way that we think? Do they feel us? Or else, it could be that the concept of absolute nothingness, which had never before gone beyond the abstract, becomes material reality only at this moment. That concept we dimly thought we had understood, which in reality we had not even begun to grasp, the particular circumstances of a life lived at absolute zero, neither flesh, soul, nor mind, that realm of space-time, could be in such a world, such a place, and since there is absolutely no way for us to perceive or be conscious of it even if it can be said to exist, it is in principle no different from that which does not exist, like the already determined future that we absolutely cannot know. Today, we saw his casket. Now, in this instant, we saw that this casket full of flesh was already buried deep in the ground at Haidhausen Cemetery. If it is obvious that the dead flesh lying here will always be him, then why do we grieve like this, here far away? What is to prevent us from simply returning to Haidhausen? But ultimately I cannot be sure whether what is lying inside there is really him, or if it is only a kind of shell and fantasy left behind by him, that at one time was known as him, but is not him anymore. Please tell me, Werner, the meaning of the specific condition known as death. When we are together with death, where do we end up? Where on earth can they be, the dead, the dead we loved?

He will become earth, Werner answered me, and although his voice was gloomy, unlike mine it was neither fevered nor confused. Take a look around at nature. Right now I am thinking of my hometown, by the Wondreb River in Obersalzberg. From childhood I grew up facing the fact that time is a coursing river, whose violence sweeps all things away. All the kinds of existence known to us, which seem to reveal themselves in this world, soon enough are unavoidably dragged away into the rough whirlpool and there ended. And when that happens, other existences appear following on behind them. But even these don't exist for very long. Before long, they too disappear in the strong current of the river. In the river, tall willows and red cedars, whole copses of white birch, are calmly carried along. Look up to the ends of the twigs of their highest branches. They stand alone, reaching toward the dim, forever far-off sky. Turn your gaze to that sky. Jörg will become earth. And in that way he returns as a part of this great cycle, this infinite whole of us. At some time in the future, we will follow him down that road. That is what people call nature, or else spirit or soul. It is quite clear that Jörg will come back to us again, as one of the numberless existences immersed in that whole. Flowers do not bloom of themselves, wind does not blow of its own strength. Within this singular nature, there has to be someone. Air freighted with rough sadness and sunlight that will touch our faces at a future moment as if brushing past by chance, gentle wind and woods and trees, all their colors in a breathtaking mix, raindrops and dew, birdsong heard suddenly in the woods, and this creation's sorrowful accent, the sun blazing up and sinking down like torchlight and November frost sitting on the branches in the early morning, the dark earth that individually and privately touches our bare feet, a river of black raindrops flowing down the glass window; Jörg will come back to us in such things. And in such things he will speak to us. And so, I've said it already, but you mustn't suffer and torment yourself just because you couldn't see him lying there at his moment of death. If you had, you would have been disturbed by a premonition of him being able to be restored to life. I also feel his absence, and am almost crazed with grief over the loss, but all the

105

same I believe that, in some form or other, some way or other, he will come to find us again. That belief is what sustains me.

No, that was nothing more than the words he offered last year. I shook my head. It is the myth of death, constructed because death is so utterly unknowable for us. Because it is too poetic and literary. Because it is such a beautiful consolation that it pains the heart. Because it is a case that will apply to all living beings indiscriminately, because ultimately it resembles that general, vague feeling of awe produced by the imagination of the living, which in the past I had obtained from things like art and music. It seems like the mysticism of the soul, which is made up of humanity's dreams and hallucinations, but in fact as no more than individuals, each of us becomes extinct within the whole, and all it does is to beautify the fate of any organism, which is to infiltrate nature's cells like a nutriment. Compromise or consolation were absolutely not his way, Werner, as you know, and so I dislike them too. It would still be good to feel that individual's existence, even if only for one last time. I want to physically sense it in reality. And if it were possible, if only for one more day, or only for another moment, I would want to turn back time. I want to walk into that time. Not the universal time of this world, I mean a sort of time that hasn't been stolen from the unconscious, time separated from an artificial world, the time of the past, which has a place in the future. Back to that time when his death was forever to lie there ahead of us, when he was suffering, when he realized he was ill, to that surreal moment in which death began to be revealed between us, forever lying in wait. If not that, if only we can at least now clearly recognize where he, the human called Jörg Trebs, is, it will be enough. That question did not leave my mind all through this week of despair, which has been the longest and gloomiest of my life. Standing at the snow-covered window I didn't know where I ought to go. To Bielefeld, where he had lived? To the hospital where he had breathed his last? To the temporary depository where his flesh was being held? To Haidhausen Cemetery where he was to be buried? Or else to Berlin, where it seemed his figure would appear at every street corner? If not any of these, then must I right now stay quietly in this place where I was put, and can I do nothing here but wait until the time when I will end up facing it? If there is no answer to this question, then this is the evidence that death is nothing more than a frightening violence, a cruel and one-sided terror which sums up life. Death is only destruction and an evil that hates us, death ruthlessly hunts us down like rabbits and, unlike what people fervently desire, gives us not so much as a drop of dew or a gust of wind as compensation, only the cold certainty that actually the dead are nowhere. The only thing we encounter after a person's death is the sharp snowstorm lashing our cheeks. Please tell me, Werner, what is death? Is it really nothing more than the one occurrence in this world that is impossible to call off? Is it only that? We, who breathed, sang, loved, read books, are we no more than that? People say that not a single happening is meaningless in this world. But where is there anything more meaningless than ourselves, we who stand in front of death? I want to know. I really want to understand how to endure this absurd absence, the most difficult thing in life.

It's no good suffering and struggling in vain to try and understand death, Werner said. To do so is useless, since death is beyond human comprehension. Just accept the things we can do, and turn your gaze toward nature and the universe. And so now be done with your sadness, keep the good memories alive within you, don't be too hard on yourself, and eventually accept the parting calmly. This is the way it will be. Since that is the way of nature, and you are a part of nature.

But that is not the way I am. Once more I shook my head firmly. A life passes, you know, Werner, a life passes, and only after and through this another life comes; if that is the way of nature then I can find peace in nature no longer. These words, "a life passes," are far weightier and more meaningful than the salvation of the entire universe and all religious truths combined. They describe a pain and destruction more oppressive than the end of the world. It means being sunk in a pit of immeasurable loss and inexhaustible sadness. Right here in this pit, the tragedy of our flesh and the utter despair of the individual twists and writhes. Great, absolute Nature only grasps us as a single unit of mother nature's ecology, merely a part within the whole, no different from plants that are born for the sake of putting down roots in the air. Not only do I not love nature, from now on I will do everything in my power to make it suffer; if I can only manage it I will willingly call down curses upon it. Now before long spring will come to call, buds will sprout from every branch and the air will be damp with humidity, deep-colored trees will exhibit their abundant flesh, but I will no longer accept this as a blessing or be moved by it. The sun's rays glance dazzlingly off the glass window in front of my desk, but even though the world of before—the kind of world which had made me think of myself as strong and independent—presents exactly the same vista as it always has as it unfolds outside the window (how I used to love that view in the past, what self-confidence I felt from being a part of it), there will be no happiness for me anymore, caught in the cycle of this world's merciless metabolism. In the future, I will compose no songs to the spring of hideously gruesome death, not one more word. A life passes, and were all kinds of young, beautiful, fresh, sweet joy to burst onto the scene, parading themselves as soon as the grave was stamped down, as if they had been waiting in the wings, I would still send no praises to the lips of fragrant spring. My first thought would probably be that those lips had fattened themselves by sucking the flesh from something's bones. Do you hear, Werner, I was sitting at my desk just like I always do when one day I saw hell open up before me, people told me that Jörg had died, that from now on he would simply not be, what is this non-being, where does this thing called non-being come from, and why on earth does non-being have to be. I have question after question. If we will soon be nothing more than non-being, then why are we here now? Now, the majestic, gaudy deathscape spreads out before my desk until the end of time. That view oppresses my whole world. And monsters that have slithered their slick bodies out from it will become the singular coffee-drinking existence that I have practiced. Only they will speak to me, and it seems that until the final moment all I can do is prick up my ears to catch what they say, and write.

Werner's answer: Don't hurry to find a solution right now, words won't clarify anything at this point. Now is the time for sadness and suffering, nothing else, time that is surely both significant and absolutely necessary. I will comfort you, and then you will be a comfort for me; that's how this time will pass, albeit slowly. He appeared in my film, so we could encounter him there sometime, if we wanted. Another time, if we wanted to, we could read about him, whenever we liked. But whether that means his existence or its opposite—that's an answer that will come to you slowly, neither from me nor from others, no, only from yourself. But it seems the harshest time for us is now. Every morning I cannot but be woken by the sound of a thorny whip flogging my heart. However, even in the saddest moments, don't forget this: what did Jörg most hope for you? He didn't hope that you would collapse. He must have hoped you would get by somehow and not suffer too much, and that you would keep on writing. And so, it's the same for me, but if you do that you'll be okay. Shed tears, bawl out your grief. Heaven's angels are no longer for us, but I will listen to your tears and you can listen to mine. But as well as tears, do as he hoped you would. If you do, now and then you will feel that he is with you. No one can rob you of his image and all that you felt for him, as long as these are kept in your heart. They will remain intact as yours and yours alone. So don't fall prey to a gradually strengthening negativity and skepticism, questioning whether that time was really and truly there, whether we truly experienced that place, whether you truly met him. Believe in him. Believe in his memory and his existence. Realistically, this is the best we can hope for, who have lost in Jörg Trebs a unique and supremely brilliant mentor.

Do you know, Werner? Jörg taught me many things over the last three years; the last of them, and the most oppressive, is precisely this: death. At the last, without any preparation whatsoever he gave me this book, without explanation or footnote or critical commentary, written in an indecipherable language, and departed. Now I am isolated and powerless, with only the book for company. When we first met he was already wearing flesh pallid with age, and for the three years I knew him he had been very close to the end of life, and all I knew was his end. But he refused to compromise with infirmity or death, he refused more firmly than anyone else in this world, and until its final moment the life he lived was greater than any other, he was someone who had wanted even more life for the sake of more life. His mind had never been exhausted for even a single moment, and his eyes would light up in front of literature. As you say, I will continue to write. If there is religion or a soul for us then it is clearly nothing other than literature, and all I can do for him now is write, but although I'm well aware that this was what he wanted above all, writing can no longer be the object of supreme happiness for me. Because from now on I am simply powerless, I cannot *but* write; that's the way it will be for me, now. A person passes, and so if we absolutely cannot accompany them to Hades, what can all a human being's mental actions be, other than vainly flirting with life, trying to win its attention?

Diary entry from the banks of the Spree River in Berlin, one day in September, 2008. We were in the middle of a long walk by the river. We passed the Berliner Ensemble at the Bode Museum and then continued walking aimlessly, our legs eventually carrying us up to the area around Bellevue railway station. It was evening, and the setting sun, though slightly obscured by clouds, was suspended above the autumn trees, which were dyed with a brilliant golden light. With the shadows of a certain hour, both a chance occurrence and a one-time-only thing. Looking at the photographs from that time, it's clear that I had been in the center of something. The center of what, exactly—that can't be expressed in a single word. But clearly the center of some particular world, made up of simple language we had already long possessed, and of simple light, of color, water, voices, footsteps, and hints of evening; some kind of opposite shore of the mind, shining fixedly, staring fixedly at all those things like their shadow or soul, water opposite water, though we can arrive at that place through a singular gesture and expression, a world that cannot be entered arbitrarily, a country of unspecific time that cannot but be called "that certain moment." Dividing our own place and time from nature and the physical world. Dividing our selves from the realism known as the present. That was something I dared to do of my own volition. I was a traveler. I was a poor uneconomical traveler who had come to that place for the sake of writing a single sentence. In that way I was an extremely self-willed traveler; still more so since my travels were not only geographical. Walk, cry, and write, I said to myself. While we ate hot cakes and coffee at a literature house cafe that afternoon, we talked about Erpenbeck's new work, *Heimsuchung*, which had come out that year. And after that, continuing the day's conversation, you had sent me an email expressing why, as a critic, you couldn't personally like the writer Martin Walser, or going further, even the person Martin Walser. This was a point of some heated debate between us, specifically relating to Martin's *Angstblüte*, a work we both knew well, but whose appraisal we had failed to come to an agreement over. Though you played the extremely pre-determined role of the perfect, "invisible" assistant, up until the time when I was able to complete my translation of that book. You set up my initial meeting with Walser, and even accompanied me in both of my two trips to meet him. At that time I recorded our conversation, along with the essay you improvised and recited in the train. The train rattles along through the landscape of Germany's southern states, and two people have their faces buried in their two arms, and two people bury their two existences in the eternally parallel tracks and in time, and station after station passed through, the monotonous fields that languidly appear and disappear, passed right through just as you realize that you are approaching them; within wind and river water that is neither a torrent nor an earthquake, neither happiness nor unhappiness, but merely adapts peacefully to the cycle of circumstances, itself soon wind and river water, but certain things in literature are different, they transcend environment and temperament, contort a face with pain, to the point that attempting to express them in words is completely meaningless, and to that extent literature was a common interest between us, of pain that had seized us both. With you, I can broach literature as a topic of conversation without embarrassment or hesitation. In that way, over the last three years we have been together with literature in various places, in various places and at the same time, we have crossed continents and have all those moments, of all kinds of places at the same time, compressed into one. Oh, but once again that particular world turns back to face the banks of the Spree, to face that moment that had suddenly flowed past through the very center of something. Because that was when, having been staring fixedly at the bridge opposite during our stroll in the Tiergarten woods, you seized my arm and blurted out "Take a good look at that road. I think I can see my mother pushing a stroller. Those are very same the woods where she would often set out for a walk with me, back in 1938 when we lived in Berlin, before the war." Until then, I had never once known you to adopt the role of surrealist. "In that case we should wait here," I said fervently, putting my whole heart into the words without even knowing why, as a kind of reflex. "Until your mother takes you for a walk, that is. I would so like to see what you looked like as a young child, and how she looked back then." Recoiling instantly, your expression startled, you gestured in agitation and reproved me, what kind of crazy idea is that? As though you were angry at yourself for having impulsively blurted out your sorrow. You made as if to dash away over the bridge, as if fleeing from something. At the time I was lost in a dream; since your eyes, which had been seeing something else, had already reddened . . .

Never have I experienced having to say a final goodbye to someone very close to me, someone corresponding to what is called, according to the general expression, one's own "flesh and blood." No, I had come to reject the premonition that there would ever be such flesh and blood for me. I was unable to grasp the essence of that thing called loss, which is both the suffering of the soul and of the flesh. Instead I said to myself: Walk, cry, and write. Since that is all I am able do in this world. Walk, cry, and write. And so, I will remain nothing more than an intermittent and uneconomical traveler, until the day I die. I was frightened. The conviction of those words: "I know." (And after it was all over, my friend who lives in Bonn sent me an email that began with exactly those words: I know what it must be like for you right now.) Now and then, without any deliberate intention, just on an impulse, I display a stubborn streak, which was what happened that day. "Wait, your mother is certain to appear, and your child-self too. I know they will. We'll be able to watch them from here. Believe me. You're a scholar of realism, but I'm a writer, one who has always been thinking up novels where this kind of thing happens, so this time I'm right." But as if struck by an invisible arrow or lightning bolt; as if that day in 1938 was truly going to pierce the wall of time and long sleep to reappear in front of your eyes; as if, though the scene was not yet visible, you could feel your mother pushing you in the stroller, walking slowly from that distant place, that day seventy years ago, toward today; as though you were suddenly struck by a frightening possibility, perhaps that no, they might actually never appear; or else as though you were furious with yourself; or else like a sorrowful penitent, looking back on their life with the agonized regret of one who knows that what they long to undo is utterly irrevocable, and with a particularly violent gesture, your lips set in a stern line as you struggled to control your emotions, you coldly rebuffed my earnest desire to wait for you and your mother, who might be going to show themselves to us, turning your back on me, and finally marched quickly away from that place, your gait agitated, and put an end to it. You walked away facing squarely in the direction of life. Without hesitation you turned your face away from the river and woods opposite us, away from that cave of time that had abruptly revealed itself to us. My heart races and the river shudders. The peaceful scenery, the calm surface turns into a burning abyss. From the brink of an enormous pitch-black hole you turn your back on me, on yourself, retreating rapidly into the distance. I follow after you, but there is no way for me to follow to your Hades.

Did you know, Werner said to me in a choked voice, his hand clutching mine, according to certain traditional beliefs passed down in Central Europe, like in Germany, when someone comes across themselves as a child, particularly as a newborn baby, it means they don't have long left to live.

The dream isn't over. A person is leaving. The body of the river wracked with slow sobs, as if all dead things are suspended in its waters. A person is leaving; I cannot see them. I can only feel that they are passing by this place. The air hazy like a suspended veil, verdant light around the edges of the woods. I sit by the river and look down into the water. A person is leaving. On their way, they pass by the village. The houses have their mouths closed, dumb; children stand in front of the doors. They look on wordlessly as the person approaches. And stare fixedly at his retreating figure.

This thing on page 65 of Franz Kafka's *Dream* is both Kafka's dream and mine. There were two reiterated heterogeneous dreams. They pile up bodies and appear. The wind often blows and if it blows their bodies over, they look out of the window immersed in yearning. We stood in front of Werner Fritsch's camera by the Wondreb River. Werner told me later that I was playing the part of one of three goddesses. And you appeared as light, dressed as the great poet Dante, walking the dark wooded paths in hooded medieval clothes. I try to see you through Werner's camera. In the final moment, light poured down over your face, bleaching it brighter than the light itself until it disappeared in the glare. Within two dreams, a person is leaving. I stare into it. But I cannot see it. Only feel that it is passing by this place.

Mouson

*T*hat night, though the taxi I shared with the model-plane collector took us along the road that ran above the river, the oil-black water was concealed by the metal guardrail and ugly flower beds. Before that, we had passed by the richer neighborhood, rows of villas with their own gardens, the central station with its lights off and shops with their doors closed, hotels and travel lodges clustered around the station, and the district of tall buildings whose glass bodies flickered in the dark; as we passed, it occurred to me that I saw people wearing white closed-top shoes running lightly along the road, their feet seeming to lift up a full palm's breadth off the ground, and each time we clattered down one of the narrow roads paved with bumpy stones, which lay to the rear of the buildings, the small-framed, stout-shouldered taxi driver spat out a mumbled, incomprehensible criticism. I thrust my head forward and strained to listen, hoping to understand what he was saying, but all I could ever make out was a strange sound like the wind whisking by, and so we fell into an auditory hallucination, imagining that a broken radio was speaking those words in his place; as predicted, the reflection in the window was that of a foreigner, with a trim moustache and hair on the backs of his hands, his skin black—when I first got into the taxi the phrase "black as coal" had sprung into my mind; his black face reminded me of the lonely African who, several years ago when I'd spent a day at the zoo in one of the cities I'd wandered to, had come up to me with his enormous old-fashioned Russian camera and asked if I would take a photo of him, at which I had hastily pressed the shutter; strangely, nothing happened, and I had to point the camera several times at the bulky African, who sat alone perseveringly in front of the thick-mesh cage the ring-tailed lemurs were shut up in. It was the middle of the day and the sunlight was dazzlingly bright, and all I could see through the lens, bafflingly enough, was the blackly shadowed mesh of the cage and a white flash of light exaggerated beyond all proportion, and when I brought my eye to the camera again, flustered as both the ring-tailed lemurs inside the cage and the African disappeared without a trace each time, it slowly became clear that they all formed a part of that dark pattern I had mistaken for a shadow. The memory of the African who had suddenly become something non-shadow every time his eyes met mine from the shadows. But the moment after the glittering headlights from an oncoming car shone full on the driver's face, the moment those beams slid off at a diagonal, that face became the same shade as a milky cappuccino, then later, once the model-plane collector had ceased to conceal his anger, gradually changed to a lifeless gray, and when the driver eventually turned to look back at us, I saw a fly crawling over the face of a Russian, hardened like lead-colored candle drippings, or we were sitting in the rear seat of a taxi whose driver was in fact a Russian.

The driver's language was made up of such a clump of vowels that it was difficult to believe, and those clumps were so huge that they felt heavy, like a gust of wind that cannot lift anything up, and the look in his eyes, so intense that it was impossible to look directly at them, was enough to make any antagonist think twice. On our way to the point which we were then at, the driver had giggled now and then for no apparent reason, and had rudely demanded to know what we did; his questions were almost incomprehensible, and because it was clear, given his inability to understand our word "literature," that he could not have understood the address we had given him at the start, we became extremely anxious. Apparently picking up on this anxiety, the driver nodded at us fervently in the mirror, though rather than serving to reassure, this action seemed to express that we were not the only ones who were worried, that the driver himself felt exactly the same.

As soon as I had gotten into the taxi, the model-plane collector explained where we were headed. It was a reading by a writer friend of his; the reading would be held at Mouson Tower, by coincidence the writer's name was also "Mouson," the title of his latest book was *Performers*, and was, the model-plane collector claimed, a very interesting work, in which the writer had collected, in the style of an encyclopedia, likenesses of all the performers with whom he was personally acquainted. The model-plane collector said that he was curious as to whether there was among these likenesses the Japanese performer who, as the founder of Aum Shinrikyo, had instigated the poison-gas terror attack on the Tokyo subway, but though he did not at this point know the answer, having not yet had a chance to take a look at the book, we would find out soon enough. Of the famous performers who appeared in the book, there was Kaspar Hauser and the Pope, the Dalai Lama and Peter Handke, Prince Charles, and Osama bin Laden of course, the model-plane collector continued. Just so you know, the model-plane collector went on, the writer goes about sporting bizarrely bright-red socks and wears his curly hair long and disheveled, and is famous for his fluttering gestures and manner of speaking as well as his threadbare attire; there's even a rumor that he eats hot noodles with his fingers, though for your information, Mouson was a successful entrepreneur. Aside from the writer Mouson whose reading we are going to, there was also the original proprietor of the "Mouson" where the reading is being held, the model-plane collector added. He is the descendent of a family who moved to Germany to escape the French oppression of the Huguenots; he gained experience working as a young soap manufacturer wandering between various cities toward the end of the eighteenth century, and on coming to this city he secured work, later took over the business in which he himself had been employed, and after establishing himself thus his business enjoyed a long period of prosperity, eventually enabling him to found a soap and cosmetics factory on the site of the current Mouson Tower. The company's most representative product is its "Creme Mouson Intensive Moisture," which was introduced directly after the First World War; the Mouson company's cosmetics factory later relocated to an area further out from the center, and a head office was built at the original factory site, including a tower thirty meters high. That tower is the tallest building in this city. Then, in 1972, after an extremely complicated process, the company was sold off and the office was torn down, with only the tower left standing. After that, it got a second life as a venue for various kinds of independent arts events, and people began to call it Mouson Tower, borrowing the name from the original founder, and Mouson Tower is an entity known to almost everyone in this city, and as it's an especially recognizable name for taxi drivers, like the White House or the Forbidden City, if you get into a taxi and say only that, Mouson Tower, every driver will glance back over his shoulder saying you'll never catch me reading a book, just the TV guide, I never set foot in the theater, never go to the ballet or book readings, but I still know what that name means, there's no way I couldn't, being a taxi driver in this city! The model-plane collector finished off this speech with an insistent gesture.

Today we had arranged to meet in front of the museum. The model-plane collector was already in something of a state when his taxi pulled up, asking if I knew the way to Mouson Tower as I was still settling myself in next to him. He'd had an errand to take care of in a different part of the city, around an hour away, and had caught the taxi from there; not only was the driver ignorant of geography in general, but the name Mouson meant absolutely nothing to him—he claimed to have never even heard the phrase "Mouson Tower" and, since he had no clue as to where a tower by such a name might be, had asked for the precise address, but the address the collector had provided didn't show up on the car's GPS, leading him to doubt whether it was accurate, but not only did the model-plane collector participate in a literary event at Mouson Tower every year without fail, he naturally took a taxi there every time, and had never yet misremembered the address, meaning there was no reason whatsoever that he might be misremembering now, and given that he was going to a reading by a famous writer, at an arts venue named after an even more famous soap-cosmetics manufacturer, there would have been no need to inform him of the address if the driver had not been a foreigner, now would there, and it's already been an hour since you said you would take us there, he emphasized. Look, if you can't find the street, can't you just ask the Center? Isn't the Center there to deal with these things? Can you understand what I'm saying? the model-plane collector said to the driver, earnestly yet coldly, courteously yet without concealing a chill note of criticism. The driver mumbled something, again with his mouth closed; to me, it sounded like someone saying that they'd already asked the Center a little while ago, but had been told that the address was not an entrance, only using a jumble of imprecise words that lacked the ability to communicate that meaning fully. But the model-plane collector cut the driver off before he had finished what he was saying, exclaiming, I know the road Mouson Tower is on, I've known about that tower since before you were even born, and I'm telling you there's no way in heaven or hell that it's this road here, Mr. Driver!

We were in the middle of a dark road. It was a backstreet, narrow enough to be called an alleyway; a row of houses with their lights off stood like high and mighty giants, lining the long, shallow curve of the pavement, and their black windows all faced outward, slightly damp from the light rain that was falling ceaselessly; now and then the raindrops were caught in the beams from passing taxis and pounced at our faces like squalling insects, and I reflexively raised my arm to shield myself, only to remember even as I did so that we were sitting inside a taxi, though in an extremely precarious situation. It strikes me that the road that curved and twisted here and there through the alleys was one of the darkest and narrowest I have encountered in this city. On top of the night being cold and bleak, the paved street was slippery, and even from inside the taxi I was all too well aware of this state of affairs; each time we inched forward it was as though the damp, black, high walls were themselves the ones approaching, looming at us as they rounded the corner, which made me think that on such a night, even if a thirty-meter-high tower were to pierce through the layers of darkness and appear right in front of our eyes, there would be absolutely no way for us to recognize it. Small shadows of a deep and wavering blue appeared briefly beyond the curve of that corner before disappearing; they had to be the lights of cars passing along a different street that leads on to an intersection. We had already circled the same address several times, having been informed that the car's GPS could provide no further information. According to an extremely peculiar memory I had of that place, one which has remained with me until today, a group of people passed by who, in spite of the night having been bitterly cold, were wearing thin, sleeveless coats, and one woman among them was wearing the white tunic of a goddess, like at the time of the spring festival, and carrying a bouquet of yellow flowers, and they all went laughing inside some apartment building; since the building's front door was a huge pane of cold glass, I was able to see, through the gap of the open door that was there just for the brief moment of them stepping inside, the black muzzle of a viciously barking dog. I recall that those people had moved as though kicking the earth with their feet. As though they were birds. Though I opened the window and stuck my head out to try and get a proper look at the shape of their shoes, the individual puddles strewn across the pavement had pooled into the single body of the night, and the swamp-thick darkness sunk down close to the ground was reflected still more blackly on the surface of the puddles, meaning nothing was visible at the bottom of this world, like a stage wreathed in black smoke so that the actors' feet cannot be seen poking out from beneath their cloaks. Like birds scratching for feed in the frozen ground, people who had walked with light leaping steps, though the shape of their shoes was not visible. As though they were birds.

For god's sake, will you call the Center or not? the model-plane collector was urging the driver again. The driver made a gesture of helplessness and, letting out an exaggerated sigh, attempted to connect with the Center; his disobedient attitude further upset the collector. In *Performers*, there are two hundred twenty-five fool-performers, from all eras; that, for whatever reason, very few of these are women—I mean, women couldn't be recorded in history even as performers or fools?—attracted the attention of feminist critics, the model-plane collector told me while the driver was telephoning the Center. This book of over a thousand pages, which has the ironic subtitle "small-scale performerology for beginners," is a record not only of the truly great performers, but also of the performativeness and foolish aspects of those commonly remembered as heroes or wise men, and would be an entertaining read for anyone interested in strange tales and far-fetched episodes, the more obscure corners of history; there, the writer's witty way with words and extensive, encyclopedic knowledge, albeit knowledge displayed as more of a miscellany, can be enjoyed together, the model-plane collector said. The driver repeated the name "Mouson" to the Center and asked for the address, at which the Center's representative seemed to relay once again the address of our current location. But it isn't here! the model-plane collector exclaimed, all but shouting. Where on earth would Mouson have founded a cosmetics factory around here? In this pitch-black backstreet? Why can't you be more specific, more concrete, when you ask for the address? We're already late, thanks to you. I mean, haven't we already driven around this block several times?! The model-plane collector put excessive emphasis on the phrase "thanks to you." The driver hunched his shoulders, the look in his eyes said "so what d'you expect me to do?", but there was no way in the world that his punctured, perforated vowel-language could produce such a sentence, and so he only mumbled inside his mouth, fretful and plaintive. You good-for-nothing, let us out here, the model-plane collector burst out, unable to restrain himself. Adding severely, there's not a single thing you did right as a taxi driver! But just then the driver pressed some button with an abrupt, resolute gesture, ensuring that the fare would not rise any higher, as though this alone lay within his power, and after this show of strength in the domain that lay under his jurisdiction, with the bearing of a dwarf sovereign parading it to the max, said: in any case I'm going to try and find it again myself. His words were pushed out from his throat with great effort, like huge rocks. Please look, I've stopped the meter so the fare won't go up any higher. You see? If we just take another turn around the area, your tower will show up, so let's give it a go. The driver spoke with difficulty, his voice thick as though with tears; his speech was relatively slow and stumbling, befitting a foreigner who couldn't manage any better, and exacerbated by the fact that the model-plane collector had been glaring at him with a look cold enough to freeze the sun. What the driver actually wanted to say was that his suggestion for a compromise was not limited to putting a cap on the fare, but was also a plea for us to consider whether in cases such as this, when the information was less than satisfactory, his ignorance of the problematic tower, which every taxi driver in the city should know, was purely his own fault, and though it was a fact, wasn't it, that the collector had not given him an exact address for this Mouson Tower, all the same the driver had not expressed any anger—at which the model-plane collector said emphatically, with the faultless pronunciation of an intellectual, as though beating out another hammer blow, that it was a trade requirement for a taxi driver of this city to know that name, the name of Mouson Tower.

We eventually ended up right in front of Mouson Tower; surprisingly, the tower was located barely a block from the winding alleyway we'd spent such a long time creeping up and down, and all that was needed to bring it into view was a turn around a gentle corner. It was in a similarly narrow and shadowed alleyway; Mouson Tower occupied almost all of the narrow plot of land that lay between two alleys, one of which was called Mouson Street, borrowing the name from the tower. And since the entrance to the tower was situated on the opposite side of the alley, people habitually thought of it as "Mouson Street's Mouson Tower," though by some mysterious means all other taxi drivers were conveying their passengers to the front of the tower without any difficulty whatsoever, at least according to the model-plane collector. The darkness spread out in all directions, with no lights on in any of the buildings, though a small restaurant sign was visible on the ground floor of the building next to the tower. It was an Italian restaurant, with glowing candles in tin candlesticks, checked tablecloths, and the din of customers tangible through the rectangular window.

Though we would trickle into that place like insects drawn to light and end up ordering two plates of pasta, though we would pick our way through the food in silence, not exchanging a single word, until the model-plane collector, still gloomy, would eventually bring himself to ask whether some action of his had made me uncomfortable, and I would answer that no, that the only thing that would make me feel uncomfortable would be to imagine that you yourself felt that way, and though after that we would end up looking sorrowfully at each other for a very brief while, ignorant of the reason that this might be, and that a look like this would be of a type that induces pain in the chest, the heart constricting, and we would have to stand up hastily in order to go to Mouson's reading, though we hadn't managed to clear even half of what was on our plates, this was still before any of this had occurred.

Mouson Tower looked like an ordinary rectangular lump of brick walls, looming tall and bulky against the black sky. This ordinariness was faintly disappointing after the history that had been recounted to me in the taxi, and had I not been aware in advance of the fact that it was a "tower," I would have thought of it as a large rectangular chimney, its shape suited to the late-autumn night. There were several cars in the parking lot, but the surroundings were quiet, with no signs of human life. As it was far too chilly a night to walk around outside, the guests all seemed to have hurried into the tower as soon as they arrived. The taxi driver pulled up by the side of the road and had to ask another driver where Mouson Tower was; the other driver gave a very concise explanation for how to get to the tower's entrance, and in this way we eventually ended up where we'd wanted to be all along, yet still the model-plane collector allowed his simmering anger to boil. My god, I'll never again be able to take a taxi with peace of mind, and I paid good money for the privilege! the model-plane collector said. On top of that, since I would have been immediately branded a hater of foreigners if I'd breathed a single word of complaint, we just had to cower in fear, never mind how distressing or uncomfortable it was! My point was simply that it's unacceptable for a taxi driver in this city to say that he doesn't know Mouson Tower; what on earth has that got to do with a hatred of foreigners? Enraged, the model-plane collector took several big strides, then, as though something had just occurred to him, turned and stared hard at me; it felt as though his staring was an attempt to identify me, my footsteps, who I was, and there was something faintly sorrowful about this, too, though it was not clear who was the cause of this sorrow. This only occurred to me later, but we would probably soon recall it in relation to something else, while eating pasta; he was not in fact sitting in a restaurant chair, but in a pilot's cockpit, his nerves made sharp due to the tension of flying, and beneath his feet the long white gleam of the mountain range was laid out like the spine of a dinosaur; his plane was in the middle of crashing, he was a sorrowful pilot who had been flying a plane that had now crashed; one day I would probably dig his spine out of the earth and brandish it in the air like a cane, and for some reason we are both aware of that while lost in insensibility; at the time I was clattering along the wet pavement, I leapt up lightly, overcome by happiness and sadness, and the model-plane collector, seeing this, opened his mouth wide and tried to say something to me, but I had slipped off my right shoe and was in the middle of shaking out the wet sand that had gotten inside it, and while I was shaking out those many grains of sand, at a loss as to where they might have come from, only then did I become aware of the bright white glow emanating from the form of my shoes, with their high heels and closed toes, like the moon in the middle of the month.

After some time has gone by, I am doing some online shopping when I come across photographs related to the model-plane exhibition held in Bern, in an article for an online magazine. Beneath the title "Largest Exhibition in Switzerland," the article states that the maiden flight of a model Airbus A380 is scheduled to take place; the model has a wingspan of eleven meters from tip to tip when fully spread, and not only that, but is fitted with four engines just like the real thing; the flight time of that model Airbus, which was around a year in the making, will be approximately twelve minutes. I stared for quite some time at photographs of those mechanical objects, studying them closely for the first time in my entire life. Twin objects, which imitate the form and function of the real thing on a smaller scale. I don't personally know any collectors of remote-controlled model planes or steam trains, square box radios, rare stamps or advertising postcards, living reptiles or butterflies. Purely by chance, I had become aware of the fact that there are many more people in the world who have a mania for collecting than I had guessed, and that there are many cases where this is not merely a youthful fad but continues throughout the course of a life, and they want to hold an exhibition of their own collection at least once, and the greatest dream of their lives is to open their own personal museum, and that there are also more such museums than I'd thought, tucked away here and there in hidden alleys. Once we have paid the small entrance fee we can step in through the front door, and if we immediately take a right we will find ourselves in the ground floor's main living room; in the center of the room, a five-meter wingspan Concorde, both the largest object on display in this museum and the proudest achievement of the collector's life, is gently touching down, wings spread, and passing along the narrow corridor that this room leads on to we encounter uncountably many miniature aircraft in a glass display case, several model planes which seem to have been brought there straight from the shop and, most striking of all, a plane made according to Leonardo da Vinci's design; looked at now in the present day, it resembles a surveillance camera installed on the side of the museum, and on the opposite wall are rare and precious black-and-white photographs of planes made by early twentieth-century inventors, photographs of the desolate expanse of runways at long-ruined airports, temporary runways for fighter planes to use in deserts and rugged mountain ranges, backwoods runways for archaeologists and explorers, or else grave looters and spies, and a photograph of the air base from which planes had transported supplies to West Berlin during the blockade; and if we go up the stairs to the first floor, stairs so narrow that for even one person it is a tight squeeze, the model planes are now displayed by period, in rooms that would once have been the owners' bedroom, study, and dining room; in the majority of cases these are miniature objects, even those that have been fitted with remote-controlled engines, and if we wander this room we will come across an even smaller room in which we can sit and watch a black-and-white film such as *History of Aviation III—1927 to 1945*, its voiceover a weary monotone, or a silent film that plays on a loop, filled with scenes of jubilation from when Charles Lindbergh arrived successfully in Paris the day after his unsteady takeoff from Roosevelt Field on May 20th, 1927, and as there are cases in which the collector's interest is not limited to the object itself, we can also discover small bookshelves holding volumes such as *Night Flight* or *Beyond the Sun—A Biography of Lindbergh*.

Wandering here and there through the rooms, we never once come face to face with another visitor, and are only able to track those who have gone ahead of us through footsteps impressed into the carpet, handwriting in the guest book, or breath condensed on the glass of the display cases; we sense shadows disappearing swiftly behind the door, low coughing in the next room or the rustling of pamphlet pages, and on stepping into a given room, we sense the body heat of the person who had just moments ago been staring, entranced, at the display-case model of a B-58 Hustler, who would clearly also have stopped in front of the pop art picture hanging on the wall, a picture done in the style of Lichtenstein, in which a woman with egg-yolk-yellow hair is clinging to a man's neck and wailing, the woman's enormously exaggerated eyes and lips, the back of the man's head, which is all we can see of him, the rough, thick outlines and exaggerated expressions, though the most intense characteristics of all are the glittering primary colors that bore into our eyes, so simple and superficial as to leave us dumbfounded, recalling manhwa or a cinema marquee, or else cosmetics posters from the 1920s, but over there, behind the man and woman, a plane stands on the runway prepared for takeoff, like a swan with its wings full-spread against the background of the blue sky, and the couple are probably in the middle of saying their final farewell. Above the head of the woman, whose fat tears are rolling down her face, is a speech bubble enclosing the words "I'll miss you . . . please write," and "Boeing 747" is clearly written on the body of the plane; in one corner of the painting, probably so that the picture could be mistaken for an advertisement rather than a work of art, is an ambiguous phrase set in black type: "We will meet again at the world's crossroads."

On the second floor is an office and workroom, so visitors are not permitted to enter; the thought that flashes into my mind as I walk down the stairs, a mixture of doubt and wonder, is why do certain people love airplanes so much, even though they've never known what it's like to be borne aloft by their own feathered wings; why do certain people love these flying machines so much that they want to make small-scale models of them to display in their homes, to stuff their homes with them until there is room for nothing else, until their homes have in a sense been bequeathed to these models, so that they can stay there together for as long as

possible, even in perpetuity, and ensure all that the models could
ever need is there for them inside their home, so that they need
never leave, the model plane's moment brought to a still-greater
perfection not only through things like runways, airports, and control towers, unidentified passengers silhouetted inside the aircraft
windows, porters, and mechanics, but even going so far as a runway attendant who, due to some abrupt calamity, when the house
is shrouded in milk-white fog, appears from somewhere and stands
there holding a flag, their face impossible to make out because of
the raincoat that covers them from head to toe.

I do not personally know any collectors of engine-fitted model
planes or of porcelain sugar bowls, of maps of the premodern
world or printed matter such as picture postcards, of glass products
infused with color, portraits of famous figures, marionette dolls,
signs with the names of streets on them, stuffed specimens of birds,
posters advertising cosmetic products, or trinkets such as bangles.
There was a period when I used to travel around to this place and
that, living in temporary accommodations, a succession of rented
rooms; after gathering together the necessary articles and packing
them into a very large suitcase, I would take taxis and buses to the
airport, stand at the end of a long line and, after going through
the departure formalities, board the plane. Small, unfamiliar rooms
arrived at in that way, rooms given to travelers who would be staying for several months, belonging to someone who had themselves
gone traveling for a similar period of time. Even when I try to
dredge up those rooms from my memory, recalling the tastes of
their owners, I never get the feeling that there was even the slightest
trace of a collecting hobby. Aside, of course, from picture frames
and travel souvenirs, insignificant dolls and one or two toy planes
suspended from the ceiling. Living for several months in rooms
where the individual traces of another person remained animate,
or else where those traces were eternally present-progressive, always

felt strange; one place I frequently stayed in was one such rented room, originally belonging to someone else or on loan just for the time being, where furniture and curtains, books and ornaments, toys and slippers and bedding, were jointly owned.

There were actually many empty rooms in the city as a whole, but because those who rented out rooms generally preferred long-term residents, obtaining a rented room for the comparatively short period of two or three months was not easy. In the worst cases, when there was no suitable room available for the period I needed it, I would have to traipse back and forth between the houses of friends and acquaintances, or even of strangers who had been introduced to me by friends, hauling my heavy suitcase from this city to that; on days when a strike or delays had left the central station all but paralyzed, I would set my bag down on the platform, perch on it with my shoulders hunched and, during the seemingly endless time spent waiting for the train, lose myself in futile doubt over whether the laborious business of struggling across the country on discount tickets really did reduce my expenses so much as to outweigh the convenience of staying in a hotel. Whatever the case, I didn't want to let the exhaustion of living overwhelm me. At such times, I would force myself to be cheerful by reminiscing over the week I'd spent in the InterContinental Hong Kong one winter. The hotel receptionist was a German woman, the white quilt cover was smooth as silk, and my room boasted a magnificent view of the New Year's Eve fireworks display, the bright night scene of Hong Kong Island between the harbors. Or else I would recall the cottage at Bodensee where I stayed for ten days one summer. The cottage had three bedrooms, two enormous living rooms, a cellar, kitchen, and dining room, and two balconies looking out over on the garden and the lake respectively. It was evening when I first set foot in its yard, and since the access road was graveled over the sound of the taxi I'd arrived in pulling away was strangely obtrusive in the midst of the silence, and as soon as that sound had disappeared I was struck by the kind of feeling you get on arriving at a solitary island, known by no one, and disembarking alone from the boat. Later, when I tried to explain to a friend how I'd felt at that time, I said that if I had such a thing as a fate, that island was the kind of exceptional place where even that fate could not have been predicted. Like dreaming once more inside a dream, the feeling of having arrived at a destination only to set out again. But there were also rented rooms where the case was exactly the opposite, such as the one whose owner had a name somehow recalling slender birds, but the overriding memory of whom is that his house was narrow and damp, with the smell of cigarette smoke permeating every nook and cranny, and of how, when I got up that first morning and went out onto the balcony, I was faced with a heap of dust and miscellaneous junk, all kinds of abandoned goods, rusted garden chairs, damp earth, and weeds that gave off a foul smell, all piled up in the courtyard overlooked by the neighboring buildings' hideous walls. I'd had to arrange my accommodations before setting out from Korea, and as it was impossible to check each little detail of every house I rented, it was only to be expected that I might meet with this kind of misfortune, at least every once in a while. Whenever anyone asked me about something to do with travel, the very first thing to jump into my mind was all the difficulties I'd had to go through in order to obtain a rented room that was cheap and otherwise suitable; rather than having to do with nature or adventure, or else being seen as a break from everyday life, what "travel" meant to me was, in a certain sense, the moving from place to place and staying with strangers, and in fact was almost a synonym for "a new rented room in which I can write," meaning I could no longer count the number of emails I'd written in order to arrange my stays, and had ended up qualified to include "extensive experience staying in all kinds of rental accommodations" in the so-called personal introductions on those websites that act as an intermediary between those looking for a place to stay and those looking to rent one out; in spite of this, all the rooms I'd ever managed to get had only ever come through friends or chance encounters, never through those websites.

One year I was lucky enough to be able to stay in a villa in Germany provided by a literary organization; as the German air traffic controllers were on strike, I experienced several complications at the airport, and didn't manage to get to the villa until after midnight. All I'd been told was that there was a safe set into one of the villa's external walls, that the code to the safe was A19***, and that if I entered the code and opened the safe I would find the key to my room inside, along with a note detailing the room's number and how to get to it. My shoes squelched into the rain-softened soil as I tugged my heavy suitcase through the garden, and I glanced nervously about in search of this "external wall"; it was totally dark aside from the faint electric light at the main entrance, the only sound was that of the ceaseless rain splashing onto the ground, loud enough to be alarming, and I stood there in silence for a while getting rained on, at the end of a twenty-hour trip; is this my house, is this my dream, I was confused, engulfed in a dreamlike fantasy state that was similar to a kind of bodily exhaustion, which is perhaps a mental disorder caused by the effects of a long plane journey, because your nerves get unstrung due to the time difference, or else the higher levels of radiation to which flight exposes you, no one lives in this huge villa, all the rooms are empty, in this place, too, this night, I will be lost, just as I was lost for a few hours in the airport that same afternoon; as though this time known as my present had seen me slip accidentally back into a dream which I had dreamed a long time ago, for a while I would be divided between the me who was going to get lost here and the me who would be watching that me, and before I had even gone up to that room I had seen it, and had the feeling that I knew the space very well, and not only that, but also knew the things that would come to pass there, the things I would end up doing; scene after scene passed slowly through my mind, as in the kaleidoscope that the lame musician used to go around with; rather than coming and going in orderly succession, these scenes recurred at unpredictable intervals, crawling fitfully in between those that appeared later, and I felt aware of things which it was not yet possible for me to know; the lonesome and oppressive fantasies of that time, which were nevertheless filled with conviction, have not completely left me even now that time has passed, and I am utterly unable to tell whether these discontinuous images that, ever since that day, have come back to me for a time and calmly possessed me before once again fading away, are purely the constructs of my imagination, dreams dreamed in a waking state, sights that I saw a long time ago, or sights from the future that, upon encountering, I would feel that I had seen before.

Among the temporary residences that I had wandered insecurely between, there was a house on Frankfurt's Holbeinstrasse that I ended up at thanks to an introduction; I stayed there last year, during the week of the book fair. The old house was very pleasant and comfortably furnished, and the owner couple gave me an empty guest bedroom. It had its own bathroom en suite; I recall that on the day I arrived russet leaves that had fallen from the huge flowerpot were scattered over the soft bathroom rug like something painted by an artist, a deliberate decoration. The owner was a retired engineer who told me that, in the past, he had gone on frequent business trips, to a number of different cities, and as there were times, especially when major expos were being held and it was very difficult to secure a hotel in the city center, he would then—as I was doing now—rent a room for a period of days from someone to whom a friend had introduced him; these rooms had not originally been intended for this purpose, but had been used by the owners' family, and so one time he stayed in the room of a young boy where all the shelves were crammed with footballs and model airplanes, and even the boxes under the bed had been filled with all kinds of models. When I woke up suddenly that night, I discovered a model-plane mobile revolving in midair like an electronic dragonfly, its faint taillight blinking, and I even seemed to hear a low, stifled burr, as though the plane were chafing its thin wings together, threading through my dreams; I remember how it felt, he said, how strange it was, even now. This was when we were talking, over cider, of the various temporary residences we had each known over the course of our respective lives.

I never rented the same room more than once. Rooms that had once been used by me appeared to have their purpose quietly disappear thanks to some third-party will. Even now when I spread out a map, the rented houses where I stayed here and there, the addresses of owners that had at one time been familiar to me and from which mail would arrive for me after my stay, plain rooms and the simple furniture inside them, windows that each wore their own expression, and the things that I had written there, together with the names of those underground stations that were the ones I'd had to get off at during the months of my stay, the sight of the ice cream shop, the bakery, the alfresco cafe where I used to eat the weekend-only brunch, will naturally rise up into my mind. I always walked the streets; on turning my head, the owners were riding by on their bicycles, watching me and waving. For many years, according to the rule I'd made for myself, whenever I had time and money I would, almost without exception, fly to a city, and live there for a time, and before returning to Korea I frequently left my bags in the cellar of the house I'd stayed in, or asked to leave in the owner's safekeeping any luggage that I didn't need to have with me, books and clothes, etc.; I did this each time with the confidence that I would come back to visit the same city again, perhaps even the following year, the owners acting with just the same sense of surety, apparently believing that, if my bag was there, I would of course come back. Despite all this, strangely enough I never did visit those same houses again, and the owners almost never got in touch to tell me to collect my belongings. There was only one time, it was late summer in Berlin and had turned unexpectedly cold, so there was nothing else to do but to contact the owner of a house I'd once stayed in, and ask their permission to come and take a few winter sweaters from the bag I'd left in the cellar. That cellar, in the house I found myself visiting again for the first time in a long while, was stuffed with the luggage of wandering renters who had stayed there after me, and I recall that in order to get to my bag, which was jammed in furthest inside, I had to move every single other bag out of the way, and all of them heavy as houses.

I lived in a Buddhist temple in Berlin, home to a single monk; a narrow, shaded brick house; a house on a Parisian street with a splendid view of the beautiful, stylish facades of the buildings opposite; an austere, rectangular socialist building that towered up in the middle of the empty street; in the vicinity of the canal where an Arab market had stood and on a street of antique dealers; right next to the Munich government and municipal offices where applicants for unemployment benefits and those reporting a change of residence turned up in droves each day from the crack of dawn; a room that had only a mattress on the floor; winter rooms I primarily remember for how unspeakably cold they were, thanks to the huge glass windows; the "house of literature" whose lodgings were accessed through the narrow, rear-door kitchen stairs; and, for one week when my luck was good, a beautiful old hotel that made me think of silent-movie era actresses, and which was opposite the "house of literature." But the rooms I generally stayed in were lonely and poorly heated. Window-seat beds where, if I opened my eyes in the middle of the night, the chilly winter constellations were spread out at my bedside. I fell asleep beneath a cold and deeply shadowed wall, and read Rilke in bed: "If I had money, the first thing I would buy before anything else would be a good stove."

The couple who owned the house on Holbeinstrasse invited me to their weekend garden. A twenty-minute walk from the house brought us to the kind of well-demarcated green spaces that were common in the city's suburbs, and the edge of the forest became visible. The weekend garden was there. As soon as you passed through the entrance you found yourself in a large space with plenty of trees, enough to have stocked a small orchard, and the ground was carpeted with pleasingly long grasses, and in the very heart of the garden where the honey-colored sunlight collected as in a crater there was a long log dining table, a set of chairs, and baskets filled with ripe apples picked from the garden, and in addition to the garden house, which had a terrace and small cooking room, there was a storehouse where bicycles and gardening tools were kept. Looking at the countless holes that pockmarked the ground, the owner woman told the man that they were going to have to do something in order to get rid of the moles. This was the very end of the book fair, in the middle of autumn. We were wearing thick shawls. The light was cold and bright, the air was clear, and in the microclimate beneath the German firs where the chill in the air, though always felt, exists alongside the warmth of the sunlight, each maintaining their separate characteristics, sitting at the log table with mugs of steaming coffee, the owner woman began her story.

A while ago we finally cleaned out the study in the house, and we ended up donating most of the books we had to the library. We'd been living there for over thirty years, and while we were sorting through all those old books, we spotted one very old box

137

stuffed away in a corner, which was clearly mine, though which
seemed to have vanished from my memory a long time ago, so that
I had probably not given it a single thought in the decades that had
passed. The box was full of letters. Letters my older brother had
sent me in the 1960s. Thinking about it, we had a very good relationship, for siblings. My brother had left home several years ahead
of me to attend university abroad, and he worried about me a lot,
was always trying to look out for me, especially as I'd just started
university myself and was living independently for the first time.
Because we were each studying in different cities, our main form
of contact was through letters, which we used to inform each other
of trivial events, our everyday doings. Our bodies may have been
far apart, but we were very close. Now, after all that time had gone
by, I had rediscovered those letters and began to read them again.
Minute bursts of feeling that we'd been ignorant of at the time, all
the things we had been blessed with in this world, things that will
not come again, things that were a matter of course and yet surprising, things that will be forgotten, things that no one will know,
matters that will come to seem no different from all the world's
other memories; through that chance reunion they pierce through
time and were revived in front of me one by one, whether memories live inside our ghosts or are forever a part of our real selves,
we will arrive at the train station at this hour and meet each other
on the platform, we'll go on a holiday or visit our parents at their
home, will make an appointment to do this and will wait for that
appointment, and I wish you good luck, I really worry about you, I
hope everything gets sorted out for you, hope your cold goes away
soon, these were the kinds of things we exchanged, that could not
have been more mundane; and our shared childhood, the happy
memories and memorable episodes that only we knew about, were
naturally touched upon here and there in the letters, and in their
revival these everyday words and scenes were replete with certain

ingredients that had not originally been there, made manifest only after a long passage of time, and recalling them now, when my brother and I are both around seventy years old, they also spark the calm premonition that we will soon vanish from each other's sight, that that moment might be near at hand; countless people of that youthful, warmhearted time have swept by in front of our eyes, and it occurs to me that we have been unable to perceive the unique and private gesture with which each must surely have parted from us, and while thinking all this I peered at those letters as though invoking a name of supreme significance, and all that now lies ahead of us will still be beautiful as the road down which we have come, and that mysterious pain and longing that those old letters stirred up again will become, at the very end of my life, a cherished happiness; this was how I came to think of it. A while later, I attended my brother's seventy-third birthday party and read out one of the letters he'd written me. A letter from a day in May 1962, the paper yellowed, my brother himself would most likely have completely forgotten its contents, and it wasn't that there was anything so very grand written there, it was just a letter in which my brother worried about my health, as I'd been suffering various aches and pains after recently moving, the earnestness held within that letter was vividly revived, the unconfessed affection, and the hearts of the penniless young brother and sister, distressed by no longer living together, beat again, and because of all this, above all because of the human feeling that had maintained an unchanging present-tense despite the great expanse of time sundering it from its first appearance, I was unable to read the letter through to the end, and equally unable to look directly at my brother as he wiped away his tears. From time to time I think of how lucky it was that I read the letter that day. If I hadn't, I would probably never have known how to properly communicate to my brother the happiness that had come to me, calm yet soundlessly intense. Because, you see, that birthday was the last my brother saw in this world, in fact his cancer was already fairly advanced at the time, and only a short while afterward he crossed over to the eternal world. And after a brief pause the owner woman turned to her husband and added, darling, we really must do something about those moles.

And then we sat in the garden for a while longer. Not talking about anything in particular, we quietly ate apples and drank coffee. Gold and red was mingled in the apples that had been picked directly from the garden's trees, and their surface was not slippery, but firm and tasty. We laughed, each sunk in our own thoughts as we bathed our faces in the sunlight and wind, then stood up from our seats praising the cider that was a specialty of the city. My suitcase was in the trunk of the owner couple's car, and I had planned to go straight to the station and take the train back to Berlin. In the car on the way to the station I described to the owner woman the dream I'd had the previous night. Because quite by chance, a person who we both knew very well had appeared in the dream, the person who had introduced me to the Holbeinstrasse couple and thus made it possible for me to stay in their house for the week of the book fair; none other than the model-plane collector himself. In the dream, the two of us were strolling along opposite banks of the Main River. I couldn't tell whether it was evening or morning, but as I had both hands stuffed into my pockets it was clearly a cold day. Walking with the width of the river between us, we each passed under the same bridge, and when I raised my head I could see huge spiderwebs strung like curtains between the supporting struts. Was this my new house, which I would come to live in in the future? The river flowed slowly, the color of steel and spider webs. I called across to the model-plane collector that it was late and we ought to return to the house on Holbeinstrasse. Though my words had no sound, I was aware of myself opening my lips and speaking, and of the model-plane collector on the far side of the river hearing the words I spoke. I was aware that that person, on the far bank of the river, wearing a black baseball cap and walking along with his head tucked unusually deeply between the lapels of his trench coat, was the model-plane collector. He walked without movement, looking like one asleep. He was there without a physical form. I continued to speak. I've wanted to say to you for a really long time now: this place is strange. All the places where I am with you are strange to me. Heterogeneous air and soil, pooled wind and flat sky and the huge bird frozen in midair, even the curious mild warmth enveloping my flesh is strange, nothing but strange. That which is outside me and which constructs me, this water and this picture, is unfamiliar. I had been living inside this peculiar irreality, I said, and had now become one with it. And since it occurred to me that he asked the cause I carried on to explain the reason. There's no way for me to know where Mouson Tower is, since I've never even heard the name before. And even after seeing it with my own two eyes, I didn't truly believe that there was such a tower, I couldn't feel the reality of a tower by the name of Mouson existing in this world, and so even when you were saying Mouson Tower, to Mouson Tower, practically bellowing it, as though you were the pilot of a plummeting plane, shouting into the wireless radio, the whole time I could only guess that it was not a tower, that you must have been confusing it with a small provincial museum somewhere in the French countryside. And yet no words came out of my mouth, since I believed that all of these scenes were simply shadows passing through the interior of the dream, and so this momentary pain or unfreedom would not hinder us any more than all the other irreality we entertain. To put it the opposite way, there is no reason to resist pain or unfreedom as these are the very things that make us dream most wonderfully. And in fact, from a certain point onward, I always felt myself to be an outsider of history or stories, a jester whose life and performances would go eternally unrecorded. But even in the middle of giving this explanation, other memories flowed by inside my head; one day I had discovered "Creme Mouson Intensive Moisture" among the cosmetics arranged in a pharmacy display counter. I'd been walking quickly down the road, both hands in my pockets; the moment I saw it I stopped in my tracks, moved close to the display case, and peered for a while at the longish tube of it, but the fact that even now, long after the Mouson company had ceased to exist, the brand was still being sold, was not something I could accept as reality, and so that moment beneath an advertising board on which a model with retro-style curly hair was smiling like an angel, accompanied by the old-fashioned slogan of "Your skin should never look tired," I seemed to have found myself in the 1950s room of a history museum. I must have wanted to tell you that story. And that I rode in a taxi with the model-plane collector along the road that ran above the river, but the oil-black water was concealed by the metal guardrail and ugly flowerbeds. Having arrived at the museum by taxi, the model-plane collector was already in a state of some anxiety; he asked if I knew the way to Mouson Tower as soon as I got in, but I didn't. I sprang lightly up into the air at each soft step I took over the ground; my shoes were white, and I was unable to see them as a layer of smoke and diluted darkness hung over the ground like a pall, but the feeling that I was floating half a hand's breadth above the ground never left me, and the model-plane collector, seeing this, spoke soundlessly with the face of one deeply asleep, without even raising his head from between his lapels; since from a certain moment onward I could no longer see his tongue or the pupils of his eyes, those words seemed to ring out from the world of his dream to the interior of mine, piercing through transparent walls and taking up residence inside me, like the three words "like a bird"—that was how I heard it.

Dignified
Kiss of
Paris Streets

*I*t began in Mao's room. Hazy, formless, faint things, things
that were neither light nor shade, yet at the same time the
illegitimate children of both, a moment of glittering black
and dark whiteness, confusion that swept down the backbone, and
then a sudden voice. Do not tell anyone about this. This feeling,
these non-sensations of leaden abstraction. But since the familiar,
mistaken attempts at talking about what cannot be said were gathered together into a single face, a montage of confusion, people
said that the face that appeared in photographs was mine.

"No, that's not me, you saw me wrong, you or your camera."

"Even if that were the case, what's certain is that this is you at
the moment the camera went off, even if it isn't you as you are now."

But photographs are taken of countless faces, uncountably many,
in the literal meaning of the phrase; there has to be some clear
reason to be able to distinguish—not indicate—this one face from
among them, this face made up of several large white holes, an
unspecific black background, and densely clustered windows of
indefinite form, as me. Mao is a photographer, which means that
taking photographs is one of the various things he does to make
a living.

We live as photographs. I imagine, we live as a performance without a stage. Or else as writing, as theater, as a writer of pamphlets, a publisher of books, a traffic-light repairer; a translator of trade documents, white goods' manuals, and medical prescriptions; a speaker at exhibition openings, a business-card designer, a magazine contributor, a maid, a writer of travel essays and critic of miscellaneous things, all possible types of freelancer, a guest lecturer at an art institute, the debtor of a bank, one unemployed by grace, thanks to all unpredictable temporary things whose forms are very different to what we had expected. I imagine. In order to further extend the life of my imagination, which is made up of everything it is possible to imagine, I want to imagine still more, to arrive eventually at the skin of what cannot be imagined, to feel it. Mao specialized in photographing certain specific parts of the human body; the money he was able to make through this unique line of business was thanks to the various women who were always completely happy to model for him without receiving a single penny in return.

I can't take this photograph home, I imagined. And I especially can't mail it to them. If I did, they would all get angry, both people I know and people I don't. They would think that I'd deliberately intended to anger them by sending them such an imprecise photograph. But Mao can get just as angry, too, so I try imagining that. In certain cases, Mao will get angry at me arbitrarily. But I don't get angry. Unless, unrelated to this photograph, a pathetic dog in a jester's costume chases after me. There's no need to go far back in time for a specific instance; it happened only yesterday. I was going about my business when someone threw a good-sized fruit at my shoulder. It was a furry brown fruit from the fruit market. When I turned around in surprise, one single laugh burst out, high and exaggeratedly loud, shrill and antagonizing, from between the other laughter that was rowdy, or rather, to be exact, rowdy yet timid. Its author was a performer, in a manner of speaking, the emperor of amusement and instigator of humor; making people laugh—making them burst out into great guffaws—was his job. This is how he made his living. All the people at the roadside cafe laughed as they stared at me. With a look in their eyes that demanded that I understand the joke as they did. But the anger was welling up inside me, and I flared up like an old woman brandishing a cane. I knew the joker. I'd fallen victim to his surprise attacks a couple of times already, always a similar trick. One time, I was crossing the square in the middle of the day when he snuck up from behind and grabbed my hand. I kept on walking, not thinking much of it as I simply assumed that the owner of the hand must be Mao. Because of course, it didn't occur to me to look and check. That time, too, it was the sound that flustered me, that impetuous, persistent, clearly malicious sound, shrill as a scream—his laughter. Only after the sound had shaken me did I become aware of the unfamiliar hand that had stealthily crept into my palm. A huge throng of tourists, gathered on the terrace of the cafe in the square's center, warm in the sun, laughed merrily as they watched us, the joker and I. Oh, that's right, tourists. An old crowd, their mood marred by fitful sleep and the hotel's tasteless food, and worn out from spending the entire day being bussed around city center sights, which were basically the same, and who had been winding down with mugs of beer in front of them, their eyes gleaming, craving some light entertainment. Entertainment of the type that, despite its lightness, would be suitable for them, tourists at a tourist destination. Humor is humor, after all, the joker said right into my ear, as I took in the big red Pierrot nose protruding from powder caked on so thick it resembled a mask. His eyes, so transparent that you almost couldn't tell what color they were, stared hard at me from frighteningly close up. Dear god, let me not have to experience this kind of humor twice in one lifetime. There's nothing wrong with playing the fool. It's not as though the idea of being made a laughingstock, helpless in a foreign land, is completely unbearable to me. But that laughter! An eardrum-shattering octave, massively exaggerated! A frantic cawing produced by the bloodied beak of an enormous bird flying hundreds of kilometers, its great wings covering the whole of the sky! The worst aria, in which the very highest notes, which ravage the singer's vocal chords, rise above each other and are forever connected, a comedy of insults mixed with ridicule in which the intention to make something inside the human body spontaneously combust through repetitive stimulation is all too clearly revealed! The insane merriment of the most cruel and excessive human beings! That acoustic assault is what's unbearable. I glared at the joker but, in the end, was unable to let myself explode with anger, as his grin told me that he was planning to wring the very last drop of laughter from the crowd by saying "the Chinese don't get humor."

All work is melancholy. No, to be precise, that work "with which we make our living" is melancholy, both in itself and in what it inevitably induces. Melancholy without any hope whatsoever, aside from that of retirement and death. For example, the ones that we know, office workers, estate agents, train crews, computer sellers, gardeners, painters, bird chasers, street entertainers, laughter instigators, aged actors, paunchy police, doctors, church doorkeepers, museum ticket-desk workers, teachers at technical colleges, unemployment benefit claimants, and the countless jobseekers who insist "still not me" or "not me anymore." If they were aware of how fatally gloomy and ashen their own countenances are. Mao, capture their captured faces and confine them in photographs. I'll come to get my photo taken again next week.

I took the tram and got off at the station for the museum. The very first thing I saw were countless pigeons blotting out the sky above the heads of wandering dogs. And the large, gorgeously colored scarabs on each leaf of the linden trees. The mutually consistent countenance of each living thing as it swims toward an unspecified bank. An exhibition of life's tenacity being held in front of the museum. After you buy your ticket and pass through the museum's entrance to go up the central stairs, you find yourself in a wide hall encircled by six bulging stone pillars, in the center of which there is a bed. An ordinary wooden bed, with a little decoration on the frame done in stone. The air in the hall is chilly, and gives off the scent of the era of stained glass and marble. A man is lying on the bed, stretched out straight underneath a white sheet, sleeping more deeply than anyone else in this world. His head and throat have the appearance of old, friable paper, and his dry puckered lips are slightly parted, his sleeping breath crawling out from between them in the form of a yellow insect. The man and I are the only ones inside the hall. Opening the newspaper one day, I came across a review that had to do with sleep. The body of a sleeping man that had been exhumed from the Parisian hills. The man had been brought here one day as though from a foreign country known as "sleep." No one knows who he is, so people named him "Sleep" and transferred him to the museum. The man is still sleeping.

"This is a part of your respiratory system." There was a monotonous gaping hole in the photograph that Mao showed me the following week. Because there was only one hole, it looked overly large, overly solitary. Its details shamelessly magnified. A reddish lump of gruesomely inflamed flesh with heinous, swollen protrusions, plump, puffy mucous membrane and pores where filthy fluid had gathered. Mysterious fine dark lines slanted here and there along the gutters of the wrinkled skin. Like metallic arrows inserted into the ugliness of an organic body. I turned my head, unable to look any longer at the brazen pitch-black lumps of flesh paraded in the photograph, a metaphor for "the shamelessness of existence." Instead, I imagined. Taking money in return for exposing the shameful viscera of human beings makes Mao the photographer no different from the butcher with the same name. I have to send in a photograph like this; that's what they'd said. A photograph that will be an official testament to my existence, a kind of proxy for me. My photograph will end up among their records. But this photograph isn't me. It is simply one in the series of "black viscera photographs" taken by Mao, its subject matter and composition determined purely by his own personal tastes. This is Mao and Mao alone. Which also means it is myself "alone." But Mao declared that "the title of this photograph is 'Dignified Kiss of Paris Streets.'"

"Even though you said that what you've photographed is my respiratory system?"

"That's right. But the title is 'Dignified Kiss of Paris Streets.'"

And with that, end of discussion.

Back to the station by the museum. A portion of the museum building was neatly covered by a milky construction cloth. The pigeons and dogs had all disappeared somewhere. Floating dust motes slipped through the wounds of open mouths and quietly took up a place inside. From that day onward I went to the museum daily. This was in order to visit the sleeping man. The man was sleeping as deeply as he always seemed to be, and in what always seemed the same position, with no way to move. At the museum entrance, audio guides resembling lunch boxes with headphones were handed out for visitors to hang around their necks. A title card reading SLEEP had been set up in front of the bed where the man was sleeping, and below that it read "serial number 228." If you keyed in 228 to the audio guide you could listen to a commentary on the work. It said that this man was sleeping in front of Mary Magdalene, who, according to myth, had just recovered her senses after witnessing the resurrected Jesus appear before her, say *noli me tangere* (touch me not), and disappear; this was clearly a lie, an invention of history. Within the vertigo taking over my mind, I imagine: the butcher of sleep, and Mao holding an ax, and the man's bed floating in midair. The square in front of the museum that greets you when you go outside. The optimum place to embrace and kiss and ask after each other's health if you bump into a former lover in the middle of the street, your high-heeled leather shoes coming to a halt as they carry you to the bus stop. The sunlight falls on beaming lips, moves away from them in a sharp red arc. Oh, how have you been, you whom I haven't seen in all this time? The street that one can walk down carrying the illusory flowers known as "the passage of time." Concentric layers of pink petals burst open to reveal their infinitely secret creases. A place where things cannot be otherwise, a place that is rare in this world. Puddles become the eyes of wild animals, scrutinizing our footsteps, and the museum's glass wall divides the image of the two of us approaching each other into billions of screens. Your former lover's hand, your former lover's lips, touch your cold and clammy forehead. A soundless voice. Didn't you come here every day to look for me? Didn't you stand here every day in front of me as I slept, key in the number for the audio guide and listen to my voice? The sky, a soft path suspended above our heads along which a plane appeared to collide with a swan as it passed. Five in the afternoon, an interview with the radio scriptwriter on the bus. Microphone and Dictaphone, hot tea in a thermos (for the throat), a spoonful of honey, cough drops, notebook, and pen.

149

Question: It's been eight years since you first came here, right?
Response: That's right.

Question: What brought you here? To put it a little differently, what, to you, is the fundamental difference between being here and being there?

Response: Questions like those. I want to wander in search of the answers to questions like those.

Question: So you're saying that you deliberately set out to wander in search?

Response: I love wandering in search. It's my job!

Question: In that case, is it fair to say that you came here (of all places) in order to wander in search of the answer to "Why did I come here (of all places)?"

Response: It's the same for the question "where did I come from?" Since, in order to wander in search of that answer, I have to have come from "somewhere or other."

Without a moment's hesitation, the bus drove right toward the center of the assembled crowd that was blocking the road. The crowd, which had been like water flowing in a smooth, continual current, startled and scattered en masse then, after the bus had gone by, reformed into a line and set off. The passengers on the bus were glassy-eyed, their gazes fixed and expressionless, looking like the heads of pigeons, visible through the bus windows as though in a display cabinet. The demonstrators who were occupying the road dragged their feet as they walked along, heads bent, supporting their foreheads with their hands. Bulky flags covered in unfamiliar letters were wrapped around their bodies, as though these were their clothes. Like monks on fire, like people who had renounced their warm hearts, like fish swimming toward the bank of some gloomy evening river. Are you a Buddhist? the radio broadcaster asked me. We were seated at the back of the bus, and I was watching the retreating figures of the crowd. Are you one of those mendicant Buddhist monks who walk barefoot over heated coals in front of some first-world embassy?

Response: I'm not a mendicant Buddhist monk; the thing is, I have this fear of coming face to face with a clown. The laughter instigator is constantly chasing me. I'm the best comedy material he's ever found. That is a stroke of luck for him, but bad luck for me. And the worse my luck is, the louder he can laugh. That's why I arranged to do this interview on a moving bus, you see. What's worse, he once suggested that we do a street performance together. I would walk along the street, pretending to just be passing by, and he would throw a furry fruit at me. I act completely enraged, taking it as a deliberate insult, and look wildly around me. Until laughter bursts forth from the spectators. Then you'll continue on your way, he said, and the performance will be over. And no one will have the slightest inkling that it was all staged. And that's not all. He frequently walks on stilts and wears long trousers, voluminous as the curtain that hangs over a stage. He wants me to be his little puppet. My performance consists of moving as though by strings attached to his hand, pretending to be a wooden doll. He is on stilts, and I am a marionette shedding ridiculous tears. He cannot understand why I refuse such an unconventional proposal for a moneymaking scheme. I am unable to bear the sound of laughter; he doesn't understand that. He also told me to follow the carnival procession, dressed up as a Mandarin coolie with a pointed straw hat and a bamboo pole balanced over my shoulders, a basket hanging from each end. I am neither an entertainer nor an actor, I've never even thought of becoming such a thing, but he cannot comprehend any of this. I've made my thoughts on this matter perfectly clear, a hundred times over, but it seems he doesn't understand a word I say. Even now he is convinced that it is only right and proper for me to accept his proposal.

Question: In that case, maybe he confused you with someone else? Perhaps a former assistant who ran away, or someone who really does perform as a marionette or Mandarin, or else with baggy trousers or stilts, or a circus clarinet. Or what if you are confusing yourself with someone else? It's highly unlikely, but there are times, now and then, when we encounter someone who knows us better than we know ourselves.

Response: There is something in what you say, but all the same, if there's one thing in this world that I'm absolutely not, it's that which the laughter performer thinks I am. That is an indisputable fact, as clear as day. As is the fact that the laughter performer is a stroke of bad luck for me.

Question: It sounds as though you need help.

Response: But can an embassy really help someone like me? Or can a Buddhist? Or a radio broadcast?

Dear listeners, this has been "Portrait of a Foreigner Who Rejects Her Own Identity as Assistant to a Clown," one of the *Portrait of a Foreigner* series, from Radio Bremen.

In the bookshop. A stranger spoke into his phone as he brushed past me . . . that will stay with me for a long time. How long? Four days more than eternity. The man moved farther away, disappearing between the stacks with his back hunched like a gorilla's. As he passed by me, his stooped profile was so similar to that of the snickering laughter performer—part of whose act was to deliberately exaggerate the curve of his back—that I came within an inch of whacking him with the Bertelsmann world atlas I was holding.

On the tram. I took a seat in a foul-smelling corner. The chair's rustling fabric gave off the smell of wet dog, mixed with the smells of damp skin, urine, and beer. As the tram rattled along, the seats swayed from side to side. A suffocating feeling. The suffocation of laboring between night and day, sleep and wakefulness, constantly swaying from one to the other as the tram swayed along its tracks, seeming to writhe in hope of escape but ultimately as bound by this mechanical repetition as the train is trapped by its tracks. But what would be different, even if you lived in a village above the Himalayan clouds? If our imagination were to remember the boundaries of memory.

I jerk awake as though having been flung forward on some impact. The sharp air of wakefulness gathered around the bed. Dust and white sunbeams rolling in through the window. The cold palm of wakefulness laid on my forehead. The curious mechanics of being wedged between being awake and having been awoken, between one sleep and another in the repeating cycle. There is no way for me, sleeping, to doubt the fact that I am asleep, but as soon as I am released from sleep, something, a sense of shock and loss that takes my conscious mind by surprise, this body surrounded by hints of forgetfulness. Have I really been asleep? Where was I while I slept? What is it that belonged to my sleeping self? Whispering: your life is made up of things you do not know and things you forget. Of things that you did not live, of your external sleep. All that you have experienced becomes alien as you experience it again through your dreams, your imagining. Thus does your life fly toward you. Fly from all that is fixed, toward a single expression within an unfixed nap. What is sleep, which is a part of real existence just the same as clocks and time are? How can I be sure that the I who is currently speaking the words is not in fact asleep? That day, there was a letter from the embassy in the mailbox. The letter opened its envelope-shaped mouth and read: Dear Frau . . . , you applied for a new identity card and documents. This letter is in response to that application. We have enclosed a copy of the registration documents that we have for you, for you to use as a temporary proof of identity. This temporary ID will be valid for one year; your new proof of identity will be mailed to you during that time.

Though Mao lives in one of adjoining buildings, the lack of a connecting passage means that to get there I have to go downstairs

and through the side door we use to take out the trash, skirt the
backyard, which is always covered with damp blue-tinged soil,
go around the corner and across the parking lot, up the external
stairwell, through the metal front door, then up to the fourth floor
again. The building comprised a cluster of artist's studios, with
rough walls of exposed concrete. Originally these had been flats
rented out by the factory workers, but they now were studio apartments. Mao had no way of locking the door; I always knocked
twice before going in. Mao was sitting at the desk in the center of
the room. He was wearing a white vest, and nothing else; his usual
attire. He was sitting with his left leg propped up on his right knee,
peering at a calendar for the following year that was spread open
on the desk. Each year, the building's Artisan Society produced a
calendar using its residents' artwork. This time, Mao had apparently been one of the participants. Mao, I called. He slowly raised
his head. Mao, I got something strange in the mail. It doesn't
make any sense, but they're saying that I'm this person. This person? Mao asked, without moving. Someone named Frau . . . Mao
waited, mouth clamped shut, for me to explain some more. He was
looking right at me. Behind his back, the window was half open
as ever. Open-mouthed, facing the darkened courtyard. What time
it was when I woke up, whether this was evening or an overcast
afternoon, the gray of damp fog: these are things I didn't know.
Have dreams always been shadowed like this? Do dreams make
all people, all objects, appear so distant? Distant scenery, patterns
of light and shade like a fixed backdrop. Mao is watching me, as
usual, without even a single twitch of his eyelashes. I feel his stare
pressing me to continue: *So?* Don't you see? They've mistaken me
for someone else. They think I'm Frau . . . , they want me to get a
new ID card using that name. An explanation so futile it made me
pluck at my sleeve. Keep this up and before I'm dead I'll have no
sleeves left worth the name. My face burned red, then immediately

cooled and stiffened. Insult? Frustration? Emptiness? No, no single word expresses an emotion. Only the emotion itself continues, shading from one to the other, imitating such words in succession. Does Frau . . . think of me? The thought made me raise my head. Is Frau . . . aware of the fact that I am thinking of Frau . . . right now? Is Frau . . . aware of the fact that I am not Frau . . . ? An imaginary candle, burning up and dripping down to its base, body and gaze, bare feet scattering, thrown into confusion by the moving bus. Then Gita, who had been wordlessly crammed into Mao's bed in a corner of the room, stood up and went to the bathroom, tramping heavily over the clothes that lay strewn across the floor. Gita's back and buttocks were white and smooth as a cleanly plucked sparrow. This Frau . . . , what was the name again? Mao asked again in a slow, calm tone, as though Gita were invisible, and as though the sound of running water, which had just started up in the bathroom, was not audible. This is her. I went over to Mao and showed him the photo on the temporary ID. Why would they have stuck someone else's photo on my documents? But the name isn't yours either. You aren't Frau . . . Well, of course not. I was still holding the temporary ID that purported to be mine. Mao took the piece of paper from my hand. What I'm saying is, if both the name and the photograph are different, that means it isn't your ID! I was still somewhat bewildered. I must have woken up at the wrong hour. Or woken up wrong altogether. Peering at the photograph, Mao continued: given that both the name and the photograph are different, given, in other words, that you are not Frau . . . and that this photograph isn't yours, they must have sent you someone else's ID by mistake. But it would usually take a fairly long time to get this kind of bureaucratic mistake sorted, especially with you being in a foreign country. An unnecessarily, pointlessly long time. Mao shrugged and turned his gaze back to the calendar. Anyway, he mumbled, I was just about to show you this . . . this is your photograph. Unlike the one on that ID. Mao pointed to the page on which the calendar had been left open. Only then did I flinch, and say, bitterly, "No, that's not me, you saw me wrong, you or your camera."

"Even if that were the case, what's certain is that this is you at the moment the camera went off, even if it isn't you as you are now."

Strange. I get the heavy feeling that I had already had this conversation, a conversation identical to this one, a long time ago or from some vantage point very close by—could it have been with Mao? It was a pain more than a conviction, like a crude medieval arrow. The unreal shock of waking abruptly from a long nap, early or late in the afternoon, at some unguessable time. The kind of shock that makes a person yield to insensibility.

"Why do you look so pale all of a sudden?" Mao asked, sounding concerned. "And sad, and like you've been sort of . . . ambushed by your frustration . . . why is that?"

"It's nothing." I turned and started toward the door. Though Mao made as if to grab my sleeve, he quickly changed his mind and lowered his hand back onto the desk, lightly, onto the calendar.

"Come next week. I don't mind taking your photo again. Then send them that photo, with a letter saying you need a new ID. It will take even longer to get it sorted that way, but how else will they be able to know your face? Since you're not there; only here."

I hurried to my familiar sleep, with one arm flung over my face, resting my heavy head on the pillow. My darkness left that place occupied. Clear, bright darkness, artificial, produced by the closing of eyes. My familiar yellow darkness where sporadic fireworks drift about, blurring through my pupils. Small sharp arrows of silver fireworks shot from a bowstring. Metaphysical and opaque scintillations. Signs harbored by my flesh, signs that will never know liberation. Lovely bloodstains.

Frau . . . of Parisian streets, my official, documented self, who is not me.

The laughter performer holding a black clarinet, how old would he have been?

Audio guide number 228: sleep is not a dream. Sleep is not a brief rest. Sleep is not black, sleep neither flows nor pools. Sleep is not dark. Sleep envelops me with thousands of limbs and eyelids, pressing down, sleep closes the thousands of windows inside me one by one. Sleep is not still. Sleep does not subside. Underneath all skin live obscene, fat-bodied larvae. Sleep is compound eyes, is blind moles. Poison poured into tunnels, to kill the moles that dig up the garden. Sleep does not knock on the door of unconsciousness. Sleep goes outside while sleeping, and sleep wakes up from me. And my imagining begins. Please tell me that I'm outside myself now, in a dreamless sleep.

Afternoons, the Parisian streets are made up of humped hills, sweat-soaked milky light, and incessantly chattering peddlers. In the past these hills were a little higher, the gently slanting sunlight a little warmer, and the peddlers a little smaller and shabbier, like tatty marionettes. My past self stood at the foot of the hills, smoking a cigarette and looking down on the Parisian streets. I was with him, but at the time, in our hearts, we each thought we were alone. Thinking about it now, even granted that none of this was ever put into words, it was precisely that thought, that feeling, that was the spirit of the times, the only thing that we felt certain of, and which we acquired internally without the influence of any particular propaganda. And it was through that feeling that we were able to know solidarity, so that we could look each other in the face without fear or anxiety. I look down from the hills at the Parisian streets. The street where peddlers produce such a clamor it's as though their entire bodies are nothing but mouths, where a performer has his back bent and contorted, where a superior but ridiculous marionette threads its creaking way between them on tall wooden legs. For me, these things defined Paris streets, and the streets I subsequently encountered them in never failed to remind me of Paris streets, to *be* Paris streets. All the hills that appeared after that day and reminded me of the Paris hills. Hilly streets shaped like prone clams. At the time, we were unable to know that we would come to imagine that day very differently from how it had been in reality, that only within this imagination would we finally come to understand each other. Not only that day, but all the days that we thought (wrongly) had gone by, will reappear and live on, without limit. We've probably already discussed this. Topics of conversation brought up inadvertently, simply because they had just popped into our heads. When twenty years or so have passed, how will the air and light and smell of this precise moment have changed? In the future, when around twenty years or so have gone by, the air and light and smell that are passing by us at this very moment—rather, we ourselves who are sweeping by this air and light and smell like a slow train, right this moment—we, or else they, or else everything, will end up flowing past what air and light and smell, to what air and light and smell? After saying the words I laughed, and answered myself: then too, as ever, we will be sitting side by side in this place and smoking. No, this exact moment might already be precisely that moment, all the moments made up of everything that will already have passed away, all the moments that will pass ahead of us. In that case, are we speaking now of the tedious cycle of eternity? Here in this station, at which the train we took by mistake just happened to arrive. At that very moment, like magic, this day of long slow youth grows unspeakably tedious, hills and unknown objects grow so familiar that it is difficult to bear, strangely enough, while crazed by the fact that yesterday, too, we were sitting like this on this very hill and listening to the siren and battle cry of the approaching police car, hideous pulped faces, soundlessly turned pages, faster and faster, the day that was eventually released from this fever, will stiffen faster and faster, without time to age, and bleed, yesterday and yesterday and yesterday, yesterday's yesterday's yesterday too . . . I say to him, at some point yesterday's me will end up meeting you. And in the future too, eternally, Salut. We will be entirely unable to step into other water, Salut. I stopped imagining. Even without imagination we were aware that tomorrow would be no different from yesterday or today. A season filled with the premonition that nothing would change. Fireworks that always come to us too late. We don't imagine. Even without surreal imagination, it was clear that the Paris streets filled with peddlers, performers, and marionettes, would live forever, constituting ourselves, Salut.

Imagining that, rather than flowing, time only gets piled up infinitely inside us.

Imagining related to Maya. At that time there was "Maya" between us. Maya was the pen name of the woman he had loved since he was in his teens. Even during that season we lived together in the Paris streets, he would read Maya's books from cover to cover, whatever the content, made an effort to attend each event at which Maya appeared, and even wrote her long letters. As far as I know, though, he never received a reply. I had no idea when he'd met Maya in person or how he'd ended up being invited to her study, her bedroom. To be frank, I didn't believe for a minute that such things were possible. We were lonely street performers, jobless, whereas Maya was a writer surrounded by admirers, someone who could even be called famous, meaning that however madly in love he was, there was too wide a gulf between them for them to meet in person, for their acquaintance to be actualized. But he talked that down. One day I read an article by Maya in a newspaper. I didn't yet count myself among her readers, but I bought her latest book because, based on the article, its male protagonist closely resembled him. At this point, quite a long time had already passed since I'd last seen him. So you're living with Maya! I thought as I read the book. You're living with Maya! You've got her for your own! You're loved! Maya had drawn him as a shadow behind a veil, but I was able to make him out quite clearly, down to each strand of hair. He appeared to have become Maya's veiled bride and leaped over old, repetitive eternity in a single step. I imagined an extremely private evening, which he shared with Maya and her young son. The planet of their quiet fireworks. I imagined Maya's soft small breasts, pillowed on my stomach. How precisely those things which are lived are worth writing about. Salut.

You might want to change your clothes, Frau . . . , Mao said, producing a gray dress flecked with gold as I stepped into the studio. I took it and was heading for the bathroom when I suddenly got the feeling that something was wrong. I turned back and stared at Mao. I'm not Frau . . . , I'm telling you. That's precisely why I need to have another ID photo taken.

"That was only a little joke. I was trying to cheer you up. So laugh. Go on, crack a smile at least."

I tried to give the appearance of laughing, but it didn't come off well.

"Mao, we've already known each other for eight years or so." I'd left the bathroom door open while I was getting changed, and raised my voice so that Mao could hear me. At the same time, I strained every nerve to ensure that those words sounded as though they carried no weight whatsoever. Which was in fact the case. Not that I strained my nerves, but that those words had no weight whatsoever.

"All because you showed up one day, as suddenly as if you'd fallen from the sky," Mao responded cheerily while he got his camera ready. "It's all your fault."

Me: Frau . . . is not some ladybug who suddenly fell from the sky. Only the innocent by-product of a bureaucratic process. No one knows where she came from, who she is, which is entirely to be expected. To put it concretely, her hometown is documents. When, at a certain point in time, fragments of documents that have lost their owner and have been wandering aimlessly ever since happen to come together and form a person, an individual by the name of Frau . . . will naturally end up being born, without anyone having intended it.

Mao: An individual who just happens to be registered at your address.

Me: My address and my profile and my proof of identity.

"I see." Mao nodded vigorously. I couldn't tell when he had taken the picture.

I imagine the day when I first met Mao. That day, Mao had a woman with him. *This is Gita, my ex-girlfriend.* Her gold and gray off-the-shoulder dress had a faint luster and looked like stripped skin; each time she took a step forward, she came off as intentionally haughty or coquettish. But Gita wore a complex facial expression as well as the dress. As though she was worried that, in the future, I would end up wearing this dress which she so liked. Since Mao only had the one dress for his female subjects to pose in.

I imagine the day when I first met Mao. I was on the Paris hills. In each small square and at each corner, peddlers had their wares laid out, and the countless people roaming what looked like Sunday's flea market, oh yes, that was it, roaming the flea market, each looked to have made themselves up like a performer, identical. A performer from a bygone age, but I can't be sure that time really does flit "past" us on its two feet. The water of memory flows, but isn't it the case that our faces submerged within it are often not our own? And so it would not have surprised me in the least if Mao were to have come toward me towering over two meters tall, holding a black circus clarinet and made up as a white-face performer in a blue gown, moving slowly through the crowd. Standing there in front of the museum I would have shown no surprise, but rather looked straight at him and even—if I'd wanted to—smiled.

What with the white makeup and white conical hat, roundish at the end, Mao's head looked like one great big chicken egg. He had painstakingly painted his lips red, and his right eyebrow was made up with the thick black-colored cosmetic characteristic of whiteface performers. His left eyebrow had been shaved so drastically as to be almost invisible. The blue gown he was wearing had sleeves whose shoulders billowed out like jars, and its neckline was decorated with artificial pearls. Waving the black clarinet like a baton as he walked in his bright gray shoes, he looked majestic, every inch the commanding officer of the performers. And so it will not surprise me even if I fall back in love with him. Because I have never seen a whiteface performer, never embraced a whiteface performer, never affectionately kissed a whiteface performer who has only one thick, black eyebrow. I moved toward him and did it all just as I had imagined. And I spoke his name, Mao, Mao, Mao, my Mao. We held hands and were quiet for a while. His expression masked by his makeup, Mao waved his hand in the direction of the museum and said, we will end up entering that place. Inside it I will take your photograph. Your sleep, called *Dignified Kiss of Paris Streets.* His mouth twitched curiously as though he was on the point of bursting into laughter. Mao, you won't photograph me in an ugly way? Promise me that you won't make me a laughingstock. I begged him like this because I was worried, but what is ugliness and what is beauty? I only ceaselessly imagine that day when I first met Mao. Each time I enter a new sleep that day reveals itself before me. Three women approach from the far side of the fields, walking side by side; each are wearing dresses, and one of them is me. We three women stretch out our arms from our sides and clasp each other's hands. Me and Gita, and—surprisingly—Maya's cold hand. The fluttering hems of our dresses are wet with the evening dew, and the sky is dense with stars. The moon is at our backs, and the camera, suspended in midair from a crane, photographs our shadows. Our faces concealed by our hanging hair. A parade of masked empresses, wings attached to our backs. We, women.

Mao, who detests the news and all media, cannot set eyes on a newspaper stand without making some cynical remark. Babbling excitedly about the bastards who, seeing that North Korea's nuclear weapons and the melting glaciers mean that we are all doomed to die, are rushing to the banks to get a low-interest long-term residency loan for two hundred years! But Mao, newspapers don't always print such nonsense. I'm reading a different article. An article that isn't fear mongering, an article about an item disappearing from a museum exhibit. Serial number 228 – Sleeping Man, a find excavated from the Paris hills, woke up one day and went off somewhere (people, I am truly not in the least surprised). He would have climbed down from the bed, crossed the deserted exhibition hall, passed through the entrance hall, and walked down the stairs. His would have been a slightly stooped and awkward gait, but no one would have been observing him carefully, so if he had slipped into the crowd as he left the museum no one would have been able to tell that he was serial number 228 (even if they had, something else would have come up to distract them). The sight of you from long ago, standing at the bus stop, absentminded as ever, with both hands thrust into the pockets of your shabby old jacket. The bus is coming. I feel my body swaying and gradually thinning out in the sunlight. I will become invisible, and all that will eventually remain in the wind are the flowers from the pot I had been carrying.

The chairs in the waiting area had bumpy plastic surfaces, so the pen made a crunching sound as it staggered over the paper. The digital clock on the wall of the government office showed twenty-five minutes past four in the afternoon. Confusing that with the date, I was on the verge of writing down April 25th on the documents for Frau . . . when I realized my mistake. But where do I have to hand in this application form? Each counter window had a number, and the numbers went up to at least 41 (Frau . . . could not see as far as the higher numbers). It seems like all the information windows in the world have gathered here! After handing in the application and getting a receipt you have to take that to the office on the first floor and get an official note of confirmation. If you come back again two weeks later with that note, you will be able to obtain a certificate of registration. When you come to get that certificate, remember to bring your old proof of identity, your newly issued temporary proof of identity, your certificate of stay in the country and the permit, a copy of your bank statement, license, registration certificate for your place of residence, written confirmation from the police, medical insurance . . . people are hovering hesitantly around chairs and sofas in the waiting area. They are all reluctant to approach the counter, wanting someone else to stride up first and grandly present their documents. Where did all these people come from? Where did they come from, and where do they want to go? The civil servants at the counter wait contentedly, sitting slightly askew, both hands in their pockets. Waiting not for the applicants to approach them, but for the end of the period during which these applicants are permitted to come for an interview. For the conclusion of a lawful and natural administration. In the glare from the electric lights their eyes gleam faintly behind spectacle lenses, beyond the glass partition bearing the government logo. "According to the constitution, all citizens have the right of residence and the right to work, with the exception only of those cases in which the base of livelihood cannot be sufficiently provided, and thus society at large ends up shouldering the burden; where there are factors that endanger the security of society at large, or where such rights must be curtailed in order to prevent infringements upon efficiency, good morals, and manners; or to soundly safeguard the institutions of marriage, family, and collective culture (from Peter Handke's 'The Three Readings of the Law')." Frau . . . peers once more at her clumsy-looking application documents. Such meager content doesn't seem likely to secure her any type of permission at all. Not even for something as trivial as getting a new photo taken, that is. Her old documents will already have been posted somewhere, and the new documents haven't even been handed in yet. This time gap, in which she doesn't exist on paper, binds her like a chain. The door opens and closes incessantly, and the congregation swells. Mute supplicants, enough to fill the hall. Applicants spanning a lifetime. Applicants who are not tall, who stand there not saying a single word, concealing their thoughts and feelings, hesitating within the commotion of silence. Breathing deeply, Frau . . . looks up. There are small ventilation holes in the ceiling at regular intervals, which look like speakers. Or are they an ordinary fire-sprinkler system? Punishing all heat with water. She imagines water pouring down from above and sweeping away her documents, sweeping away the documents of all the people gathered there, sweeping away the smiles of the civil servants sitting at the counter windows, extinguishing the hard fossils of faces that wanted to keep living, the electricity wires and electric storage equipment, the telephones and telegram stationery, filling up the hall of time and overflowing without limit. If that happened, my documents would be free of me. They would be able to go wherever they want. To be whatever they want to be. Frau . . . put her name and signature at the bottom of the document. As soon as the tears spill from my eyes, lascivious laughter bursts out from among tired, bored tourists with mugs of yellow beer set in front of them, as though they had been waiting for something of the sort. They who have suddenly grown ancient in this moment, their hair turning gray and their teeth falling out. Where did they come from, and where do they want to go? Twilight is falling outside the window, and the civil servants are preparing to go home.

How Can One
Day Be Different
from the Rest?

"How can one day be different from the rest? Or, how can one day be just like all the others?" This was the title of the play Mrs. Kim wrote. The performance was to be on as large a scale as the title itself. The play called for a huge semi-circular stage to be divided up as many times as possible, each tier packed with countless small rooms. As the arrangement of these rooms describes a huge semi-circular curve, it will be difficult for those in the audience who aren't seated right in the middle to see more than just a fraction of these rooms, but that doesn't matter in this case. The more rooms the better. When Mrs. Kim first wrote the play she had the stage divided up into three hundred sixty-five rooms, one for each day of the year, but while the performance was in production this was adjusted to the more realistic number of a little over one hundred.

Each room was intended to signify a day. The rooms appeared similar at first glance, but less so upon closer inspection. One room had a blue kettle by the window, another had an empty vase on the table, etc.; some rooms had beds and some had sofas. And then there were rooms that were bathrooms, others that were living rooms or entrance halls. There was not a single word of fixed dialogue. The actors were free to go into whichever room took their fancy and improvise a performance that encompassed a single day, whatever they felt was appropriate to the particular room. They could come in bearing flowers and put them in a vase, and then the actor who came in after them could toss those flowers into the trash. If there wasn't a trash can, they could even throw them out of the window. If there was coffee in the room and they drank it, if they curled up on the bed or sofa for a nap, it's all fine. Once the performance of a single room was felt to be sufficient, in other words once the performance of a day was concluded, the actor moved to a different room. That was the whole play: hypothetical days filled with each actor's own arbitrary actions. Just like ordinary people, that is, who spend their own days as they please. If two actors happen to end up in the same room, they fall in love with a sense of inevitability, then when this mutual harmony has been completely exhausted they end the day without regret by leaving the room. There is no way to ensure that all loves come to an end when a day has gone by, and of course, there were cases when lovers encountered each other again in their aimless wanderings between the rooms and picked up their love where it had last left off, though this was less common. And though the director strictly forbade it, there were also instances in which one actor caught another's eye during rehearsals and the two would plan to meet on stage in a particular room. Still, normally they would meet other partners in other rooms and fall in love all over again.

Sometimes, the lights would go off in a room midway through the performance; this meant that, at that moment, the actor in that room had died. This would be the end of her performance. She couldn't go into another room, or even leave the one in which the lights had gone out. The actor who had at one time been their lover would never be able to meet her again, no matter how long they spent searching among the rooms on that huge stage. Because no one can enter a room where the lights are off. It was not determined in advance which rooms will have their lights turned off or when, so none of the actors knew when they might die. They died suddenly, like being struck by an invisible arrow. At a table where they had written something worthy of being counted as great literature; by the window box, wondering how today would be different from other days; changing their trousers; on the phone; making passionate love; attempting suicide; sleeping; getting undressed to go to bed; yawning with boredom; in some pit of sadness or despair, or else in some moment of happiness, wanting, earnestly, to live.

But a serious problem was discovered once rehearsals began. Mrs. Kim had not prescribed how long each day should be. Each actor regulated the tempo of the day according to their mood; when their internal clock told them that the day was up, they promptly changed rooms. And so it was frequently the case that morning would be beginning in one room while, in the very next room, it was afternoon or evening. This confusion was exacerbated when two people ended up in the same room. One person would be living the morning, and the other would be living a different time of that same day. This was a problem when it came to love. The words love speaks in the morning are different from the glance it proffers at night. Moreover, one person would want to begin love then and there, while the other would be preparing to perform the end of love against the backdrop of the setting sun that only he could see. And if, having finished that day's love, he went ahead and left the room, the other would be left behind, at a loss, feel abandoned, and fall victim to frustration or resentment. Often the actors were sufficiently absorbed in their improvisation that these emotions were not performed, but actually felt, and impromptu fights sometimes broke out on stage. Another problem was that, despite there being far more rooms than there were actors, there were still times when three or even four people would end up in the same room, in which case there was nothing for it but for them to give themselves over to an extremely complicated and confusing three- or four-way love. In a single room, as in reality, there was nowhere to hide oneself away, nowhere to avoid a partner's gaze, so these tangled and unruly love affairs would give birth to quarrels and wounded pride. And so not long after rehearsals had begun, days of tumult and pandemonium were no longer a rare occurrence.

If things went on like this it was clear that the play would be criticized as an incoherent mess, so the director felt it necessary to implement some kind of control. She hit upon the bright idea of regulating the days by the tolling of a bell. When the first bell is rung, the actors all begin their mornings. Then when the second bell rings, the day concludes. But though this method seemed such a perfect solution, the actors didn't take to it at all. In the world of the play, time does not flow as it does in reality, and the actors could not base their days on the clock of reality; are you saying we'll be able to anticipate when the second bell will ring? That, as soon as it rings, we'll have to end the day, unfinished, even if we've just begun performing the afternoon? How can a performance be improvised if all the day's hours are standardized? It's physically impossible to immerse yourself in an improvisation while at the same time diligently measuring the hours. In some rooms we encounter a strange woman wearing lace underwear and fishnet stockings, and in some rooms we end up sleeping alone—how can such days all be performed in the same amount of time? Will days that start and end simultaneously at the sound of a bell really suit this type of performance? The actors complained that they were not tin-headed soldiers moving their limbs in accordance with commands, not mice trained to change rooms automatically each time the bell rang. But the director held out, stubbornly insisting that this was the only way to make the play performable.

The director also proposed that, were an actor to enter a room where two other actors were already engaged in a relationship, the unwitting intruder should instantly step back out of the room, pretending not to have seen anything. This provoked an even greater backlash than the idea of the bell. The actors' opposition went beyond scorn and ridicule. They had no intention of being characters in some pre-programmed computer game, they said; they had to perform all the possible variations reality allows for, not comply with some foolish decree to ignore them. This play's fundamental nature is that it is an improvisation; neither its lines nor its fingerprints are fixed. So why does the third person have to retreat obediently, pretending to be blind? All they need is the impulse, and a thrillingly risky three-way relationship, the sweetness of a private tête-à-tête in a closet, hiding from a lover's eyes, adultery tainted with bare-faced lies and betrayal, the unalloyed pleasure enjoyed by three in one bed, or some more base hedonism, will be spread out in full color, in whatever way and to whatever degree they choose. Taking this opportunity to resurrect old debates, the actors questioned why they couldn't leave their respective rooms while the day that had begun there was still going on. We often visit other people, or have them visit us. Why should love and friendship be permitted only between those who happen to enter the same room in the same day? And why do we absolutely have to change rooms when a day is said to have ended, and why does the actor who was there with us have to choose a different room to move to? With such a way of doing things, the actors cannot but enact scenes from a prison, a mental hospital, a detention camp. Angered by the actors' apparent desire to place themselves above him, and convinced that such a degree of chaos and improvisation would only serve to further obscure the play's intention, the director snapped that if it were performed in such a way then their actions would become incomprehensible not only to the audience but to the actors themselves, causing the play to descend into a hopelessly tumultuous melee, and asked how their demands were different from claiming that neither the rehearsals nor even the director himself were necessary to the production? Did audiences flock to the theater to be presented with a mere state of anarchy?

Their differences of opinion deepened to the point where the discord between the director and the actors reached the point of no return, and the worst-case scenario became reality: the actors who had been scheduled to take part in the first night's performance all chose to boycott the theater. Only one person turned up—Mrs. Kim. Mrs. Kim had also been going to appear as an actor in the play. When curtain time drew near and still none of the actors had shown up, Mrs. Kim turned to the director and, with the generosity of a lifetime, said, "I should be able to perform on my own. I don't need anyone else. Besides, no one in the audience will be able to see all of the rooms, so there's no need to fill the stage. I'll go from one room to another. This way, there'll be none of the confusion you've always worried about, and at least one major problem will have been solved, no?" As an actor, she might fail, but this was a risk she was willing to take if it meant that her play, at least, might triumph.

But the director treated this proposal a little more coolly. The newspapers and media had shown an interest in the play's experimental form, and because they had already mentioned several times, albeit in a fairly critical tone, that what was going to be performed was an orchestra of improvisation, a self-portrait of everyday life with deliberately exacerbated tedium and latent madness showing through, they couldn't change the very nature of the play at such a late stage. Besides which, the stage was absurdly large for a single actor, meaning the audience would have to spend a lot of time simply locating the one room among over one hundred in which the performance was going on. Granted, you could solve the problem by putting a spotlight on that one room, but that wouldn't be appropriate for the one visible theme that the play advocated—countless days running in parallel. Plus, the individual rooms were far too small in comparison with the stage as a whole, so there would be those in the audience who would watch carefully what went on in this one room, thinking that it was the entire plot of the play, and there would be sections of the audience who could only see those empty rooms in which, accordingly, nothing was happening. More than anything else, though, the play was never intended to be a one-man production; it was the type of play that clearly couldn't work with a single actor, which shouldn't unfold based on any individual actor's spoken lines or personality. The play had been constructed in order to present a countless number of meaninglessly random human beings in parallel to each other; it wouldn't work for the audience to concentrate their attention on any single actor. The kind of play whose very nature rejected any form of spotlighting. For all of these reasons, the director swore, it would be impossible even—or perhaps especially—for the most gifted actor to perform this play solo. "After all, the most impor-tant thing is that this play cannot have a main character. No one can have a name or a face, isn't that right? Here, individuality is made identical with large-scale anonymity—nothing less will do." At this, the director pressed his lips firmly together and adopted an expression of courage in the face of insurmountable odds. Feeling that he was over-egging the tragic heroism somewhat, Mrs. Kim flinched. How strange it was. Wasn't the author of the play none other than Mrs. Kim herself? So why did she find it so difficult to accept all this? "Even if two actors encounter one another in the same room, as soon as they are each in separate rooms they become, as a matter of course, entirely unable to remember each other; not only that, but when they encounter a totally different actor they have to carry on with their performance, pretending,

173

no, truly believing, that this new actor is the one they knew before. Believing so much that it soon becomes a fact rather than a delusion. Even though they have created this performance themselves, it's not 'their' story. That's the way it has to be—at least, if we're talking about the play that I'm directing. Since that's my interpretation. The audience, and of course the actors too, have to be born again in a world in which awareness, perception, is remade." The director's delivery struck Mrs. Kim as unnecessarily emphatic, even obstinate. Though he was not, in principle, mistaken. As the author of the original play, Mrs. Kim was best placed to know this. And though the director had not alluded directly to this, in the decade-plus during which she had worked as an actor, Mrs. Kim had rarely moved beyond run-of-the-mill supporting roles in which, far from being lauded for her superior talent, there had never been the opportunity for her to win even a respectable level of acclaim.

As the director continued to enumerate the many reasons why the play could not possibly be put on as a one-man performance, Mrs. Kim suddenly felt that he was onto her—that he'd figured out her desire to be a playwright. Though this was not such a difficult thing to guess at, given that she had written her own play, the idea that someone else might have gotten wind of the intensity and urgency of her desire, betrayed by her offering to step into the breach and perform the play alone, so desperate for it to go ahead that she would even betray its unique and representative characteristics, provoked such an enormous sense of shame in her that it hurt her to the core. Desire that goes beyond circumstance and degree is another name for vanity, and vanity means hunger and want—these, at least, must have been the director's thoughts. And this must have been why he put such a strong emphasis on the importance of anonymity in this play. Mrs. Kim could read the questions in the director's contorted expression. Why did this woman need over a hundred rooms and almost the same number of actors, if they were ultimately to be no more than ghost-images of herself? What was the point of such large-scale anonymity? If she'd imagined that she could simply substitute her own solo performance, why write a play of this chaotic magnitude, that had led to the actors causing such a scene? This woman is willing to overturn the play's very subject, themes—oblivion, anonymity, repetition, reproduction, dispersion, isolation—which she herself gave birth to and which I as director have defended against considerable opposition, all due to her desire to be a heroine; isn't that the long and short of it? If so—if the whole purpose of the play is null and void, and if all this time my efforts to keep its essence alive have merely condemned it to failure, and if that essence had never been anything more than a means to carry out the exact opposite of its purpose—there's no reason on earth that things had to turn out like this.

Ultimately the play foundered; the criticism of the mass media poured in, strengthened by the actors' protests, so the curtain fell even before it had been raised, and the production was notorious, known far and wide as a disgraceful scandal, an egregiously expensive undertaking. Worse, a certain critic commented scathingly that if the work had actually been staged as planned, the audience would have been helpless in their seats, forced to watch as pandemonium broke out, exaggeratedly chaotic yet tediously monotone, and of which they could understand nothing, so that in that sense one could even call the production's foundering a "stroke of luck." In actual fact, the critic in question had dropped by the theater during one of the rehearsals and had seen it all, in addition to the problems the director himself had already foreseen; the actors hurrying back and forth down the narrow corridors, searching for the room that had taken their fancy, bumping into each other and knocking each other over, two actors of the same sex fighting over the same room, which each insisted that he needed to perform in alone; actors of the same sex finding themselves in the same room and, without coming to an agreement as to whether they ought to dramatize their relationship with romantic feelings rather than limiting it to friendship or discord, share a meaningless conversation of ludicrous misunderstandings, then bring the day to a non-committal close; actors who spent the entire day lazily picking their nose in the same room; other actors who, at the start of the rehearsal, found a room with a bed and promptly spent the rest of the time sleeping off the previous night's hangover, insisting that this was a performance of important realism; worst of all, several quick-witted actors who used the rehearsal time to work on various side-projects, pretending that this was all a part of their performance. Thus did Mrs. Kim's dream of being a playwright crumble into dust. It was to be her first and last play. She would never write another.

Mrs. Kim saw. She liked what she saw. Colors and shapes which always appeared with different tones and different shading, even sound and touch, forms that, without exception, impressed her with their elegance, people, people of all body types, significant movements, gestures pregnant with or concealing meaning, vague things and defined things, visible things and invisible things, all things. Mrs. Kim was living in three rooms at the same time. She enjoyed the varied countenances of three different rooms, three wordless scenes, three countries that weren't each other's substitutes. Each of her three rooms was in a different city, and each city was far away from the others. Of course, this was all in her imagination. Had she wanted to make it a reality, though, it would not have been altogether impossible. She could have gone to a distant city, rented a room, and arranged for the rent to be automatically withdrawn from her account. Then she would be given the key to that room, and would be able to drop by whenever she felt so inclined. Not only would that be much cheaper than renting an entire house, but she would avoid the hassle of managing an empty house from a distance. She wouldn't have to install a separate phone line, and if she was lucky there might also be a communal television that she could use.

Having her own room to go to was different from staying in tourist accommodations. Hotels were the same the world over, whether in Singapore or Seoul, Bogota or Damascus. People called it international standard. And naturally you couldn't leave your luggage in a hotel room when your stay was over, you had to take everything with you, even down to the smallest pin. One year, Mrs. Kim had lost her favorite sunglasses while on a city break. She wore her sunglasses everywhere in that city, as the autumn sunlight had been unusually dazzling. To restaurants and service stations, theaters and florists, newspaper stands and ice cream parlors, and to the cafes where she went to give her aching legs a rest. She must have left her sunglasses in one of these places, but there were too many of them for her to determine the precise one. She almost certainly hadn't left them in her hotel room, but she telephoned the front desk just on the off chance. On informing the receptionist that she had lost her sunglasses, Mrs. Kim received an extremely sluggish reply: "It's a shame, but there are no butterfly-shaped sunglasses with white frames among the lost-and-found items registered at this hotel. What we do have is a blue-and-brown patterned umbrella, a white bathrobe with a print of bamboo and Japanese women, an almost-full bottle of anti-dandruff shampoo, baggy pajama pants, a single black leather glove, for the right hand, a toiletries kit containing men's shaving equipment, a handkerchief and socks, a camera, a ring, an earring, clear spectacles, a towel not belonging to the hotel, it hasn't been looked after properly so the color's faded, and two books in Chinese, I don't know about what but they don't look like Bibles. Something to do with Buddhism, perhaps? Then a map of the city center, a museum discount coupon, a set of postcards bought at the marionette theater, and . . ." The hotel was a neat little establishment, quite historic, in the small city's old town, facing a square with a little fountain. The guest rooms were also small, without televisions or anything similar; there was a single step at the entrance to each room, and despite the "mind the step" notice hanging from the ceiling cautioning them, if a guest was even mildly incautious they would, without exception, embarrass themselves by stumbling. No one was sure why the step was there; it must have been a relic from the days when the building had had another use, before it had been remodeled as a hotel. But right by the bed was a long, narrow window that looked down on the square, which was as beautiful as old squares tend to be, and if you left the window open in the evenings you could hear musicians playing the accordion, and watch Protestant nuns in curiously-shaped gray-and-white hooded robes passing by in pairs.

Listening to the hotel employee reciting the lost-and-found list like some epic poem, Mrs. Kim couldn't suppress the laughter that bubbled up inside her; she clapped her hand over her mouth and, unable to regain her composure, was forced to hang up. She had never imagined that so many items would get left behind in a hotel, and of such variety too. And she thought of her own rooms. Rooms in which she was living, in this city and that; the room situated in a narrow alley of the city that was her destination, no, her point of departure; no, both, which she would set out from in order to travel to the city where that room was located. There, Mrs. Kim would be able to lose, or leave behind without worrying about someone else stealing them, not only sunglasses but old pajamas and shampoo, shaving equipment and umbrellas, summer shoes with the heels worn down, corn ointment or leg razors. Like former lovers, these items would age as they waited there for her, waiting in case she ever chose to come back.

One of her rooms was in Seoul, the second was in Shanghai, where she had gone on her honeymoon, and the third was in a distant city where she had wanted to live but had never yet been able to. As there was no definite name for this third, distant city, it would change name and shape as though the city itself had become a vagabond, forever in transit. Each morning in her imagination she flung the windows of the three rooms wide open to drink in the sunlight and noise of each of the three different cities. After beating the dust from the three quilts, she boiled rice or sliced bread and made tea in three kitchens. She shared breakfast with three sets of companions, landlords and fellow renters, and turned up the radio, sat at the desk and wrote a letter to someone far away, or read one that had come from a similar distance. Mrs. Kim had a different name and ID for each room. Separate names even while all three were the same, and the same day even while all three were different; it took a secret magic to make this possible. The news was broadcast in a different language on the radio in each of the three rooms, indeed every sound was composed of a different language: that of the short-stay travelers in the next room flicking through maps and travel guides, the low voices of strangers, a ringing telephone, an unknown voice reading a fortune found in a book, lovers' whispered confidences, footsteps crossing wooden floorboards, the feeble mewling of cats. Even the dreams dreamt in the separate rooms were each governed by different languages. The gorgeous patterns of rugs woven from mutually unintelligible languages fluttered about in three rooms. Three imaginings whispered to Mrs. Kim.

Mrs. Kim saw. Yellow walls and deep-brick-colored roofs, long rectangular windows and rain gutters, and the cooing of a pigeon perched on a chimney, gently craning its neck. As with all beings that live in the air, an invisible root can be felt in the pigeon's cries, which the wind scatters far and wide. Sunday morning wakes abruptly to find itself spread out beneath a taut and shadowless swathe of blue sky. In that place there is a window. And beyond it is the scenery of the world. "Tell me your address," whispers a voice from outside the window. Mrs. Kim sees the voice. The pigeon flies away and there in its place is the voice, perched on the chimney. The voice looks like a tall, willowy acrobat, dressed in black, who is just about to start a performance.

"I'll send a letter as soon as the performance is given the go-ahead. Whether or not we'll be able to meet on Highway A92 that day . . . my guess is that you're still wavering. Thinking that it's far too quick, and far too unpredictable, and far too different from the world as you've always known it. You remember the proverb I told you, right? 'There are things we are able to do, but nothing that we are compelled to do.' These words apply to many things in our lives. So set your mind at ease. Let your thoughts be as peaceful as lily pads on tranquil water . . ."

Though the sun will not have to rise much higher before the day warms up, at this hour of the morning the air coming through the open window is extremely chilly. Cozy, lazy tossing, and then the brief 6 A.M. news on the radio. When is it, this moment after I have woken from sleep? When is it, that time first thing in the day when you absentmindedly open a book and the story it contains becomes your own? Things that are the me I am already, or the me I will be in the future. A woman who used to tell fortunes as a game rather than for money had a method she called "book fortunes"; selecting a volume from the books you brought with you, opening it and choosing a sentence, all done arbitrarily, she would insist that that sentence told the person's fate. And after all, why would the "personality" of a sentence in a book be fundamentally any different from that of the picture on a card or the movement of the constellations? Of course there was a lot that seemed absurd or meaningless in believing that sentences chosen through such a method can reveal a person's fate, but the fortune teller had a wonderful way of speaking, like flowing water, packaging simple sentences with obscure hints and garlanding them with gorgeous rhetoric. At the time Mrs. Kim was struggling with the role of the beautiful widow Lé-Ou, who appears in Jules Verne's *Tribulations of a Chinaman in China*; on the book's inside cover was a large paper umbrella floating in the sky, with the title and author's name written on it in calligraphy, and below that was the nineteenth-century Chinese landmass, sunk in turmoil.

A battle was taking place on the bamboo-thick river; surrounded by people fighting and risking their lives, a farmer walked slowly along the riverbank, carrying a water-toting device over his shoulders, and in the distance there was a stone tower soaring up into the sky, and a huge lion brilliantly picked out by the moonlight. Scholars with long hair and round glasses debated around a table while ghost-like people sank in the water, their expressions blank as they were swept to their deaths. The script had been cobbled together from several of Jules Verne's stories, and was one of the scant handful of works in which Mrs. Kim had been given the role of co-star, though it was, admittedly, a student production put on at a university. The scriptwriter was also a student, a bibliophile who was currently around halfway through Jules Verne's sci-fi adventures. The woman who told "book fortunes" rented a room in his family's home, and it was among her things that the bibliophile had discovered the Jules Verne series in the 1967 edition put out by the Swiss publishing house Diogenes, and had put its stylish illustrations to use in his own theatrical staging. The illustrations were all strange and outlandish. When Mrs. Kim first glanced at the picture on the inside cover she was more taken by the apocalyptic scenery, the backdrop depicting the crumbling

Chinese empire, than with the Occidental looks of the beautiful widow Lé-Ou, whom she was to play. Enormous masts in the claws of the wind, the black river, assassins swimming through that dark water, each carrying a knife in his mouth, the round moon floating on the water's surface, a philosopher on a boat, and the densely clustered bamboo leaves that seemed to hem him in, stabbing in from the edges of the picture like sharp sawteeth. The woman who told book fortunes naturally made use of this Jules Verne series in her line of work; it was obvious that these ink drawings, with their elaborate detail and ruinous atmosphere, would for the most part substantiate her prophecies with the dramatic hints and unreal colors that permeated them.

When was it, that time when she had woken from a long, dream-filled sleep and was lost in thought wondering about that dream; when that drawn-out, static scene of herself lost in thought had been a dream in itself. Mrs. Kim groped by her pillow for paper and pen. Her cleanly laundered and neatly ironed bedlinens, the smell of the cold tea she had been drinking the previous night, and the smell of sleep not yet completely dissipated hung around the bed. Lying down nestled among these smells, Mrs. Kim slowly wrote the following words.

"And so, I received the letter you sent and was flooded with happiness. It's true that our first encounter was of an intensity rarely seen. Once our gazes had become entangled, there was no way for us to pull them apart. Considered in a certain light, it was precisely the kind of gaze that I'd thought I'd be captured by, that I'd always dreamed of, but I'd never imagined I would encounter in reality. On actually experiencing it, I felt sure that the pain would have been too much to bear had I lived, aged, and died in ignorance of it, but of course this doesn't make any sense, because how could I be hurt by something I was ignorant of? And in any case, no pain could surpass that of knowing you but being unable to have you, being unable to be with you, of you just grazing by. Right this moment, I can think of nothing but how I might run to you. But you are too far away, and in the future, too, you will always be on tour, performing in various cities. I wonder how I can explain it, as all emotions progress so quickly, far faster than I can put them into writing . . . even if we cannot see each other a single time during this whole month, when August comes we'll be able to film together at least for one day, somehow or other. I already gave the director my consent. I heard that you are also scheduled to appear. The director told me that this time, it will all go ahead as planned. And so, if the world were to end before then, the despair would kill me before anything else. We will end up meeting. I must be the only performer who hasn't read the original work, which will soon become obvious to everyone, but I don't care a bit. The only important thing is that, one way or another, we will end up meeting."

There are also mornings that take a different form. Dense black rainclouds come crowding in and fat raindrops fall from the sky. Everyone bows his head at a similar angle, simultaneously, as though choreographed, and opens black umbrellas. Were they in some third-world country, it would have looked like a mass demonstration conducted in silence. People indoors hurriedly close their windows to prevent the rainwater from blowing in. Mrs. Kim, who had been choosing a peach at a street stall, raises her head the instant the first raindrop falls onto the nape of her neck. It occurs to her she has already witnessed this exact scene at some point in the past. There is nothing at all surprising about this, since always, at all times, Mrs. Kim is seeing many things. A line of bicycles passing through sodden streets, reflected shadows produced by puddles, the shadows of shadows, slow, failed shadows that have lost their way in the instantly absent sunlight, wildly fluttering newspaper, the flustered gestures of someone enjoying himself yet feeling awkward, racing quickly in through the door together with the thick scent rising from dog fur, a lump of strawberry ice cream abandoned on the ground outside. Unique scenes that seem only coincidental and momentary and innumerably repeated, in which such things take shape.

. . . And the paper on the desk and the paperweight shaped like a dog's head that has been set on it, and the document paper fluttering all through the room where no one had remembered to close the window, scraps on which memos had been jotted down. Damp white butterflies of rainy days. Slanted potted-flower petals where rainwater gathers.

Because Mrs. Kim had so many memories of the countless things she had seen, it took her such a long time to bring them back one by one that a well-remembered scene would take as long to recall as to drink an entire cup of tea, while those whose edges had worn away with the passing of time morphed into vague, incoherent masses, and at times this process of slow extinguishing transformed them into other, absolutely unknowable forms. In some instances, the memory would be riddled with huge white holes, naturally obscuring its face. Holes that become the memory itself.

At times, Mrs. Kim finds strange scenarios occupying a room in her memory, despite the fact that, as far as she knows, she has never witnessed them firsthand or even imagined them. She can't tell where they have come from. Mrs. Kim guesses that they are the memories or imaginings of other people which, having lost their owners and drifted in the empty air, at some point entered and took up a place with her. In such cases Mrs. Kim is taken by the thought that she has escaped the world of her own experience and dreamed instead the dream of a mysterious sage. A dream of the previous night, or else of a night twenty years ago. In such dreams she sees a white donkey upside down in a deserted country, treading the night sky as it walks along. The stars crunch like sugar underfoot.

Standing in front of the door with her hands in her pockets, despite having come to the realization that she doesn't have the key she needs, Mrs. Kim merely feels dispassionate. Because she feels that the missing key is someone else's rather than her own, the idea that she has briefly entered the memory of another person—the person who had at some point lost the key—was far more intense than her awareness of having lost it herself. To her, that feeling was caused by a vague conviction that some actual event—something like having lost a key—will arise. It will not come about, or had it come about, it would have done so only within a certain hypothetical domain. Loss is a phenomenon that leads to a temporary delusion—the idea that the lost thing has vanished, has become invisible. This is fundamentally different from the idea of that same object not being in a particular place. In actuality, it is simply that the room where the key is has momentarily ceased to correspond to the room in which you yourself are. Were someone—Mrs. Kim had, as always, slipped into an imagining that unspooled like a skein of thread—to have "actually" lost a key, there would be no dreamy sense of unreality. Instead, they would feel physical unrest: headache and vertigo, worry or hysteria, and finally an uncomfortable and gloomy emotion that could be called unhappiness—the direct opposite of the disinterest that Mrs. Kim was currently experiencing. But unhappiness or despair were words expressing an unsurpassably vivid world, one that went far beyond simple imagining. Here, Mrs. Kim's own imagining wavered. If imagining were like reading a book, Mrs. Kim might have given up and closed it at this juncture. So that it could not speak to her prophetically. But despair . . . that was a body without a skin. Even without deliberate stimulation, the universe itself becomes suffering. Despair was a

185

black picture governed by a feeling of paralysis, an acute impotent craving. The kind of despair that would be described to us by a fish that had been washed ashore, had it been taught to communicate using human language.

And yet still we are ignorant of it, Mrs. Kim thought. And will remain so forever, as fish do not know to speak.

I seem to have heard such words at some point or other . . . that's right, a very long time ago . . . it seems that her parents had spoken such words, right before Mrs. Kim had packed her bags and left home, announcing that she had quit university and was going abroad to live with an older man with whom she'd become involved, a theater actor who was also a penniless womanizer. Some figure of speech related to the unhappiness and despair that set in toward the end of a human being's life. A long allegory warning of the result of thoughtlessness or irresponsibility. Ending with a phrase of resignation and reproof, *you will forever be in the dark.* When, as a university student, Mrs. Kim first saw the man, he was on stage reciting the lines given below. The entire play was just a one-man monologue.

But I'm someone who's always enjoyed adventure, I've always lived as a wanderer, without ties or commitments, and never possessed more than a musical instrument, a T-shirt and a pair of trousers, I've gone around many poor countries barefoot, met many friends on the road, all contemplative travelers like me, I went to Annapurna and met a love goddess who let me nestle in her bosom. I'm a musician and a puppet-theater performer, I also appear in and compose music for plays and films, but I generally support myself by putting on performances in theaters and fairgrounds, by playing violin and accordion and riding the unicycle. I'm especially fond of the accordion, which, more than any other instrument, gives me the feeling that I'm performing with my whole body. Our friendship, which will begin from this point, will embrace all of these things. Along with all the aspects of your own life I don't yet know. But that doesn't make me hesitate for even a moment as I write these sentences. None of those unknown factors will make me take a single step backward from this point at which we've arrived. I'm prepared for everything of ours that we are aware of, and also everything of which we aren't, to be an accepted part of our relationship. And I want to help you do the same . . . but first I should clarify that I fear this might wound you, that I fear that the all-encompassing and adventurous friendship that lies ahead of us, this near future that will demand all possible kinds of human intimacy, will be a wound to you . . .

In the library, Mrs. Kim came across a short story that had to do with keys. It was contained in the 1979 *Weekly Chosun*.

"In 197X, our family was living in Beijing, where my father had been posted as a newspaper correspondent. One Sunday that November, a French diplomat with whom my parents were friend-ly invited us to lunch. The weather had been overcast and drizzly since the morning. My parents, my two siblings, and I drove to the French diplomat's house, which was about half an hour from ours. After lunch was over, our two families went to the national theater, which wasn't very far away, to see a traditional Chinese play. We probably came out of the theater around five o'clock in the afternoon. The sun was setting and it was already dark; the sky was as cloudy as ever, and the rain had grown a little stronger. Only after we had arrived home and were at the front door did my father realize that his key was nowhere to be found. We waited uneasily in the car while he telephoned the French diplomat's house and asked if the key had by any chance been left there. The French diplomat said that he didn't see the key after a cursory glance so would make a more thorough search, and we were to call back in around ten minutes. For ten minutes we sat watching the fat raindrops, in front of the door to the house that we couldn't enter. But the key never did get found. My father must have dropped it in the theater, or on the way there. And so we had to give it up for lost. But there were two keys to the house; one kept by my father, and one by the maid.

The maid wouldn't be coming to the house that day as it was a Sunday. We didn't know where she lived. But the person who'd introduced her to us was a man called "Gao," a squat man with a fleshy face and white, feminine, lovely skin, whom my father had met several times through his work at the Chinese Foreign Office. My father telephoned the Chinese Foreign Office, explained the situation to the person on duty, and obtained Gao's contact details. After, that is, he'd been to the French embassy to get the number for the Chinese Foreign Office.

Luckily, he was able to get a hold of Gao. But Gao didn't inform us of the maid's address straight out. Instead, he claimed that he didn't know the address himself and would have to ask someone else. But that was clearly a lie. It was an open secret that the maids who worked for foreign families were all regulated by the Chinese Foreign Office. We just had to wait, sitting in the embassy's reception room where the heating didn't work, staring into the darkness of the cold damp outside. I don't know how much time passed. My youngest sibling lay down on the sofa and fell asleep. Father tried phoning Gao again. But this time Gao wasn't at home. His wife didn't know where he was either. Just as we were wondering whether it might be better to give up on this line of enquiry, go to spend the night at a friend's house nearby and wait for the maid to come to ours the following day, someone came to the embassy to find us.

This someone was not Gao. In fact, it was a they—two soldiers we'd never seen before. One was short and wearing a large hat; the face revealed in the dim lamplight was outlandishly gaunt, with protruding cheekbones, and his eyes were cold and expressionless as ice. The kind of face whose glare would sting like a slap. Though the other seemed a little more human, his attitude was no less drilled and brusque than his companion's. Waiting in the car was a uniformed interpreter, whose appearance and attitude was the least noteworthy of the three. Difficult to explain, then, why my father felt the most threatened by that ordinary-looking figure. Even while he was smiling at you or shaking your hand, the interpreter's eyes never lost their sharpness. Later, when he would reminisce about that time, my father would say "he had a snake's eyes. As soon as I saw him, I drew in my neck instinctively, to be out of the range of his strike." Though my father could speak passable Mandarin, the soldiers insisted on conducting the conversation through the interpreter. As it progressed, my father gradually came to sense that the interpreter's role was not to facilitate the conversation but to keep an eye out for something. The object of his scrutiny might equally have been my father or the two soldiers, or even the maid herself, though it was difficult to guess the reason for this, or even the whole unexpected situation, which encompassed all of these. They listened quietly as my father explained how he had come to lose the key, though they must have already known the whole story, as it had been told to the Chinese Foreign Office and then to Gao. They told us that they would guide us to the place where the maid lived, and we got into our car and followed theirs deep into Beijing's lower-class district, where we had never before set foot.

A line of identical houses ran on from one another. Houses whose wooden boards gleamed black in the rain and whose roofs were sparsely tiled. You would think you were looking at a single house, then realize that it was in fact dozens of houses huddled together, a hill of blackly soaked rags, no, dozens of hills clustered into a mountain. At first I'd thought that there was no one in the darkness outside the car, but I soon became aware that the darkness was itself made up of myriad expressionless black eyes, gleaming like fish eggs, eyes that concealed thought and feeling, which slowly softened and dispersed as though flowing into the rain, revealing the darkness little by little, revealing a long line of figures wearing coats and trousers of a similar cut, like ghosts passing by between the metallic black streaks of rain. Though nothing was actually audible aside from the sound of the rain, each time their shoes met the stony ground I experienced the splashing sound of the water and its slippery feel as though these things were happening against my own skin. Like their vague stares, which had seemed to bore into us each time they flitted past our car, for a very brief moment, as though stealing a glance at something secret . . .

This is exactly the scene I saw in a dream a long time ago, Mrs. Kim thought reflexively. But as to whether it was genuinely a "dream," or something she'd seen occur in a certain city, a certain room, something described in an unintentionally overheard telephone conversation or in a book she'd absentmindedly flicked through, she couldn't be certain. How like a mirage this thing we call "memory" is! Far beyond the horizon of a deserted stony wasteland, a variety of orange flowers that has never grown before blooms in a riot of gold. In fact, there are several varieties. Is that true, or was it once true, or will it be, in the future, a thing that once was true? Mrs. Kim was happiest when she felt that she was living in a reality that did not belong anywhere.

"We couldn't tell where we were anymore. We'd thought that the forest in front of us, black as wet coal, was an enormous sloping mountain, then realized that it was in fact an endless mass of houses stuck together cheek by jowl, a narrow watercourse giving off a foul stench, alleyways paved with blackish stones, and the shadows of countless rain-soaked people. Everything was entangled with darkness. And those entangled things formed a harmony as perfect as that of a musical scale, endowing the scene with a certain equilibrium. The streets were now too narrow for the cars to go any further, so we sat in our car and watched the two soldiers vanish into the rain. The interpreter remained in the car. Why are they going to such trouble? Surely they could have just given us the maid's address. I could picture her only hazily, the small figure of the maid, possibly in her mid-forties, who had only a smattering of English and French and so communicated through a series of nods, shakes, and tilts of the head, whom we had always called 'Nan.' The only reason I could think of was that her government did not want its citizens to have any unregulated contact with foreigners, especially not contact that would be impromptu and out of the ordinary, as this was. Though it was a simple matter of retrieving a spare key."

Mrs. Kim closed the magazine, disappointed that nothing more was said about the key. When it comes down to it, she thought to herself, this is a story about China, not about keys at all! So we'll never be told whether they ended up getting the spare key, whether this led the maid to be accused of being a spy for a foreign country, whether she was publicly punished, or where my own key is. That was as far as her train of thought could carry her, because all she knew of China was the InterContinental Shanghai hotel and its immediate surroundings, where she had gone on her honeymoon. And besides, if it were 1970s China, wasn't that the time when people hadn't called China, China? Mrs. Kim recalled that she had read *China's Red Star*, as many others had at the time. But she couldn't remember a single thing aside from the title. There had also been Jules Verne's *The Tribulations of a Chinaman in China*, hadn't there. Something about a widow called Lé-Ou . . . naturally, Mrs. Kim was ignorant as to the precise nature of the Chinaman's tribulations, having never read the book itself, only a play script quoting an episode from it, and the illustration, of course. But the book's title and the scene from the illustration were engraved in Mrs. Kim's mind in such sharp relief, convincing her that she had in fact read the whole thing. More than that, convincing her that she remembered it. By contrast, everything about *China's Red Star,* which she genuinely had read, was mired in doubt.

"I'm sorry, but right now I don't have the key to the office. I must have given it to the manager! Would it have been last year? I worked in Shanghai for six months last year. For a Swiss construction company based in Shanghai, to be precise. That's right, I handed everything over before I left for Shanghai. Everything. I definitely wasn't working there last year; I was in Shanghai."

Ah, a key story! Mrs. Kim pricked up her ears.

"No, I'm not going back. My contract didn't get renewed after the first six months, you see. When I left for Shanghai I was excited about obtaining a position in 'rising Asia,' but I guess my luck must have been bad, because I just kept landing the worst jobs. Pay was fixed at a lower level than what I'd received at the main office in Geneva, plus the work itself was harder than I'd thought. It began from the very first day; someone was waiting for me at the airport, to take me straight to the office. I didn't even get the chance to unpack my luggage first. I was tasked with managing the rental apartments of European residents in Shanghai. But I couldn't speak Chinese, no one explained Chinese law to me . . . There weren't even any documents translated into English. How was I expected to be able to set up an apartment management guide when I didn't know the local laws and regulations? Though others seemed to just ignore such things and focus on keeping it all running, it caused me a great deal of confusion, you know. It was very different from how I'd always done things, even at school. I couldn't shake the feeling that everything was done by pure guesswork, without any definite governing principle. And that's no way to run things. Eventually, something horrible happened."

The speaker was Philip, who lived next door. He was talking to someone on the phone. Mrs. Kim could see him through his half-open door, standing with his back to her. Since it was the only phone in the house, whenever someone wanted to use it they had to pull the cord into their room, or else stand and talk in the corridor. It was a communal line, so each time one of the residents made a call they would write down the number, date, and time on the itemized list posted in the corridor, then the landlord would calculate everything at the end of the month when he received the phone bill, and ask for individual payments. Mrs. Kim decided that she ought to ask whether Philip had seen her key, or whether he had taken hers from the kitchen thinking it was his, put it into his bag with his other things, and taken it with him to Shanghai. Once he had finished his conversation, of course.

"A Chinese worker fell off the roof he was cleaning."

Poor Philip. Mrs. Kim had heard the sentence as "Something horrible happened; while working in China, I fell off the roof I was cleaning." Experience is made up of things that fall under "making a living," and things that fall outside it. That also looked like two personalities that constitute making a living. Mrs. Kim was sitting in the hospital waiting room. It would have been the exact moment when, for Mrs. Kim, menstruation ceased to be one of those things from which she was "making a living." There is a checkpoint at every national border. They want a certificate, or tax, or a bribe. She would have had to pay something. Medical insurance card, travel insurance card, passport, or simply credit card? Mrs. Kim had just had an injection; since no one had told her what the injection was, she was simply enduring its effect in ignorance. As she closed her eyes and leaned back against the chair, she saw a seaside where she felt as though she had stayed at one time, but was clearly a foreign resort she had never set eyes on; in spite of that the thought ran through her mind that she had once been in that place, whose form and colors looked curiously altered, no, the thought that she was there right now, ran through her mind. It was a bow-shaped beach made up of narrow bays, beneath a low blue sky. The air was a mix of turbid brown and pale pink. Mrs. Kim saw. The people strolling along the beach were all unmoving photographs or paintings. They were brilliantly colored tin or strawboard or colored paper or balls of yarn or scraps of cloth attached to buttons. Happy smiles and contented expressions, hems hitched up for splashing through the shallows, dogs on leads and opened parasols, even the sound of their laughter and the cheerful atmosphere all fixed, unmoving, to the screen of the backdrop. Only the waves were moving, surging up onto the beach at a regular tempo. Each time a wave washed up, the weight of the water would tip Mrs. Kim's head to one side. Rather than retreating back to the open sea, the waves piled up inside her. A certain part of her was fated to drown. The water gradually rising inside her corresponded to the level of her sadness. It was far too heavy a sadness for her body to resist. It was an enraged feeling, not of her heart sinking or becoming depressed, but of flaring up as in an explosion, a feeling that she was riding the uncontrollable waves, surging frantically toward an extreme shore. Mrs. Kim turned and muttered to the person next to her before she realized what she was doing, "I don't know why I'm so sad."

Her neighbor glared at her briefly then turned away without responding. But a nurse happened to be passing by who heard her and did respond.

"Quite a few people say their mood lifts as soon as they have that injection. They even come to the hospital complaining of depression, swearing that they're going to get the injection."

"There's this scene that's coming back to me, like a memory from long ago, and although it didn't make any particular impression on me, so there's no reason whatsoever for me to become emotional, it feels like I'll die of sadness. I'm crying so much I can barely see."

"Just wait, and in a little while all those emotions will fade. It's a temporary side effect. Later, the only feelings left will be happiness and contentment. Honestly," the nurse told her kindly, then went away into one of the wards.

Sitting on the waiting room chair, Mrs. Kim cried her eyes out. She couldn't help it. Each time a wave surged up the beach, riding a regular rhythm, her heart contracted as though being squeezed in a vice. Like a soft sponge being wrung out. But strangely enough, the sadness was empty. She keened in the face of a white hole of memory. She hadn't made such a sound since her time in the secondary school choir.

"If you use soap," the landlady explained, "you have to wring the sponge out afterward, like this. Otherwise it will stink."

Mrs. Kim simply nodded.

"And since there's only one key per person, you have to be very careful not to lose it. If one key gets lost, all the locks have to be changed, you see. For everyone. For security, you know. And for the front door as well. Just imagine what a hassle that would be! And the person who lost the key would have to cover the full cost, you know."

"No, he wasn't a real employee, just some guy from the sticks who did occasional handyman jobs. The company had no obligation to take out insurance for him, which was precisely why they hired him, because it was cheap. He was taken to hospital, but there wasn't much that could be done. Who would have paid the hospital fees? The nine mouths he had to feed all descended on the hospital, bawling their eyes out, not worried about him, but about how they themselves were going to manage. Which was probably what the man would have been thinking about, too."

Still with the receiver pressed to his ear, Philip went into the kitchen to get some water. The phone cable trailed after him like a faithful dog. Using gestures only, Mrs. Kim asked Philip if he'd seen her key. In order to indicate the word "key," Mrs. Kim moved her lips exaggeratedly to make the shape of the word. But Philip couldn't understand right away so, covering the mouthpiece with his hand, responded by mouthing "what?" When Mrs. Kim pointed at the key box attached to the front door, Philip then shook his head to say that he hadn't seen it. All the while, a rapid stream of words could be heard coming from the person on the other end of the line. So Mrs. Kim wasn't able to ask him anything else.

"You're asking why he fell from the roof? I don't know. How would I know whether he deliberately let himself fall, or just happened to be less careful that day? I know nothing about him. Whether he was a trained roof cleaner or a novice who'd crawled up onto a roof for the first time that day. It had nothing to do with my work, my position. The Chinese employees were the ones in charge of hiring Chinese laborers. Was he wearing protective equipment? How would I know that? Didn't I tell you I didn't even know if the use of protective equipment was prescribed by law? The Chinese employees might have known, but not me. But it's correct that, though he was the first to fall while cleaning the roof, it certainly wasn't the first time the roof had been cleaned. The company said it was entirely the fault of the worker's carelessness and therefore not their responsibility. Perhaps no one had ever used any kind of protective equipment. I mean, I'd never heard of anything being used . . . What sort of shape do Chinese-style roofs have? Well, they're good . . . but the houses we managed were all communal villas for the exclusive use of foreigners, only for

Europeans. The roofs of those houses were all red, in that horned-saddle shape that Europeans prefer . . . I felt I should to go to my boss and bring up the topic of the value of life. Not that I expected him to pay any attention. And I was proved right. None of the other employees batted an eyelid, either. The Chinese were cooler still. They simply said that a Japanese patient had already arrived in the very next ward, and that he would be receiving the Chinese worker's internal organs at any moment."

Why would people pretend to be talking about keys before shifting the topic to China? You only have to open up a newspaper to come across some special article on China, whether in the financial, culture, or travel section, or wander down any street at random to see a poster for an exhibition on Chinese culture to celebrate the Beijing Olympics, alongside one for a lecture by the Dalai Lama. China will even have a starring role in the pamphlet of an aid organization that allows people to sponsor unfortunate third-world children, providing them with a fixed amount of money each month in exchange for a letter or photograph. People enjoy talking about China. But they each talk about a different China. Countryside and metropolis, this city and that, the southern provinces and the northern, the east and the west, this ethnic group and that, Buddhists and Muslims and shamanism, summer and winter, airplanes and trains, desert and marshland, rich and poor, spread out in a panorama where each has its own wavelength, separate and discrete. But the stories that Mrs. Kim was seeing all had the same backdrop. High mountains capped with white clouds, a remote cave where an old dragon lives, a waterfall flowing over a remote cliff, and a vast forest of bamboo that shivers with each gust of wind to produce a mysterious sound. In the emperor's palace in Beijing, envoys flock from vassal states scattered far and wide, squabbling to present their offerings. China controlled its vassal states through having them perform such commercial transactions,

197

rather than choosing to build an empire through waging war. And then there are the media's guaranteed crowd-pleasers: an elderly woman with bound feet, the blackened fabric fused with the skin; helpless young girls, victims of human trafficking and of sexual abuse; the merciless Cultural Revolution and the sayings of Chairman Mao . . .

"The Shanghai I saw was a figment," Philip was saying. China is a country made up of things that get seen by people who are all different from one another. So it stands to reason that the things those people see are also all different. A long time ago people said that Marco Polo was a liar, but he too would only have been able to see that which was made visible to him. Just as the China that appears in *China's Red Star* was different from the China of *The Tribulations of a Chinaman,* and both of these were different again from the China of her honeymoon. Such was the conclusion that Mrs. Kim, who hadn't left downtown Shanghai once during her honeymoon, and hadn't read *Tribulations* either, came to regarding China.

But the key was right there in Mrs. Kim's pocket. This discovery did not shock her. It could have been a dragon in her pocket instead, and she would have still remained unruffled. Mrs. Kim used the key to open the door and stepped inside with her head stiffly raised, pulling her bag behind her. The small room she found herself in gave off a smell of withering petals, damp moss, and wax. On one wall there was a door leading straight through into another room, and this other room led through to yet another. Each of these rooms was decorated with cheap furniture, chairs covered with sheets, Chinese paper lamps, etc., there were several books in the bookcase, a map and train timetable on the desk—but neither sight nor sound of any other human being. Mrs. Kim passed through the rooms until she reached a kitchen; there she found several tables with people seated around them, drinking tea or beer or reading the newspaper. These people all looked extremely tired, and regarded Mrs. Kim with blank stares. Stares that skimmed their object briefly, as though reflexively prompted by the mere fact of something entering their field of vision rather than stemming from any actual interest. After all, there was already plenty going on around them in this room that was no bigger than any of the others, with a man in a red waistcoat bringing drinks or food to those seated at the tables, while another red-waistcoated man fried eggs at an electric stove or made sandwiches or poured coffee. Mrs. Kim had to thread her way through them very carefully while pulling her suitcase behind. The kitchen was all steamed up, its air damp and sticky, and the smells of food and oil and coffee dregs hung in a thick fug. This is like the toilet on a train when the ventilator's broken! Mrs. Kim thought as she hurriedly slipped out of the kitchen. She was careful, but couldn't avoid rolling her suitcase over several unsuspecting pairs of feet, whose owners made their discomfiture known. There was another room after the kitchen. A continuous succession of empty rooms. Mrs. Kim walked ahead, pulling her suitcase. This time the rooms were laid out in a row, one leading through into another. Because the connecting doors had all been left open, the long line of rooms appeared to Mrs. Kim like a straight highway stretching out in front of her. There were windows on both sides, through which a green river could be seen, a lake with swans swimming leisurely, a Japanese garden of exquisite pine trees, suburbs of drab, nondescript commercial districts, the wave-tossed sea, fields, women wearing hats, vases, and fruits, all flowing by . . . From some point onward the rooms seemed to become a long glass gallery, the floors shining like brass, with no end in sight. Mrs. Kim was there in its interior, an interior flooded with suffocating white light. With each step Mrs. Kim took, the light morphed into a different form, casting nets and lattices like flickering sunbeams over the surface of the water of which Mrs. Kim's body now seemed to be made, in a vain attempt to imprison her. The body of the light, which was transparent and had no density, mingled with her own. At some point, Mrs. Kim spotted a man standing on the threshold between one room and another, far in front of her. The man's face was not clearly visible, not because of the distance but because he had his back to the light, so that he was visible only as a dark silhouette with light trying to break through. Still, Mrs. Kim could tell that he was wearing a red waistcoat like the men in the kitchen, and was holding what looked like one of those handheld payment devices that waiters carry. The whole place was a world unknown to Mrs. Kim. This succession of rooms, those rooms where the scenery outside the window shifted from forest to city, from summer to winter, and passed beyond the boundaries of light and water, was what Mrs. Kim had in Seoul, in Shanghai, or even in that third city whose name was unfixed. They formed a rattling train, and the man was a ticket inspector making his rounds. Having eventually arrived in front of him, Mrs. Kim held her letter out for inspection. At that, the light that was surrounding them grew gradually more faint. The train was entering a dark tunnel.

When, after a fifteen-hour flight, Mrs. Kim caught the bus from the airport to the train station, she was only just in time to catch the train. According to the timetable she'd checked in advance, the train was due to depart at a quarter past five in the afternoon, and if she missed that one she would have had to take one with two changes, both in unfamiliar cities in the middle of the night, or else wait until the next day. Dragging her large wheeled suitcase—because she'd been planning not to go back to the house again, she'd wanted an especially large bag that could hold as many of her things as possible—and also with a heavy bag slung over her shoulder containing basic necessities and several books including

Goethe's *Faust*, still feeling as though she were suffocating thanks to having been trapped for a long time in the cramped economy seat, constantly deafened and unable to sleep, grumbling over the fact of having spent almost half a day on a plane, yet unable to register this as something she had really experienced, still, Mrs. Kim managed to find an empty seat on the train. She had the letter in the front pocket of her bag, so that she would be able to get it out and read it whenever she might have the time. It was the letter she had received barely a month ago.

The letter was from the unicycle performer who had fallen madly in love with Mrs. Kim, one he'd been supposed to send a long time ago in order to let her know his performance schedule. But in the meantime something unexpected had happened, an explanation for which had been added to the letter. He wrote that his wife had decided to leave. According to the letter, though she had not actually left yet, her decision was made; she wanted to go back to India and stay with her family to study classical Indian music. And he wrote that he had no intention whatsoever of opposing his wife's decision, that he was planning to spend the next month touring cities in the border regions, doing street performances.

Nan, the street performer called Mrs. Kim in the letter. He called her that several times. He liked that single syllable, which shortened the final syllable in her name. He addressed her in a way that no one else did. His deep, beautiful voice set him apart from everyone else. He was also a magician wrapped in a black manteau. His voice was able to make the words he spoke into a living bird and send them flying up into the sky. He was able to make the wooden duck he pulled out of his bag cry. He could even get the duck to open a black book with its bill, to the page that would tell the onlooker's fate. And if he read the sentence that was written on that page, it became poetry. Unwittingly captivated, the audience

201

gave a chest-trembling sigh. He had a beautiful body, elegantly slender as a youth's, and beautiful silver-colored hair. And a face that, though admittedly wrinkled, produced a smile as beautiful as ever. Even when he donned his Pierrot nose and got up onto stilts to play the fool, he was a beautiful actor. That was revealed in his gestures. Even if he performed in a room where the lights were off, so that no one could see him standing on the stage, still no one in the audience would doubt that at that precise moment, a moment that was set apart, he "looked beautiful." Beautiful, in a way that was ever constant. He was a definite being formed of indefinite cravings, of whom Mrs. Kim had always dreamed when she was young. Mrs. Kim understood that. And they were carried away. They fell in love. It was a brief, dazzling moment of miracle.

Suddenly the train clattered to a stop in the black darkness. It was not a scheduled stop; it had broken down, the cause unknown, and could not go on any farther, meaning that the passengers all had to get off and change trains there. On top of that, the announcement clarified that because this was a small station, not especially well connected, the passengers should examine the timetable carefully to get to the closest city with a connection to their destination. Though Mrs. Kim was so tired and exhausted she could have sunk to the ground and fallen asleep then and there, she got down from the train along with the rest, pulling her suitcase behind onto the desolate platform. Pallid stars were clustered in the sky like droplets of milk, above the stationary train, the track stretching on, and Mrs. Kim. The stars were looking down on them. They were at a small village station almost forty kilometers from the city where, at that very moment, the street performer would be giving an evening performance at a restaurant downtown.

A uniformed station worker came up to Mrs. Kim, who stood there blankly, and asked her where she was going. He advised her that if she waited just half an hour she would be able to catch a train to her destination. While he was speaking, a train pulled in, remained briefly, then carried on its way. Mrs. Kim only needed to wait "half an hour," he said, and then she could catch the train. The timetable on the platform said the same. But what if the train was delayed? The train that Mrs. Kim had originally been on had arrived around fifteen minutes later than scheduled at the station before this. So, after the promised "half an hour," how would she know whether or not the train that arrived at the platform was the one she needed to take? What if the route or train number was not written somewhere on the body of the train? Or if there was something like that in the front window, but Mrs. Kim missed it as the train pulled in? In that case, Mrs. Kim would have to haul her heavy, cumbersome bags all the way to the front of the train, check the sign, then drag the bags back down the platform to the nearest passenger door. But would the train stop for a long enough time at as small a station as this? Why, the last train hadn't stopped for much more than thirty seconds. The biggest problem was that Mrs. Kim had no idea where the train was going, or how to ascertain such a thing, or where she needed to look when the train arrived, this train that was actually now pulling into the platform. Of whether the destination would appear as an electric sign at the very front of the train, or on a notice board in the passenger windows. All she had to go on was the timetable. If she'd been in a major city station where each platform had its own electronic information board there would have been no need to worry, but no such thing existed in this small station, which had only the one platform. Only then did Mrs. Kim's chest tighten with the fear that suddenly crowded in. What if she missed the last train of the day? No, what if she got onto the wrong train and ended up even farther from her destination? If that happened, the street performer would think that Mrs. Kim had had a change of heart and decided not to come. He would believe that she had succumbed to fear.

My Nan, I know full well that you are afraid. I understand.
The street performer had written such things several times.

For a long time, Mrs. Kim practically forgot about her play. Rather than the idea of it having passed into oblivion, she simply kept it from rising to the surface of her consciousness. Though perhaps it was only natural that the play would be forgotten, given that it could be neither published nor performed. And so when, after several years had passed, she happened to meet someone who remembered the play, Mrs. Kim experienced surprise, faint palpitations, and even the reflexive wish that the person in question had done her the favor of not remembering that the performance had been thwarted. But such a wish was doomed from the first, given that the person in question was none other than the play's director, whose relationship with the actors had broken down and ultimately caused the production to be cancelled, and worse, who had uncovered Mrs. Kim's secret desire; a person, in other words, whom she had earnestly hoped never to meet again. Mrs. Kim had continued to be involved with the theater, though this involvement was fairly infrequent, and as the director had continued to work as a director, their bumping into each other wasn't necessarily that big a coincidence. What did make it so was that the director had since emigrated to South America, and had had nothing to do with Korea or its theater scene for some time. He was visiting Korea for the first time in a long while, had made time to come and see a play, and had by chance bumped into Mrs. Kim, who had come to see the same performance, also on her own. Mrs. Kim's uneasiness was not unfounded; predictably, after the usual bland pleasantries had been exchanged, he launched straight into the subject of their play.

At first Mrs. Kim was unable to find the appropriate responses, and as the conversation progressed she blushed from embarrassment. After praising Mrs. Kim's play as one of the works that had left the greatest impression out of all those he had worked on, the director asked if she had written anything else since. Has he forgotten what a difficult time it was for all of us who were involved with that play? The investors got burned, the government organization who'd funded us gave us a huge lecture, several fights broke out among the actors, leaving them irrevocably estranged; I couldn't even think of writing another play. But instead of enumerating these facts, Mrs. Kim decided just to respond with a vague smile. In an unpleasant fashion, though this hadn't been his intention, the director had brought to light Mrs. Kim's grand dream of passing beyond the borders of her own imagination, as an actress who, when the lights in all the other rooms flicked off simultaneously due to some accident, leaving only her own room illuminated, had momentarily forgotten her own anonymity, an anonymity which she had always carefully maintained but which had needed to be hidden inside countless other selves, inside a room that was only a small part of an enormous overall staging, so terrified was she of revealing so much as a sliver of her dream. The director had also recalled to her that she had a responsibility to that anonymity. Mrs. Kim found being with him uncomfortable, forcing her as it did to recollect the incident—as Mrs. Kim referred to it—which connected them, leaving her quite helpless. But in this, too, the director's feelings were quite different from Mrs. Kim's. He wanted to talk with her for a long time. Especially about that play. What they should have done to prevent it from getting in such a fix, for the performance to have gone ahead and been successful, was there really no way to give the actors a little more agency while still ensuring that their performance remained within the bounds of the play's creative constraints, wasn't there a more effective way to stage that monotone panorama, one we just didn't think of in time? If only it had been successful, what a huge opportunity for the both of us! The director's monologue rattled on ceaselessly.

Shaking his head, he said, "Coming up with such crazy schemes, there's no doubting we had our heads screwed on funny back then! All those rooms! All those actors! We worked so hard to prove that it was all meaningless!" or "if the critics had actually seen the performance they might have been even more scathing, ha ha!," and even burst into laughter while slapping his knees. Then, as though something had suddenly occurred to him, he bowed his head in Mrs. Kim's direction and said, in a low, grave voice, "I must confess that back then, after the whole production had fizzled out, I started to wonder, belatedly, how things would have turned out if I'd agreed to your proposal. You as the only real actor on stage, inside a single room among many. Since it's not that the remaining rooms are all dead, there's no need for their lights to be turned off. In each of the other rooms, there would be a marionette posed in place of an actor. The dolls have a simple mechanism fitted inside them so they spin around or dance or sit or stand, repeating simple actions, and now and then two dolls in the same room are made to lie down in a pose of lovemaking. At first glance, the audience cannot tell who is a doll and who a real actor, but after a certain amount of time has passed, the difference would become clear to them, right? Since, rather than performing naturally, like the sophisticated robots that appear in films, the marionettes will only crane their necks or dangle their limbs loosely like ordinary dolls. And so those dolls are not intended to cheat the eye. The opposite, in fact; they are tools for discovering what is real. From the perspective of the audience, you see, the real play begins the moment they recognize you. Just like you, the dolls all change rooms after a fixed amount of time. But the role of the dolls does not in any respect go beyond that of dolls, and the real performance, the main action on the stage, is something that you improvise alone. Rather than just passively watching the stage, the audience is responsible for identifying 'you' among the many marionettes. Of course, for such a performance the stage will need to have a special mechanical device, but how about it, don't you feel that it would be worth trying? Why couldn't we have thought like that from the beginning?"

Mrs. Kim couldn't remember exactly at what point she had come to love the director, who at first had only made her feel uncomfortable. They met up every day until he was due to return to South America. They talked and talked for hours about the theater and plays, especially about the play Mrs. Kim had written, and how they might have been able to put it on successfully. They returned to the same subject again and again. Then at a certain moment Mrs. Kim realized that what they were longing for, or at least reminiscing over, was not her play itself but the director's energetic, challenging youth, which had gone by and would not return again. The moment she became aware of that, her heart became so light it felt like a rubber ball bouncing up, and she was relieved that she no longer had to sit in front of him on pins and needles, feeling as though she had committed some crime and not knowing when the charges might jump out of his mouth. From that point onward Mrs. Kim was able to show him a far softer, more generous, and affectionate smile. It was not the vague or evasive smile of before, or the smile of defense or entreaty, or the obsequious smile of one who senses that their weakness has been detected. It was the unreserved, wholly positive smile given only by those who are truly enjoying their role as listener. It was the smile of a girl expressing pure admiration, untainted by humiliation. That particular smile captivated the director, who was sunk deep in nostalgia. He slipped into the fantasy that he was as young and passionate as he had ever been, unafraid of risk or madness as he had been in days gone by, that he was not flattering himself in this, that he was able to transmit such passion to others too, that his own passion could make fireworks of equal intensity burst in their hearts. It was a fantasy that Mrs. Kim's smile made possible.

Mrs. Kim saw. That the look in the director's eyes had grown gradually more clear and intense, his thinning, disheveled hair and dry lips were now gleaming with luster, he was making an effort to straighten his shoulders and the back of his neck, having previously been stooped, appearing shrunken and cowering, and that even his manner of speech had recovered its former impertinent decisiveness. That the conceited expression with which he had once scorned compromise, believing that he could stand up to one hundred actors and single-handedly put them in their place, was slowly surfacing on his face. Mrs. Kim felt a corner of her heart growing heated. Unlike things that had never existed, forgotten things remained forgotten, and that wasn't right. Such things were charged with the mission to revive in one form or another. Their initial question, "Why couldn't we have thought like that from the first?" was changing into the question "Why couldn't we recognize each other from the start? We spent such a lot of time together . . ."

However filled with eternal light it might have been, their love was fated to be short-lived. The director had to go back to South America, could not avoid the ties of family, especially as he had become a grandfather only a few months ago, besides which they themselves were instinctively putting up defensive walls, saying that this was not something that could last. What they wanted were all the brilliant, shining things that fill the eyes of a fish that washed ashore, for that brief moment at the end of its life. Things expressed through the warmth, the fragrance of flowers, a parrot flying through the sky, a fiery volcano, a butterfly fluttering in a heat wave, and scenes of legend that are absolutely incommunicable because they can be experienced only at the border between the air and the body of just such a fish, only at that precise moment. Things that are, in this way, unique. Moreover, it is quite clear that love that consents to the lovers' parting is already no more than the dregs of itself. Already they were frantically wondering how they might prevent love's character from slowly withering and deteriorating, keep its inspiration from dying off, as though this were the key to them staying alive.

The street performer continued his recital.

But the truly frightening thing, the uneasy possibility is that fear might make us stop as we are, without ever attempting anything. And in the midst of all this we might get off the train, and not be able to understand the timetable, and find the station worker's words equally incomprehensible, and lose an important letter or train ticket, so that instead of pressing forward, forging on to our destination, we fall victim to despair, deciding that it has all been in vain, clamp our lips shut, and go back the way we came. If, our tongue having stiffened when confronted with a strange language, we lost even those magical gestures with which nature had endowed us. We would quickly turn into a fragment of yarn or rag, strawboard or thin tin. We would become colored paper and scatter in all directions. Even so, one day we will go on an outing to the beach. We will laugh happily there. It might even happen that, in that moment of mutual happiness, we become strolling figures in a painting, skimming past, and there will no longer be you and I, and there will be no particular future.

209

I've been a witness to countless fears in my life, and a prisoner to fear more times than I can count. I built a huge castle of my fear and imprisoned myself inside it. Before I left for Nepal, before my law studies were completely suspended, before I climbed up to Annapurna . . . had I, in confronting fear, always made the right choice? And your choice? Regrettably, I couldn't teach you how to choose. I'm not your teacher . . . at least, if you wanted to learn something, it couldn't be through aphorisms, and that includes my own. But since the only thing that is clear is that such fear will block our road, I cannot help, though I am afraid, but continue to talk about it. If we couldn't sing anymore, my Nan, or understand that wordless, bright song that soared up inside us, this letter would be the most meaningless and brazen lie in the world. And brazen things are worse than those that are simply untrue. Because brazen things use lies. And in that case it might have been better for this letter never to have been written. We who are entranced by fear will fly straight into the grave that is silence and lie there. Nothing whatsoever will happen there, there will be no songs, no difference between this and that person's face—people will likely append the word "fundamentally" there—this and that person's memory, or at least no reason for them to be so different. My Nan, does the word "grave" make you cower? My Nan, even if fear drove you back as it did me in my younger days, I would not berate you or demand that you go forward. I learned how the living must understand fear. In other words, that what is my own is also another's. And so, my Nan, I understand you. I am not trying to frighten you. I am not pressing you, I will not resent or curse you, no matter what decision you might come to. Even if you forget me and retreat, you would still be able to stand on stage as you have been, and maybe even continue writing scripts. You would both give love and receive it. You might be happy, for a very long time!

What I imagine is slightly different. Now my eyes are looking into the far distance. Looking, after much time has passed, at the foul stench given off by our death, which hovers over the city dump that is itself made up of countless deaths, then disappears in the underground watercourse of a different, newly-founded city. At a river and smoke forming a world, then making a place for a different river and smoke. Looking, an incredibly long time from now, at such time flowing by, in which even the air itself will disappear. My Ophelia, one day there will be another time so dazzling it is difficult to believe, as certain days were when we were alive, and a distant snow-covered mountain will form above the grave, and above that a clear lake, and we will surge through that water without mass or volume. Pilgrims of the future will peer wordlessly into our eyes in the water. As though we peered at each other in the past. At that time, however beautiful in all directions, however much like a dream, however clear and bright the dew in heaven and earth, though there will be nothing more than the silence, which has already dissolved back into the mists of time, we will peer quietly at them, the pilgrims in the water, their suffering-filled eyes, as though they are our own, as though they had at one time been our own.

And what we see is the stuff of a future when you have grown old as I am now and I have already disappeared from this world. In that future, when your zest for life has cooled and your blood grown dark and viscous, you will end up seeing many things, and among the objects you see will be one that jogs your memory, so that memory will end up hanging around us, and you will recall the time when you read this letter, that afternoon when you went on an aimless walk, and you will wander the whole afternoon, unable to remember what it is you have forgotten—perhaps you might even think it is a key—yet searching all the same. You will move slowly through this room and that, gazing out of the window at times in the vain hope that someone might help you. And then the consciousness and memory of other people, that had always formed you, the characters you performed, the characters who performed you, will appear in turn at the window, their identity concealed, and disappear. Because that appearing and disappearing has a fixed speed, you might think that you are on board a moving train. Those that appear at the window will be lost in thought as they flit by you, just as you will be, riding a train coming from the opposite direction. That you sometimes find yourself genuinely unfamiliar is due to your unusually high sensitivity and responsiveness to such imaginary characters. But you will wander among them in vain your whole life. You will consider them as intimate and secretly pitiful as though they are you yourself. I will not say anything about the kind of decision you will have made when you, my Nan, who must now be facing deep, dark anxiety and fear, finally greet that day. But that day too, your deep womb of memory will release the smell of kindling that has failed to catch fire, having withered itself to death and collapsed over the long passage of time.

Bae Suah, one of the most highly acclaimed contemporary Korean authors, has published more than a dozen works and won several prestigious awards. She has also translated several books from the German, including works by W. G. Sebald, Franz Kafka, and Jenny Erpenbeck. Her first book to appear in English, *Nowhere to Be Found*, was longlisted for a PEN Translation Prize and the Best Translated Book Award.

Deborah Smith's other literary translations from the Korean include two novels by Han Kang (*The Vegetarian* and *Human Acts*), and two by Bae Suah (*A Greater Music* and *Recitation*). She also founded Tilted Axis Press to bring more works from Africa, Asia, and the Middle East into English.

**OPEN
LETTER**

**OPEN
LETTER**

WWW.OPENLETTERBOOKS.ORG